3 5 C E N T S
M A T T Y L E E

suspect thoughts press
www.suspectthoughtspress.com

Author photograph by Jennifer Bua
Cover design by Shane Luitjens/Torquere Creative
Book design by Greg Wharton/Suspect Thoughts Press

First Edition: August 2006
10 9 8 7 6 5 4 3 2 1

Library of Congress Cataloging-in-Publication Data

Lee, Matty, 1969-
    35 cents / by Matty Lee.
       p. cm.
    ISBN-13: 978-0-9771582-2-5 (pbk.)
    ISBN-10: 0-9771582-2-5 (pbk.)
    1. Male prostitutes--United States--Biography.   I. Title. II. Title:
Thirty-five cents.
HQ144.L44 2006
306.76'620973--dc22

                                        2006015697

Suspect Thoughts Press
2215-R Market Street, #544
San Francisco, CA 94114-1612
www.suspectthoughtspress.com

Suspect Thoughts Press is a terrible infant hell-bent to burn the envelope by publishing dangerous books by contemporary authors and poets exploring provocative social, political, spiritual, queer, and sexual themes.

for my sweet Lucia

Special thanks to Lucy, Richard, Wash, Todd, Billy for keeping me sane, Jon Raymond & everyone at *Tin House*, Darin Klein, Kevin & everyone at Skylight Books, Sean Meriwether & *Velvet Mafia*, Christopher Russell, Dean & Gina, Lola & Tito, Beulah Mae & Riffat (RIP), Sabrina Lee for getting me started, Greg & Ian, Julio, Scott & Trak, Mouse & Minimouse, Alex, Donald, and most of all Ralph and all the caseworkers, cops, teachers, therapists, shrinks, and people in general who just give a damn.

Portions of *35 Cents* originally appeared in slightly different forms in *Tin House* and *Velvet Mafia* (www.velvetmafia.com).

The Past is a lie.
—Ralph

L I G H T N I N G
B U G S

They tell me I used to run naked through our neighborhood all the time, but I can't remember. The only time I can remember was the night we left my dad. He came home drunk from work as usual and started right in on my mother. Where had she been and who had she seen while he was at work? My oldest sister, Stephanie, told him that Mom had been home with us all day, of course, but that only earned her a smack in the face.

"Now you've got the kids lying for you too!"

"Leave them out of it," my mother pleaded.

"Are you raising your voice to me?"

"Just leave them out of it, Charlie. Please."

"Go to your rooms," he screamed at us, "and don't come out!"

My sisters got up and ran for their bedroom. I sat paralyzed on the couch.

"Did you hear what I said, Matthew?" He started moving toward me and removing his belt, but my mother stepped in between us.

"He's scared, Charlie!"

"I'll give him something to be scared about if he doesn't get moving!"

Mom bent down and scooped me off the couch, then carried me quickly to my room. She put me down in front of the open door and ushered me in, closing the door behind me and whispering, "It's all right, Matthew, just go to bed now."

I honestly did try to sleep, but the yelling was just too loud and then came the sound of things breaking: wood things, glass things, and then human things too. I was four, and I guess I was scared, but I don't remember. I got out of bed and stood in front of the only window in my room. It was just getting dark outside, and I could see the lightning bugs were starting to blink on and off. I used to love lightning bugs.

Our house had been built partially underground, so the bottom of my window sill was at ground level. It seemed so peaceful outside, all quiet and dark, so I opened the window and climbed out into the cool night air. The lightning bugs were everywhere. I walked around the vacant lot next door trying to catch them but without any luck. I sat down on a rock pile and watched them blinking on, then disappearing like magic, only to reappear again a few seconds later somewhere else. One landed on the knee of my baby-blue pajamas. Its ass began to glow bright yellow; it was beautiful and then it just disappeared. I wanted to disappear too.

I got up and took off my pajamas. I looked over my shoulder at my ass and concentrated on trying to make it glow. And it did! Not at first, but after concentrating very hard for a minute or two, my ass started glowing bright yellow just like the lightning bugs! I had never been so happy or excited in my life. I just started running; running and laughing. At first just in the vacant lot, and then out into the street and down the block, with my ass blinking bright yellow every thirty seconds or so. When the light would go out, I imagined I was invisible like the lightning bugs. It was an amazing feeling, to be present only for an instant and then disappear again back into the night. I felt free and beautiful, like a lightning bug.

I heard tires screech loudly behind me, but I wasn't scared. I knew I would disappear again in an instant. I turned around and was blinded by the headlights. I heard a familiar voice, a warm and friendly voice.

"Matty, what in tarnation are you doing running down the street buck naked, boy?"

"Look, Mr. Davis, I can glow like the lightning bugs!" I turned around again to show him my glowing ass.

"Lightning bugs, huh? Well, you sure enough almost ended up stuck to my grill like a lightning bug," he laughed. He had a deep, self-assured laugh that came all the way up from his belly. Mr. Davis was my friend. That spring he had taken me to Kmart and bought me my first-ever pair of Workerman boots for my birthday. He let me pick them out myself. I chose the tan ones with the yellow laces just like his, only smaller.

"Come on, Matty, we better get you home before you do turn into a lightning bug. Damn, boy, your butt's so white, I do believe it is glowing!"

I ran over to him, and he picked me up and put me into his pickup truck. He was dirty and sweaty from work, and he smelled like work too, not booze. He smelled salty and sweet at the same time. I loved the smell of Mr. Davis, and I imagined I would smell like that too one day after a hard day's construction work. He climbed into the truck after me and closed the door. The dome light in the cab of his truck went out, and Mr. Davis disappeared just like a lightning bug. Then he looked over and smiled, and all I could see were his enormous white teeth. He drove me the half block to my house, not because he was lazy and didn't want to walk, but because he knew how much I loved riding in his truck.

When we pulled up in the driveway he cut the engine and climbed out. I stayed where I was.

"Well, come on, boy, get out," Mr. Davis said. When I still didn't move Mr. Davis leaned in and whispered quietly to me, "Ain't nothing going to happen to you, Matthew, I'll make sure of that."

I slowly climbed over to the driver's seat where Mr. Davis grabbed me under my armpits and swung me out of the truck and then in a huge arc up over his head. He put me down, took my hand and led me up onto the front porch. He was about to knock on the door when he stopped like he had just gotten an idea. He leaned down and whispered in my ear. "Did you leave your clothes outside or inside," he asked.

"Outside," I answered.

"Well you may be crazy, boy, but at least you ain't stupid. Now show me where you left your clothes."

I led him to the side of the house where my pajamas were still lying on the rock pile. He helped me to get dressed and then walked me back to the front door again. The house was silent. We rang the bell and waited. After a few minutes, my mother opened the door. She had a red handprint across her entire face. She looked exhausted.

"Oh, Mr. Davis, I'm sorry, he must have climbed out the window again. Thanks for bringing him back."

"Who is it?" my dad yelled from his easy chair.

"It's Mr. Davis. He found Matthew outside again."

"Well, bring him in here and close the door now!"

"Thanks again, Mr. Davis," Mom said, pulling me inside and closing the door. Mr. Davis put his foot in the door before she could close it all the way.

"Is everything okay, Cindy?" he asked in a whisper.

"Well, okay as always, I guess," she answered.

"Well, all right then, if you ever need anything, Cindy, I'm right across the street."

"Get in here and shut that door," my dad yelled. Mr. Davis removed his foot from the door.

"Good night," he said as my mom was closing the door, but he looked like he wasn't so sure how good it really was.

My mom picked me up and headed straight for my bedroom, but we never made it.

"Just where in the hell do you think you're taking him," Dad hollered from his easy chair.

"To bed," Mom answered. "It's been a long night, Charlie."

"Bring him here," my dad said gravely. I started to cry as my mom carried me into the living room.

"Put him down."

She deposited me in front of his big easy chair.

"Don't worry, Matthew," he said, "I'm not going to hurt you. I'm just going to teach you a lesson."

That was a lie, and I knew it. Like Mr. Davis said, I was crazy, not stupid. He took off his belt and told me to drop my pants. I did as I was told. He told me to lie down across his lap, and I did as I was told. I didn't learn anything that night except that after a while it stops hurting and you need to pretend that it still does or you'll really get him pissed. I guess that might have been the lesson I was supposed to learn. If someone wants you to feel something and you don't, it's easier just to pretend you do.

I went to bed crying and wishing Mr. Davis was my dad. The last thing my dad told me that night was, "Stay away from that nigger Davis from now on, Matthew."

And I did, too; I never spoke to Mr. Davis again. Later that night, after I had fallen asleep, I was awakened by a loud crashing sound, then more crashing, then broken glass. I found out later from my sisters that the first crash had been my mother's head as it broke through the wall into their bedroom. The broken glass was the window in the living room, which had surrendered to my dad's fist. But like I said, that's all just hearsay from my sisters; all I remember were the sounds. I looked out my window and the lightning bugs had all gone—to bed I guess.

My door burst open, and my mom rushed in and picked me up in her arms. We ran through the living room where I saw my sisters half-dressed, and they were running too. We all ran together out the front door, down the steps and into the car. Mom jumped into the front seat with me, and my sisters got in back.

"Lock your doors," Mom screamed.

She was fumbling with the keys when he smashed the driver-side window with a brick from the driveway. Kristen and Stephanie screamed, and I froze like I always do in a bad situation. My dad reached his bloody fist into the car and grabbed my mother by the hair, and then she was screaming too. Then everything went crazy. Everyone was screaming, and I was lost and paralyzed. My vision was like a strobe light. I could just see flashes of light and chaotic horror-show images of people screaming and fighting and then darkness again. Like the lightning bugs were in charge of the lights, but these lightning bugs were the evil ones. My ears were killing me, and I thought I was going to be sick, and then...

"Step away from the car, Charlie," came a deep and familiar voice. It was Mr. Davis.

"Mind your own business, nigger," my dad screamed.

"This is my business, Charlie. You making it the whole street's business. Now step back from the car, Charlie, I'm serious." And from the tone of his voice you could tell he was. My dad let go of my mom and stepped away from the car.

"I'm gonna kill you, nigger," my father said under his breath.

"Now that may be true, Charlie, but not tonight you ain't. Now go on back inside and get some sleep."

Mr. Davis was so much bigger and stronger than my old man. I would have liked to see them fight, but Mr. Davis was right, not tonight. Dad went inside and slammed the door closed behind him.

"You got people to go to?" Mr. Davis asked my mom.

"Yes," she said. "Thank you, Leroy, for everything."

"Never mind about that, you just look after those kids now, Cindy."

D U M P S T E R
D I V I N G

That night we went to my grandparents' house where we stayed for a year or so. After that, it was a few of my mother's friends' houses for a while until we finally ended up in a tiny apartment about an hour away from Philadelphia. The building we lived in was called the Shady Terrace Apartments, and it was indistinguishable from the thousand or so other apartment buildings in the area. The first few months we were there I got lost all the time. It seemed to me like an endless sea of concrete blocks. Some were red brick and some were white cinder block, but they were all menacing. It was a suburban prison where the fences and bars were no less real simply because you couldn't see them. I felt trapped as soon as we moved in, and I think my sisters and my mother felt it too. The mood was gray as we carried our brown boxes in from my grandfather's station wagon. I think everyone who lived in that area felt the same as us. We were all trapped in one way or another. Nobody would live in a place like that by choice.

My mom tried to brighten it up at first with a lot of plants and stuff. We drove down to a local power station where the linemen gave us a giant wooden spool that my mom and I rolled home and painted lime green. Then she bought some matching lime green fabric and recovered our old couch. With the plants and a lot of wicker baskets it gave the apartment a sort of ghetto-tropical motif, which was nice and brightened things up a bit.

By then she had started working nights as a cocktail waitress and going to school during the days, giving me plenty of unsupervised time to get into trouble. One of the first new habits I picked up was dumpster diving. There were thousands of apartment buildings, and each one had at least two dumpsters. On the day we moved in, my mom asked me to throw some empty boxes in the dumpster out back. I was only six pushing seven, and I couldn't reach the lid, so I just put the boxes down next to it, but I wondered why anyone needed such a huge secure-looking container just for their trash. I made a mental note to find a way to look into that dumpster as soon as I got the chance.

A few months later the opportunity presented itself. One night I was taking out the trash as usual. Still being too short to open the lid, I would just throw the garbage bag up into the dumpster if the lid was open or just throw it on top if it was closed. That night I found someone had left an old couch sitting right next to the dumpster. So I climbed up on the couch and peered into the innards of a dumpster for the first time.

It was so dark that I could barely see inside, but I knew I had found something special, something secret. I went inside and got the flashlight from under the kitchen sink and then headed straight back to the dumpster. I stood on the old couch with my little red flashlight illuminating all the trash in a perfect little circle, and I knew right away that this was going to require further investigation. I leaned forward and pressed my stomach on the side of the dumpster to try and reach some of the trash on top. As I began to fall forward and my legs lifted into the air, I realized I had made a huge mistake. I probably should have dug one sneaker in between the seat cushions so I would've been anchored a bit.

I didn't panic; I just flipped completely over and landed on my back in a heap of stinking trash. Did I say heap of stinking trash? I meant to say secret cave of discovery and exploration! For a moment, lying there on all that trash, I felt just like an astronaut floating in zero gravity. It was dark and damp and stinky and completely opposite from what I was supposed to like. My Aunt Carroll, who was a born-again Christian, used to say that cleanliness was next to godliness. What I discovered that night was that I would never be next to God.

I must have lain there on my back for a half an hour just staring up at the stars and letting that stench fill my nostrils and my lungs. Eventually the corner of a cardboard box that was digging into my back forced me to move. I got to my feet and with flashlight in hand I began to explore.

I was as methodical as an archaeologist on a dig. I went through every box and bag and examined its contents, no matter how gross. After digging for a few minutes, I found my first little treasure. It was a little plastic doll wearing a brown dress. It was supposed to be a monk, which I knew about because I had seen them in the stained-glass windows of my aunt's church. I picked it up and noticed that its neck was too long. I thought that the head was coming off so I tried to push it back on. When I pushed it down, this large penis sprung up from between the monk's legs and shot out the front of his dress.

Shit! My flashlight was dying. I banged it against my leg to squeeze some more life out of the batteries. When the light came back on, only a little less bright then before, there it was sure enough: a plastic penis sticking right out of the monk's dress between his legs. I didn't really understand that, but I knew it was wrong for me to have it. I knew it was an adult thing and that it was bad for sure. It was my first "bad" thing, and needless to say, I treasured it forever.

After that, I was hooked. I started rummaging through the dumpsters every day after school. I found so many things. It was like shopping with no money but even better because it was more like exploring. It also gave me the feeling of putting something over on someone else. I felt as if the things I found were discarded by careless or stupid people and that I was smarter than they were because I could see the full potential of what they considered trash.

Of course, the best things were always the "adult" things. Besides the monk, I found a lot of cool sex stuff. One time I was with this older neighbor kid and I found this long red bag with goo in it. I pulled it out and shouted, "Hey, check it out!"

"Oh gross, man, get that away from me," he shouted.

"Why, what is it?"

"Man, you don't know what that is?"

"No, what is it?"

He was laughing like crazy.

"Come on, tell me what it is, man!"

"It's a jizz bag."

"What's that?"

"A rubber."

"What's a rubber?"

"Dude, it's what you wear when you're fucking a chick and you don't want to get her pregnant. The guy's dick goes in there and then it catches the cum."

"Gross!"

"I told you."

I threw the rubber as far as I could and resumed digging. I wondered if men's penises were all different colors too.

I also found a lot of magazines with pictures of naked ladies. These I would take into the woods by my house and look at for hours. It gave me a warm feeling inside to look at them and sometimes to touch their private parts too. I liked how the magazines would show them all dressed up like a cowgirl or a mechanic in the first pictures, and then slowly they would get more undressed in each picture. Sometimes after touching their private parts I would touch my private parts too. And sometime I would even rub the pictures of their privates up against my privates. And that was exactly how he found me.

One day I found a magazine and went into the woods to look at it. I was sitting on a rock by the creek flipping the pages when I heard a voice come from up in the trees.

"Nice magazine."

I looked up and saw a man sitting on a branch of a tree. "It's not mine, I just found it...I was gonna throw it away!"

"Don't worry, I won't tell anybody. Do you like looking at dirty magazines?"

"No!"

"Then why are you looking at it?"

"I don't know."

"I like looking at them. Can I look at yours?"

"It's not mine!"

"Well, can I look at it anyway?"

"I guess so. Sure."

He climbed down from the tree and came over to me. He sat down next to me and began flipping through the magazine. "Wow, this makes me horny. What about you?"

"What?"

"Does it make you horny?"

"What's horny?"

"Does it make you hard?"

"What?"

"Your dick, does it make your dick hard?"

I knew what a dick was, but I was so embarrassed I couldn't answer.

"It makes me really hard, wanna see?"

"I don't care."

He unzipped his jeans and reached in and took out his dick.

It was hard, like the monk's. "Do you want to touch it?"

"No."

"Can I see yours?"

"No."

"Come on, I showed you mine."

"So?"

"Listen, I'm not gonna do anything, I just want to see it."

"I don't want to."

"I know where you live. If you don't show me I'll tell your mom what you were doing out here."

"I wasn't doing anything!"

"Okay, but if she sees this magazine she might get pissed, right?"

"Yes."

"Just show me yours, and I won't tell anybody. Okay?"

"Okay."

And so I showed him. But of course he lied when he said that was all. After I showed him, he wanted to touch it, and I let him do that too. He was rubbing his really fast and just touching mine lightly.

"What are you doing?" I asked.

"It feels good," he said. "If you rub it enough it gets dry and then it will lubricate itself."

"What does that mean?"

"Watch."

I watched, and it did lubricate itself, I guess. When he was done lubricating himself he told me to try. I tried to rub myself the way I saw him do it, but it wasn't working. I got scared and wanted to leave.

"I have to go now. My mom is waiting for me."

"Your mom's not even home yet."

"I have to go anyway!" I got up and ran away leaving the magazine with him.

Every time I went into the woods after that he was there. He made me watch him touch himself a few more times, which I didn't mind. He said he'd tell my mom what we were doing if I didn't. Then one time he tried to get me to kiss his dick. I didn't want to, but he forced my head down onto it. Then he lubricated himself onto my face. When he let go, I got up and ran. I never went back into the woods again.

But I didn't need to; they were everywhere. When I started second grade the following year, the janitor of my school followed me into the bathroom one day. While I was peeing he stood at the urinal next to me, which made me uncomfortable.

"You need to shake it more," he said.

"What?"

"Here like this," he said reaching for me. He grabbed my dick and started stroking it. He was fat and ugly, and I was scared. He wouldn't let go.

"I have to go now," I said.

"Try shaking mine first."

So, I just did what he wanted. I grabbed him the way the guy in the woods taught me and the janitor lubricated himself too. I guess my lubrication system was broken or something, 'cause all I could ever do with mine was pee.

Afterward he told me not to tell anyone, or I would get into a lot of trouble. I never did tell anyone, and I tried not to use the bathroom at school anymore. But, there were more. Everywhere I went they were there: at the bathrooms in the park, at the YMCA, at family gatherings, everywhere. Every time I was alone for five minutes or more, one of them would turn up. Always the same game, touch me, let me touch you. When we moved back into Philly a couple of years later, the list was already way too long to remember.

C H E E V I E

I don't know why we called him Cheevie. His real name was Stephen, but nobody called him that, not even his parents. When we moved back into the city Cheevie became my best friend. He was a year or two older than me and somehow the responsibility of looking after me just fell to him. The first time he saved me was only the second day after we moved into the neighborhood.

I was walking around the new neighborhood, checking it out, when this old man sitting on his porch asked me if I liked trains.

"You mean real trains or model trains?"

"Model trains."

"I've seen them at the hobby store."

"Well, how'd you like to see one up close? You could drive it too!"

"Okay."

"Well, come on in. I have one down in my basement."

"Okay," I said and ran up onto his porch.

"Hey, man, don't go in there!"

"What?" I turned around. There was a little scruffy kid standing on the sidewalk.

"I said, don't go in there, man," he said.

"Mind your own business," the old man shouted at him, but the kid kept talking as if the old man weren't there.

"That's old One Lung Mulligan. He's a pervert. He'll take you downstairs to show you his trains and then rape you. You'll be lucky if you even get out of there alive!"

"Get away from my house, you punk," One Lung yelled.

"Fuck you, pervert," the kid yelled back.

And that was amazing! A kid yelling "fuck you" at an adult! I couldn't believe it. I ran down the stairs and stood next to him.

"Fuck you, pervert," I yelled. "Fuck you, fuck you, and fuck you!"

And that felt good! I think I had wanted to say that for a long time. Fuck you, pervert! We ran away laughing, and after that, I rarely left Cheevie's side. He was my first best friend and still

18

one of the best I've ever had. He looked after me, and I looked up to him. A lot of people looked up to Cheevie. There was something special about him, and everyone knew it. We were in a going-nowhere sort of neighborhood but everyone knew he was going somewhere; there was just something different about him.

So Cheevie and I did everything together, and I didn't have any more problems with adults touching me. Well, except at family gatherings where I couldn't take him along. We got into a lot of trouble together, but it was "kid" trouble and it was fun. If we were downtown and some old man asked us if we wanted to look at magazines with him, our answer was always the same: "FUCK YOU!"

Another good thing was that Cheevie had an older brother, Ricky, who was seventeen, and Ricky's best friend, Pete, became like my older brother. They were the tough guys of the neighborhood. The only one tougher than Ricky and Pete was Pepper, and nobody fucked with her. Cheevie and I could get away with just about anything. If any of the older kids fucked with us, Ricky and Pete would kick their asses good. If Ricky and Pete weren't around, we would tell Pepper that the kids were picking on us and making fun of my scar, and she would fuck them up quick. Pepper had a nasty scar on her face too, only she got hers in a street fight, and I got mine in a domestic disturbance.

The worst thing about fighting Pepper was that she was a girl. You really couldn't win. If you kicked her ass, which was highly unlikely, you ended up looking like a pussy that beats up girls. But if she whipped you, then forget about it. You might as well move to the Midwest, 'cause you weren't getting any respect in Philly again.

One day we were sitting on the corner stoop, and Pepper was standing on the curb talking shit, when this car drove up behind her. A guy whom she had beaten up at the fair the week before jumped out of the car and smashed her on the head with a beer bottle. I thought Pepper was dead. There was blood and glass everywhere, and she just stood there a little wobbly like she was gonna collapse. The guy who hit her just stood there watching with his mouth hanging open like he couldn't believe what he'd just done. That was a mistake. His friends in the car, who were already starting to drive away, were yelling at him to get back in the car. They were too late. Just as Pepper started to regain her balance, Ricky and Pete came around the corner. They had the driver by the neck in like three seconds and were yanking him out of the car. Once they had him out, Pete jumped in the car and took the keys and then all hell broke loose.

Pepper wiped the blood out of her eyes and started closing in on the guy who hit her. He just stood there like he was frozen. Mistake number two. Even Cheevie and I wanted the guy to run. When she finally got to him, I closed my eyes. It was just after five, and all the men in the neighborhood were getting back from work. A huge crowd formed, and when they found out what happened they decided to take the action out behind the bar so no cops would break it up. The worst thing you can do in Philly is go into someone else's neighborhood to fight a local. Even the grandmas would come out to make sure you got the message not to come back around again. And I can assure you that none of those guys ever came back again.

Me, I was never into violence, and I felt bad for the idiots, but I also felt safe for the first time in my life. In the suburbs, anyone could get a hold of you and pretty much do what they liked; there's more privacy out there. In the city, there were the neighbors to answer to, and I loved that tribal feeling. If someone fucked with me, all I had to do was point them out and they were going to pay. It's funny how people move out to the suburbs to protect their kids. Talk about leading the lamb to the slaughter; that's where all the fucking perverts live!

So for the first time in a long time I felt safe and protected. I did all the things that other city kids did: shoplifting, skipping school, throwing rocks at cars, fighting, graffiti, and running from girls, but my favorite thing was just hanging out on the corner with Cheevie. He was a good kid, and like I said, he was headed somewhere. Despite all the trouble we got into, Cheevie was always trying hard in school and getting good grades. He was the hoodlum version of a teacher's pet. At a very young age he figured out that school was his way out. His dad worked in the refinery and drank all night. His brother Ricky was biding his time, but we all knew he'd be at the refinery sooner or later. In fact, almost everyone in our neighborhood would end up at that refinery.

One day I took Cheevie over to my grandma's place for lunch, and they hit it off from the start. Nobody at Cheevie's house gave a rat's ass what he was up to in school or anywhere else for that matter. But my grandma seemed sincerely interested in Cheevie. Pretty soon I'd run into Cheevie on the street and ask him where he'd been.

"I went by Millie's place to show her my report card."

"Who the fuck is Millie?"

"Your grandmother, stupid!"

I was a little jealous at first, but I got over it. My grandma was still nice to me, and I liked it that she liked my friend.

Things were so much better in the city and for a while there I almost thought I was normal. I almost forgot about all the perverts. Almost.

Then one night Cheevie knocked on my door. My mom had taken the night off from work so she answered it. I heard them in the hallway.

"What happened, Stephen?"

"My dad threw a Masterlock at me."

"Come in here quick. Matthew, go get me some washcloths right away!"

Cheevie looked terrible; the lock had hit him on the forehead just above his right eye. The swelling was so bad you couldn't even see his eye anymore. My mother cleaned the wound and put ice on his head, and then we drove him to the emergency room. When we got there she told them that Cheevie was me so we could use her insurance. That was cool of her. I was frightened when he knocked on the door because I thought she would be the typical mom and tell him to go away. Most nights she was working when Cheevie came over, so they had only met once or twice. But that night my mom made me proud. She was very nice to Cheevie and after he got ten stitches in his head she took us to I-Hop for pancakes.

It was a nice night, but it didn't last. When we got home she made a bed for Cheevie on the couch and then took me upstairs to bed.

"I don't want you to hang around with him anymore," she said.

"What, why not?"

"Because I don't want you exposed to that. We left your dad to get away from all that."

"But it's not Cheevie's fault!"

"I know that, and I feel sorry for him, but I still don't want you hanging around him anymore. That's final."

"That sucks!"

"Good night."

I still hung around Cheevie, but I think that night changed my mom. She had a new boyfriend, and they started talking about getting away from Philly. They mentioned Florida. Six weeks later, just after Cheevie had gotten his stitches out, my mom and her new boyfriend were gone. They had bought a truck, packed in all our furniture, and left for Florida. My sisters and I stayed at my grandma's for the summer and then one day a letter arrived from my mom with three airline tickets in it. A week later we were gone too.

Cheevie stayed in touch with my grandma for the next eight years. Every semester he would show up at her door like clockwork with his report card. Straight As all the way through high school too. Then one day he showed up with a letter from some college saying they would grant him a scholarship and after that they lost touch.

As for me, I was now eleven, and once again, I was on my own. With no more Cheevie and Pepper to protect me, I started slipping back into my old shyness again. When I was with Cheevie I was tough and could tell anyone to fuck off. But alone, I became softer, more pliable. And it wasn't just that I was afraid to tell people no. I think it might have been that I missed all the adult attention, even if it was only from perverts; maybe even because it was from perverts. I still don't know. But I think mostly in life, you get what you're looking for. My mom got Florida and palm trees, sunshine and coconuts, and I got...well, something else.

M U L A T T O

Paco Salmeron was definitely not one to be fucked with. He was taller than all the other kids by a foot, muscular, and *mulatto*. That was a new word I learned upon moving to Florida. It meant half black and half white, but in a school full of rich little white kids, it meant 100 percent bad motherfucker. I had been in Florida, at this new school, for two weeks without even seeing this bad motherfucker Paco Salmeron. He had been suspended from school for a month for killing a teacher. Well, maybe he didn't actually kill a teacher, but the rumors had him doing a lot worse than that. From day one at the school some dorks took me aside and told me to watch out for Mitchell Freedman, who was the school bully, and to never, under any circumstances, look at Paco Salmeron. Mitchell Freedman was a bully, but he was popular and well liked/hated by everyone. But Paco Salmeron was an outcast. He was unpredictable and wild and nobody was certain what he was capable of.

It turns out that I wasn't that popular either. Kids were calling my sister and me "hillbillies" after only two days there. I guess the jeans-and-flannel-shirt look hadn't made a big splash in Florida, but hillbillies? We were from fucking Philadelphia; they were the fucking hillbillies! But that was the eighties, and super-tight jeans and golf shirts were the shit in Miami. In Miami, I was the one out of fashion. I also had broken front teeth, a ghoulish scar on my lip, and a serious speech impediment. All that didn't add up to Mr. Popularity.

The only one more out of style than me was my teacher. His name was Mr. Schneider. On my third day in class he was wearing these skintight black polyester pants, Italian leather boots, and a bright red silk blouse. Somewhere in my back brain, my survival instincts kicked in. I was tired of all the hillbilly shit, and I had to do something fast to gain acceptance at this new school. In Philly I was the class clown, so I made some stupid joke involving Mr. Schneider and his sense of style. It worked. Everybody cracked up. I thought I had it made. Then Schneider cleared his throat very loudly, and the room became silent. It would be putting it mildly to say that Schneider was offended.

Looking back now, I think I must have truly wounded his pride because he quit his job as a teacher immediately. His new job, for the remainder of the school year, was humiliating that dirty, wretched little hillbilly kid.

He really got his back into his work too. For the rest of the year I had to sit in a desk at the front of the room facing the blackboard on the front wall. At lunch I had to eat on the stage behind a curtain—the school's theater doubled as a cafeteria. I was not allowed to talk to other kids, eat with other kids, exercise with other kids, or breathe the same air as the other "good" kids. Up until that time I had always thought adults were just mean by accident. Schneider showed me just how premeditated they could be. He was vicious, and he stayed that way. At first I thought he would get over it in a few weeks, but it never happened. He was truly devoted to fucking with me all day, every day. He would look for ways to set me apart, to make me look stupid, to humiliate me. I often wonder now what he did with his free time after I left.

Being singled out as the fuck-up of the school didn't help my social standing in the least. It did earn me a few acquaintances of the freak and outcast variety, and a few little ugly-duckling smart girls with glasses looked at me with pity every now and again. But for the most part I was "that bad kid" or "that weird hillbilly kid who sits behind the curtain at lunch." And that was pretty much how things went. I started to settle into my new role and even to enjoy it sometimes. I didn't have many friends, but somehow being the bad kid with the wicked scar on his face kept the older kids and the bullies off my back. I mean, they would fuck with me, but not that much. I was slowly becoming like Paco Salmeron. Even Mitchell Freedman pretty much left me alone. The rumors started flying around about what I had done to Schneider to get him so mad at me, and I have to admit the truth was boring in comparison.

Paco Salmeron came back to school, and I saw him one day in the halls. He was tall, dark, and intimidating-looking, but we didn't have any classes together so he never bothered me. I figured that he had heard the rumors about me and I had gained his respect. You know, the way two outlaws respect each other. So the last thing I was expecting when I was taking a piss in the boys' bathroom after school one day was for Paco Salmeron to walk in and declare, "I'm gonna fuck you up, hillbilly!"

I guess I would have pissed my pants if I hadn't already had my dick out. I just couldn't stop pissing, if you could call it that. What was previously a vicious stream of piss had suddenly turned into a tiny trickle of pee-pee.

Those were the first words ever spoken between us and I suddenly found myself doing what so many grandmas call "tinkling." And it was at that very moment in my life that I realized what "tinkling" meant: I stood there, for what seemed like an eternity, in total humiliation, with little sprinkles of pee-pee sputtering out of my pathetic little wee-wee. It was as if my dick had decided that if we never finished that piss we could possibly avoid the ass-kicking that was coming. Maybe we could wait him out? In the end though, I couldn't stand the humiliation of the pitiful sound of my own urine trickling into the urinal and I decided to override my dick and just put it away still dripping. Begging for a stay of execution, it left a wet stain on my pants when I turned to face him.

There was Paco, still waiting. I was about to say something to try to limit the damage, but he grabbed my throat so fast I didn't get the chance. And then I was back in the urinal, only backward this time. The porcelain was cold against the back of my arms, and the stainless-steel flusher handle was jammed into my back, and I couldn't help but notice that now the back of my pants were getting wet too. Paco had one hand still around my throat and he slowly raised his other hand back by his head and balled up his fist.

I don't know what I was thinking about then. It's strange; in a crisis I just don't think. I tell everyone afterward what I thought I should have been thinking, but in the actual crisis, my mind is always blank. If I had been thinking, I would have thought of something better to do than what I actually did. Anything at all would have been better than that. I was scared, and so I started to cry.

And the next thing I knew, Paco was hugging me. Not some guy hug with pats on the back and all that bullshit. He was more like holding me, tenderly, like a mother would, or as I imagined a mother would. My mother never held me like that. And then I was really crying. I was sobbing and having trouble breathing and my whole face and neck were covered with tears, and Paco was just holding me there, so tightly, so close to him. And then he was crying too, and I could taste his tears in my mouth. Because he was so much taller than me, his tears were all running down onto my face. I can't even tell you how long we stood there like that. If felt like hours. I had never before in my life felt so close to another human being. It was a moment between two outcasts, and we weren't just crying for the present, but for the future too. It was like, in that moment, we both knew this was just the beginning for both of us. The road we were on was not going to be filled with academic scholarships and blue ribbons, and we both knew it. That was my first real intimate experience with another human being and probably still the most poignant.

Then we were breathing heavy for a few seconds, and the crying stopped and the moment was gone. Both of us knew better than to say anything. We just stopped hugging and walked out of the bathroom together. He walked me home, and we talked a little about sports and girls and shit and then I asked him if he wanted to crash at my place because it was getting late, and he said all right in the coolest way I had ever heard: "Aw-ight."

We spent the next couple of days hanging out together. Paco told me how he got his bully reputation. Turns out Mitchell Freedman used to call him names and beat him up a lot, and one day on the way home from school Mitchell threw a rock at him and said, "Paco's mom is like a refrigerator, everybody's always sticking their meat inside her!"

Paco just turned around and broke Mitchell's fucking nose with one punch. Then, he got on top of Mitchell and proceeded to beat the living shit out of him. That was on a Tuesday and half the school was there to see it. Paco hadn't been at school on Monday; he was at his mother's funeral. She had died of cancer on Friday night. I was the first person Paco ever talked to about it in the two years since it had happened, and I was beginning to understand how alone he really was and why he hugged me instead of kicking my ass. I was also beginning to understand how a "badass" was made.

That first night at my house, he showed me a picture of his mom that he carried in his wallet, and I thought he was going to cry again. A few days later I met his dad; well, sort of. He was passed out in an easy chair in front of the TV. We stole his cigarettes and the rest of his beer and drank and smoked in the park all night long, two more American hoodlums in the making.

Paco went away to some summer boot camp for dysfunctional kids a few weeks later. When he got back, we were moving on to junior high school. At junior high, they bussed in kids from everywhere, and there were a lot more black kids. Paco started to drift their way. I guess he had given up on trying to get his white half accepted. Things went better for him in junior high, and pretty soon he had a lot of black friends, and he was a pretty badass football player. He still tried keeping in touch with me, but we slowly drifted apart. We were never mean to each other, and we always said hey when we met and shit, but we weren't tight anymore. I started running with the drug crowd, and he hung out with the jocks. I guess we both started to "fit in." I still can't hear the word *mulatto* without thinking about Paco Salmeron and wondering what he's doing now.

As for myself, I went on to bigger and better things. I didn't know it then, but very shortly my life was about to change.

3 5 C E N T S

In the summer of 1982, southern Miami Beach was a very different place than it is today. Before it was reduced to the detestable acronym SOBE, it was simply called South Beach. The mere mention of the name brought to mind shirtless and sweating Cuban refugees drinking coladas on a street corner, or smoking crack in decrepit old buildings that blushed in modesty when they were lovingly referred to as "Art Deco." Those were the days of the Habana Hotel for ten dollars a night, where the rooms had chain-link fence on the windows instead of screens. The patrons didn't mind the mosquitoes, but they drew the line at pigeons. That tired old whore of a city is the South Beach I remember.

Does anyone remember El Loco? No, El Loco wasn't some trendy new underground club or a restaurant where all the waiters were in drag. El Loco was a man, a Cuban refugee to be exact. He was wanted for murdering a cop. In 1982, he was public enemy number one, and every night on the local news the anchors spoke of the manhunt that was under way to find him. El Loco was to be considered armed and extremely dangerous. He was easily identifiable by a tattoo on his forehead that read, of course, EL LOCO.

So one hot summer day, a small boy was trying to buy cigarettes at the bodega on 21st Street and Collins Avenue, but the owner refused to sell the smokes to him without ID. The kid started cursing, and he was about to storm away when a deep voice with a heavy Cuban accent spoke up behind him.

"Oye, puta, dale un paquete de Marlboro a este chico!"

The owner of the bodega reluctantly placed the cigarettes on the counter, and the kid snatched them up and put down the money. When he turned to leave, he came face-to-face with a lanky Cuban man in dirty jeans and a white wifebeater under-shirt. On the man's head was a red bandanna worn gang-style. The kid said gracias with a bad Spanish accent and started walking away, but the man called after him, "Oye, flaco, mira aqui!" Then he lifted the front of the bandanna to expose a jailhouse tattoo. The kid departed knowing his life was forever changed. He'd met his first outlaw, the great El Loco!

Of course the kid was me, and that was my South Beach in 1982. I had just turned thirteen and was living in midtown around 71st Street. At that time, when most of the kids my age were playing spin the bottle and truth or dare, I was slightly advanced sexually. My early fantasies had progressed from seeing Heather's panties in math class to starring in my very own child porn film. I remember one night watching a made-for-television movie about little kids being abducted and forced to star in pornographic movies, after which I rushed right to bed for a quick beat-off session with a sock. *If only I could locate a kidnapper/child pornographer*, I thought. I spent the next several days skulking around parks trying to look abandoned, but unfortunately without any results. I guess my neighborhood was too normal for that, or possibly not normal enough.

At about that time, two friends of mine got summer jobs at the Butterflake Bakery on 11th and Washington, then the heart of degenerate South Beach. They asked me to fill in one week when they were going to Disney World, and as luck would have it, they never came back to work. What I found was a little Disney World of my own.

On my very first day at work, a man with a striking resemblance to Jesus walked in the door completely naked. He just stood there staring at me.

"Can I help you, sir?"

He didn't answer, but his eyes said no. Later, when the police had carted him away, the old Cuban ladies who worked in the back told me that he used to be a professor of anthropology at the university in Cuba, but he had recently lost his mind. Apparently he had misplaced his clothing as well.

That was just the beginning. In the weeks that followed I watched a slow-moving train of human wreckage pass by the bakery window. Hustlers, pimps, perverts, junkies, crackheads, psychos, and occasionally someone looking for good fresh challah bread. I felt at home for the first time in my life. For once I wasn't the "bad" kid surrounded by little angels; I was a dirty little boy in a crowd of dirty people, just like me and even worse. When I took my lunch break, I would just go to the beach, sit on a bench, and watch the freak show go by. One full hour of heaven, one full hour where I didn't have to impress anyone or fit in. It felt poetic, if that's a feeling. Just sitting there watching, reading, laughing, and occasionally interacting. My first speaking roles were quite limited.

"Oye, flocco, dame un cigarillo?"

And my response, a humble "Si."

"Hey, man, can you spare sixty cents?"

To which my answer was always, "Sorry, man."

From these humble beginnings I rapidly progressed to more than just an extra. My first few major interactions were mostly buying weed. That seemed like a good way to break the ice, and it worked. In a couple of weeks, people knew me, and asked if I was all right when they passed by my bench.

"Hey flocco, you all right, you need anything?"

And my lines grew as well.

"Hola, Pepe, como esta?" and "Buenos días, Maria. Had a rough night?"

Even my Spanglish was improving. I didn't have to wait long for my starring role. It came after only three weeks, and it couldn't have happened at a better time. I was flat broke, and if I didn't get some money I was going to have to walk sixty blocks home in the ninety-degree heat. I was sitting at my usual bench on the beach, smoking cigarettes and drinking a Coke, when some extremely skinny Latino guy sat down next to me and asked me if I liked movies.

That was it. No romance, no pleasantries, just did I like movies. But I knew what he was really asking, and my heart started to race immediately. I was going to get the chance to have an orgasm in the company of another human being! It was that quick. Things just added up in my head, and I knew who he was and what he wanted. Don't ask me what he looked like or what he was wearing. I don't remember. Nor do I remember what set him apart from all the other people who sat next to me on that bench. I just knew. Not just him, but all the others after him, too. I knew them all, and I could pick them out of a crowd from a mile away. It was like some instinct that had been sleeping inside me was now wide awake, and it would never go back to sleep again. We went through what I would learn was the *ritual*.

"Do you like movies?"

"Yeah, I guess so."

"Do you want to come over to my house and watch some movies?"

"I don't know. Where do you live?"

"Right down the street, at the Habana Hotel."

"Okay."

And I was on my way. When we got to his house, more ritual:

"Oops, that's the wrong movie!"

"No, that's okay, leave it."

"Oh, do you like porn?"

"I don't know. I haven't seen that much."

"Are you comfortable?"

"Yeah."

"Those jeans look too tight."

"Yeah, they are kind of tight."

"So why don't you take them off?"

"Okay."

And that was how it went. *Okay* became my mantra. Okay to this, okay to that. Okay to everything. It's easy once you get the hang of it. You just pretty much say okay and then deal with the situation as it comes. I remember the only thing I was worried about was sitting naked on his filthy fucking couch. The couch and the bed were the scariest parts. I mean, weren't all gay men supposed to be clean and tasteful?

So he gave me my first consensual blow job while I watched the movie, and while it wasn't the girl I had been hoping for, it wasn't that bad either. I came in like thirty seconds and got up to go, but he wasn't having any of it.

"Oye, where do jew think jew are going?" he asked.

"I have to get back to work."

"Oh, please don't go yet, papi, por favor!"

"Okay."

We moved to the bedroom, where he got naked, too. The two of us together must have weighed like ninety pounds. He asked me to lie on the bed and then he climbed on top of me and started sucking my dick again and rubbing his cock between my calves. This made me slightly uncomfortable, but it was nothing compared to the sock. I don't even know where he got it. One minute he was giving me head, and the next time I looked down my dick was all covered up in this dirty black dress sock.

I was a little shocked. I mean, I had beat off into a sock before to avoid the messy cleanup, but I had never seen the sock as a sexual toy. This guy was all about it. He was kissing the sock and then sucking my dick through the sock, which by the way, I could barely feel. Then he took the sock off and started tying up my dick and balls. I wanted him to stop, but I was too afraid to say anything. He kept tying and retying the sock, tighter and tighter, until it started to hurt. He straddled my waist and put my hand on his dick and then took the end of the sock into his mouth and started jerking me off by pulling on the sock with his mouth. I could barely reach his dick, but I just tried my hardest to jerk him off. I figured that the sooner he came, the sooner I could leave. He had this totally frantic look on his face. I was a little scared and my balls were hurting but I couldn't seem to say anything. The words just wouldn't come. Then I felt his cum on my stomach and it was over. After he climbed off of me, I instinctively knew to ask for money.

"Do you think I can borrow some bus fare?"

"Okay," he said.

And that's how I earned my first thirty-five cents hustling. I could tell from the way he responded to the money question so quickly that I could get more the next time. I mean, shit; I didn't even have any pubic hair back then. That should've been worth at least ten bucks! When I first took off my jeans he stared at me forever saying things like, "Aye, Dio gracias" and "Que lindo!"

After I left his apartment, though, the guilt flooded in on me. I was a faggot! I was dirty! I was going to hell for sure! I didn't see how I could take back what I had just done. Not his...in my... and my...in his...

Oh, God, forgive me! Dio, por favor!

But it felt good!

Shut up, you faggot, you filthy little prick!

What confusion. What mixed feelings. What a mess. I was pretty worried for a while, until I got off work and caught the bus back uptown. That made it all a little better. After all, at least I wasn't walking.

When I got home, I smoked a joint and planned my next move. As soon as I started to think about doing it again, the guilt went away and all I was left with was the heat, the desire, and the fucking anonymity of it all. So fucking hot! My second time was that very same night, less than ten hours after my first. I

3 5 C E N T S

found myself sitting alone at a bus stop that night and the world and everything in it seemed like a whole new place.

T H E   L I B R A R Y

It wasn't that I liked reading; it was more like I just hated school. I would do anything to get out of school. Mostly I just waited for my mom to go to work, and then I would head over to the beach. I used to stop at the supermarket on the way over and spend my lunch money on two loaves of day-old bread for ninety-nine cents. Then I would just go to the beach and feed the pigeons and sometimes the seagulls too, although I have to admit I preferred the pigeons. I've always liked pigeons; they are the scum of the sky. "Flying rats" is what most people call them. So I spent most mornings feeding the pink-eyed flying rats down by the beach. Later, I would just stare at the ocean and daydream about my mother and her new boyfriend running away to Europe and abandoning me. I can't even count how many peaceful days I spent down on the beach just daydreaming and feeding the pigeons.

One day I was feeding the pigeons at my usual spot on the beach at 75th Street, when I noticed this three-wheeled motorcycle coming at me pretty fast. By the time I noticed it was a cop, it was almost too late. I got up and ran as fast as I could toward the parking lot of the library. There was a three-foot wall surrounding the parking lot. I jumped over it and ran as fast as I could toward the library. The cop had to go around the wall, so I gained a little distance on him. I ran right past the library and straight across Collins Avenue without even stopping to look both ways. There was an apartment complex across the street that had a courtyard that ran right through the middle and opened onto the alley out back. I was about ten steps into the courtyard when I saw the blue lights in the alley and I knew I wasn't going to make it.

I turned around and ran right back out of the building and across Collins Avenue, again without even looking. I ran around to the back of the library and stopped dead in my tracks. There was nowhere to run to. I could hear his siren coming back up 75th and all the condemned hotels where I could hide out were on the other side. South of the library there were some light woods but I would have to make it all the way across the parking lot again and that was impossible. From the sound of his siren I guessed he'd be coming around the corner any second. I flung open the library door and ran inside, almost knocking down an elderly woman with a walker.

"Excuse me, young man!"

Shit! I was busted. I turned around and saw an attractive young woman standing behind the counter.

"Yes," I said tentatively.

"We appreciate your enthusiasm for reading, but please don't run in here."

I just stood there panting and waiting for the rest of her speech. Waiting for that cop to storm in and bust me, waiting for her to tell me to leave.

"Well," she said.

"Well, what?" I asked.

"Well, run along. Wait, I mean walk along," she said, chuckling.

And that was that. That stupid cop never found me, and the librarians never threw me out either. I spent the day in peace just wandering around the library, and I loved it. I felt safe in there, safe and protected. That first day I checked it out pretty good. The couches were comfortable, the bathrooms were clean, and there were thousands of things to look at. I wasn't all that into reading, but they had a lot of books with pictures and magazines too. After a while I picked out some *National Geographic* magazines and went to the couch to look at the pictures. I really enjoyed it; it was like daydreaming at the beach, only now with pictures too. I imagined I was on an Arctic exploration or on safari in Africa.

"Excuse me, young man."

Someone was poking me in the shoulder. I looked up and knew right off I was in trouble again. It was that same pretty lady from the front desk.

"Yes?"

"You've been asleep for hours, honey, and we thought someone might be worried about you."

"Oh, thanks. What time is it?"

"It's three thirty, dear."

"Wow, I have to go. Sorry about falling asleep on your couch."

"It's all right, honey. It happens all the time."

I put the magazines back and went out the front door this time just in case that cop was the patient type. On my way home I kept hearing that pretty librarian's voice over and over in my head. She called me "honey" and "dear." She was probably the nicest adult I had met since my third-grade teacher, Mrs. Miller. I was in love and I couldn't wait to go back to the library the next day. I forgot all about my flying rats. As soon as my mom left the house the next morning, I headed straight for the library.

That day went even better than the first. No cops and no questions asked. After that, I went every weekday. I don't know if the librarians thought I was some home-school kid or on vacation with my parents or what, but they never asked any questions.

And so that library became my first *place*. My own place, where I could be alone and not have to deal with my friends, the cops, the schools, teachers, and worst of all, my family. It was the one place where I could establish some sort of identity on my own, and that's exactly what I did. I wasn't even really reading at first, I was just pretending to read. I would collect a bunch of books on the same subject, like World War II or nuclear physics; the more complicated the better. I especially liked books with technical diagrams and complex theorems. Then I would find a table in the back and open all the books to pages I thought looked "intelligent." And I would just sit there and pretend to read and study, the whole time observing my surroundings, watching the people there, and more importantly, watching to see if they were watching me.

Mostly people just ignored me, but every once in a while I'd see someone peer over my shoulder and shake their heads. Then they'd walk away with one of those impressed looks like they just saw Bobby Fisher or some other child prodigy. I knew I was a fraud and all, but it felt so good anyway, having anonymous people thinking I was smart and shit. Like the hustling, I guess. That first time on the bench, I didn't think or wonder if I was wanted, I knew it. He wanted me so bad it was killing him. When I agreed to come back to his place, I think he nearly fainted. That felt good, and so did the way people treated me like I was smart at the library.

Pretty soon the librarians were coming over regularly to

check on me and see what I was studying. I suspect some of them knew what I was up to and that I wasn't really studying at all, but librarians are cool, so none of them let on. They started calling me pet names like "bookworm" or "boy genius," and I was eating it up. I had a whole new separate identity there. At home I was the fuck-up, in school I was the underachiever, with my friends I was the clown. But at the library, I was that cute little smart kid who reads all the time. Eventually I even did start reading the books and educating myself in some haphazard fashion, but that's another story.

So the first good thing about the library was the escape it offered me, the chance to be someone else. The second good thing I discovered unexpectedly. I was wandering through the aisles of books one day when I came across an unattended lady's handbag with the change purse visible right at the top. It was just sitting there, abandoned on the floor. I don't know what possessed me, as I was never really a thief, but I just reached down and picked the change purse out and kept walking. My heart was beating a million times a second as I headed straight for the bathroom. I went immediately to a vacant stall where I sat down and opened the change purse. Holy shit if there weren't four twenties sitting folded up right on top. Jackpot!

So I stuffed the four twenties into my pocket plus about twelve dollars in assorted small bills and a dollar or so in change, and I was about to try to flush the change purse when I got all guilty. I mean I liked the library, and I didn't want to stop going there, but if I stole this money then I wouldn't be able to show my face around there anymore. I put the money back in the change purse and walked back to the place where I found the handbag. I was about to drop the change purse back in when I just couldn't resist anymore. I took one twenty out, then dropped it back into the handbag, and returned to my fake reading.

That night I scored some weed and some cigarettes and things were good. The next day I went back to the library and I was slightly apprehensive as I got near the door, but it was just me being paranoid. Nobody was any wiser. All the librarians treated me the same as any other day. There was no WANTED poster with my picture on it. And what's more, that very same lady's handbag was sitting on a chair not forty feet away from my regular table. It was a dream come true. I guessed that the owner of the bag hadn't even noticed that any money was missing. Pretty soon, it was my regular routine. Just like walking the dog, every morning I went to the library, only now I wasn't just watching people watching me, but also keeping an eye out for stray lady's handbags. And there was no end to them. I guess most people just feel safe at the library.

I set up some ground rules right from the start. Rule number one: don't get greedy! I never took more than a twenty, and if they had less than twenty then I wouldn't take anything. Rule number two: don't ruin a good thing by blabbing about it. I'm proud to say that, until this very moment, I have never broken rule number two.

And so that was how I found myself in front of the library the evening after my first trick. I was feeling guilty about that afternoon, but still horny for more. Since the thirty-five cents was already spent, I thought I'd head over to the library and see if I could score some more cash before closing. The only problem was that I ran into a friend on the way over, and he slowed me down so much that when I got to the library, they had already closed for the night. I was pretty bummed and pretty stoned, so I just sat out in front of the library at the bus stop sort of pulling myself together. After all, it had been a long day, and I had a lot to think about. So there I was, wondering if the friend I had run into could tell if I was gay or not. Had I changed? Was there some telltale sign about me now? He was acting a little strange, wasn't he?

"Hey, you wanna make some money?"

I hadn't even noticed that the car had pulled up to the curb. I was a little shocked. It had grown dark while I was sitting there thinking and now there was some fat Latin guy in a beat-up, silver Chevy Chevette with the passenger window rolled down, asking me something about money. My first thought, given that I was sitting right in front of the library, was that he was the husband of some old lady whose purse I had fleeced.

"What?"

"Do you wanna make some money?"

"For what?"

"For what," he said. "I suck your dick is for what!"

"Okay."

What else? Then, as I was walking toward the car, I remembered the thirty-five cents of that afternoon.

"Wait a minute, how much money?"

"Ten bucks."

Fuck, yeah, I was thinking, *now that's more like it!* But all I said was, "Okay" and got into the car...

He had his hands on me the second I got in. Hand on my knee like some junior high school chum or something. But then he kind of had a problem with his coordination and his hand ended up in my crotch. He tried to pretend it was an accident until he noticed I was hard.

"Wow, you got a big pinga, my friend!" His hand kept moving, stroking me over my jeans, then under my jeans but above my underwear, then under the underwear. And isn't that where it's all about anyway — under the underwear? The difference is how they get there and how long it takes; for me, the longer the better. Call me a romantic, I guess. So he took his time, but he was getting pretty damn excited and his driving was becoming suspect at best.

"Do you wanna go to the park with me?" he asked.

"Okay."

We went to a park close by and got out of the car. He led me over to a huge banyan tree and pushed me back in between two of its enormous roots.

He kneeled before me and undid the button on my jeans and then zipped the zipper down. Then he just put his face up against my underwear and started sobbing. I found this a little weird, but the whole thing was weird to me anyway. I mean, it wasn't like I was an old hand at this. So I just stood there quietly while he kneeled in front of me sobbing into my drawers for what seemed like hours, and all I was thinking was how I'd like to tell him that I was just reading about banyan trees at the library the other day.

And right while I was thinking that, some yuppie couple in his and her Fila sweatsuits went jogging though the park about thirty feet from us.

"Hey man, there are too many people here. I'm getting a little nervous," I said. I just wanted to stop him from crying.

"I know a safer place where we can be alone. Do you want to check it out?"

"Okay."

Ten minutes later we were in a maintenance closet next to some apartment building where a few kids from my school lived. There were fucking brooms and old mops and shit that stunk everywhere, and I couldn't see a fucking thing, but I liked it in a way, and at least he'd stopped crying.

He started all over again. Rubbing my dick through my jeans, and then undoing my fly, but fuck if he didn't get right back to rubbing his face against my underwear and bawling again. I was getting a little freaked out by all this.

The last time I saw my real dad, he cried on my stomach for an hour. I had never even seen him cry before, but the day after we left him he came over to my grandma's house and nobody was home but me and her. Dad just sort of collapsed on the steps, but when he saw me at the top of the stairs he started crawling up them to me. I guess he was drunk, but I didn't know that back then, I was only four. I was terrified! What in the hell was he doing? He looked so beaten. He never made it to the top of the stairs, not even to my shoulder. The best he could manage was three steps down from me with his head on my stomach and his arms around my waist and then came the bawling. I've still never seen anyone bawl like that. He just cried and cried until my T-shirt and my shorts were soaking wet and my legs started to itch like I had peed myself. I didn't know what to do, so I just stood there and said "Okay."

"Are you still my boy?"

"Okay."

"You wanna stay with me, right?"

"Okay."

And I had never been more fascinated or detached in my life. That was just how I was feeling with this obese man crying on my underwear in the broom closet; detached, yet fascinated. I was thinking of my dad and of Paco, and it didn't take me long to start getting depressed. But just when I thought I had to stop this before I ended up bawling too, he came to his senses and suddenly stopped crying.

In an instant he had my dick out and it disappeared just as quickly down his throat. I still couldn't see anything, which probably helped, but it felt so good. I mean, he had my dick and he was not planning on giving it back. It's like he was trying to swallow it or something. And no matter what, no matter how awful it was or how guilty I felt, I liked it. I just couldn't help but smile. It was like I found my calling, my place in life and my method of dealing all at once.

It's hard to explain the feelings I went through back then. It wasn't just sexual; it was the way these men wanted me and the power and importance that they made me feel. It was something I had never felt before. Like I was truly desirable. Maybe I was a piece-of-shit perverted and dirty little boy, but they wanted me anyway, and they were willing to pay ten bucks to get me.

Ain't that close to love?

So slurp, slurp, choke, swallow, and that was that. He handed me a ten-dollar bill and asked me if I wanted to do that again sometime.

"But don't get me wrong," he added. "I ain't no faggot."

"Okay," I said. "I'm out in front of the library most nights at the bus stop where you found me."

And so I was.

Now ain't that close to love?

P E D R O
& E R I C

After that I spent every day at the library until closing and then every night at the bus stop in front of the library. The crying guy came back a few times and then he disappeared, only to be replaced by another. You know, the butcher, the baker, the candlestick maker. It was all pretty routine, and sometimes it even got boring.

"Roll up your sleeve and make a muscle!"

"Oh, that's good, just keep that up."

"Rub your ass on my face, man!"

"Yeah, that's great!"

Sometimes I didn't even have to get undressed. One guy just wanted my drawers. He'd actually fucking pay me five bucks for them. The first time he pulled up and asked me if he could buy my underwear for five dollars, I thought he was crazy. Turns out I was right, he was completely fucking nuts, but that didn't make him poor, right? I gave him my drawers, and he gave me five dollars. I saw him at least twice a month for a year or so. Another guy just wanted me to whack off in his front seat while he watched, and I figured that I was doing it all day anyway, so why not get paid for it? Then there was this one freak who didn't even want to watch. He would pull up in his expensive and immaculately clean white Mercedes and just roll down that power window and hand me a Ziploc bag. I would take the bag behind the library into the bushes and whack off into it, seal it up, and bring it back. Then he would snatch up that bag and hand me a crisp new ten-dollar bill, and I wouldn't see him again for a month. We never even spoke. The first time was the trickiest—trying to figure out what he wanted and all.

Most of them were creepy but harmless, so I found the whole scene pretty cool. But when I said it got boring, that was a lie. I do that sometimes. It was a lot of things, but never boring. Of course there were standouts. The ones who wanted me to do something totally bizarre, or the ones who were just different from all the rest. Pedro was one of those, different from the rest; a real standout.

The first time I saw him he drove by in a brand-spanking-new Chevy Berlinetta. There were two guys in the car, one dark-haired and Latin and the other blond with blue eyes. I noticed them slowing down and staring right away, but wasn't sure about them as they were in their early-to-midtwenties.

Up until then the youngest person that had ever picked me up was a doctor in his late fifties. But they made the turn. Making the turn right after the bus stop was pretty much a sure sign that they'd be back around the corner in a minute. And they were, but now only the dark-haired Latin guy was in the car. He slowed down and pulled up to the curb in front of me with the power window sliding down slowly. And that killed me every time. I loved watching those power windows slide down silently. I knew what was coming next.

"Need a ride?"

"Yeah, thanks."

"Where are you going?"

"Nowhere."

"Do you want to party?"

"Okay."

"What's your name?"

"Matty."

I told the truth, because I do that sometimes too and because I didn't even know you could use an alias back then.

"Oh, in Spanish it's Mateo. Well, don't worry, Mateo. We're just gonna party a little bit. Everything is gonna be cool. Do you want to get some beer?"

"Okay."

"Do you want to get high?"

"Okay."

"Do you mind if we go back and pickup my friend Eric?"

"Okay. Wait a minute, what did you just say?"

"Is it okay if we go back and get my friend Eric?"

And then I was thinking, *Oh shit, then there'll be two of them and only one of me, and that's not a good thing. What if they get rough, what if they try to force me into something?*

I think Pedro could sense my apprehension.

"It's okay. We're not gonna do anything you don't want to do."

I wasn't really listening to him. I was just looking into his eyes, and I didn't see anything that looked violent so I said,

"Okay."

We went back around the corner and picked up Eric who was waiting at my bus stop now, and then they drove me to some oceanfront apartment in midtown. Up in the apartment we smoked some more pot, drank some more beer, and just basically relaxed and had a good time for a couple of hours. It was pretty cool, and I even started to forget why they had picked me up. For a while there, we were just three friends hanging out, getting high and talking. They both seemed really interested in me and what I was saying, and I liked them too. Pedro was from Argentina but lived in Miami Beach now; Eric was from Berlin and was just visiting Pedro for a couple of weeks. I was having a good time, just relaxing and feeling good and then...

We got back to business. Eric said he had to go to the bathroom and disappeared for a while. When he was gone, Pedro asked if I wanted a massage.

"Okay."

"Take off your clothes, Mateo."

"Okay."

And the next thing I knew I was on the floor on my stomach naked, and he was rubbing my back. He was also naked. After a while he rolled me over.

"Aye Madonna!"

"What?"

"Nada. How old are you, Mateo?"

"Thirteen."

"Aye, que lindo. You have no hair!"

My pride got a little hurt. "Sorry" was all I could say.

"Oh, Mateo, don't be sorry, I like you like this, without any hair. It's sexy. Don't worry. You'll get hair down there soon enough."

He wasn't lying about that either. Then we went through the run-of-the-mill stuff. He was sucking my dick, licking my balls, et cetera, and then out of nowhere, BAM!

He kissed me right on the mouth! I was totally freaked out by that too. I mean, none of the older dudes had tried that before. But like I said, this guy was different and definitely a little more intense than most of the older guys. He was cool and young, and it was his dime, so I just went along with it. And even though it was a bit gross at first, it wasn't all that bad, and I was getting the hang of it and then...BAM!

Just like that he's pushing my head down into his crotch! Nobody ever did that before either. In fact I wasn't so sure I liked young guys all that much after all. But, you know, I'll try anything once, right? And it wasn't so bad. Can't say I loved it, but I didn't hate it as much as I thought either. Kinda like spinach, I guess.

I was trying hard to do it right. God knows I had seen it done enough by then. I knew what felt good and what I liked, and so that's what I did. But I couldn't help thinking, *Shit, man, you're sucking a dick!* Was that going to change me somehow? Would I still like girls, or was I going start acting like a fairy now? Every once in a while I would take a step back and look at myself from outside, and I was appalled.

Holy shit, try not to act *so well, you faggot!* It was pretty scary to see myself acting so well and all.

Then suddenly I was back on my stomach with a mouthful of carpet. Pedro was pretty strong; he was strong and fast and on my back, pinning me down. I was munching carpet, only that wasn't really what I had in mind when I thought about carpet munching. So maybe at that point I was starting to panic a little. Just a little though. Did I mention the size of him? Pedro had a lot of things going for him, I guess. I could feel his pretty-fucking-gigantic cock rubbing between my asscheeks, and then I really started to panic. I mean I couldn't fucking move at all. He was holding my wrists and pinning my legs under him, and I was just completely fucking helpless.

Flashback to when I'm six. Have I told you this one before? We'd been away from my dad for about two years, and we were living in the Shady Terrace apartment complex, which was just filled to the brim with perverts and pedophiles. But like I said, for the most part what they did to me was quick and painless, and although I didn't understand what they were doing, I knew if I went along with them and just shut up, it would be over pretty quick.

So that's why I went that night with the freaky neighbor guy when he asked me up to his apartment. I knew he probably wanted to see me naked or make me touch him or something like that. So I just went along, silently saying okay. When we got up there he started taking off my clothes immediately. He was twenty-seven or -eight and so much bigger than me that I didn't resist at all. I figured he just wanted to look at me naked and touch himself like all the rest.

That's not exactly what he had in mind, though. Once I was naked he undressed too—sort of. He didn't take off his shirt or shoes; he just pulled his pants down to his knees. Then he grabbed me really fucking hard and threw me facedown on this fucking smelly old sofa and told me to shut the fuck up or he would kill me. I felt him climb up on my back and start rubbing against me. And he kept that up for like ten minutes, just rubbing his dick between my asscheeks, and then he stopped and started to climb off me. I was so fucking relieved, and I made a mental note to stay way the fuck out of his path next time.

But he didn't let me up. Instead he started spitting on my ass! I was freaked out by that.

"What the fuck are you doing?" I screamed.

In reply, he slammed his fist into the back of my head, and that hurt like shit. I felt real dizzy and sick, like I was going to puke, and I couldn't remember where I was and then I felt this fucking searing pain in my ass and then...

I don't know if I fainted or he stopped or what. All I remember was that a John Denver song was playing in the background. *Take Me Home, Country Roads.*

At first it was real faint and I could barely make out the words, but then it got louder and louder. I realized it was coming from the bedroom and I hadn't remembered it playing when we had gotten there. I couldn't feel him on top of me anymore either. So I slowly turned around and looked at the room. Mack Truck bulldogs, Budweiser ashtrays, bowling and Little League trophies, but no fucked-up neighbor guy. I never asked him his name, but I'm pretty sure it was Alan. Anyway, he wasn't there. I can still remember the rank smell of his dried spit all over me. To this day when I smell spit on the sidewalk I still think of that fucker.

Almost Heaven...

The music was blaring out of the bedroom, and I could see the light under the door and his shadow moving around in there. So I got up and grabbed my clothes and ran out into the hallway and got dressed in the dark at the top of the stairs. Then I ran home and went to bed. I never told anyone. I know how to keep a secret. My ass hurt and my shit was red for a couple of days, and then life went on. I never forgot about it, but I never thought about it either. Until...

There was Pedro on top of me, rubbing his cock harder and harder against my ass. And it all came back: the neighbor guy, the John Denver song, everything. I was more than a little scared then. I opened my eyes and saw Eric in the doorway staring at us with his dick in his hand, leering. It's like everything was cool and then suddenly I was in some horrible carnival sideshow nightmare.

And the strange thing was that, despite thinking I was about to get raped and being scared out of my mind, I couldn't utter a single word of protest. Not a fucking peep.

Country roads...

I was in a panic and about to fucking scream. The walls were really closing in on me. And just then, SPLAT!

I felt his hot cum landing all over my ass and on my back. And I have to say that it was pretty sexy too. I mean I was just about to freak the fuck out, and all of a sudden I was a little turned on again. And then it was Eric's turn and then both and then...and then...I was sucking one dick, then another, then both. I was losing count and they weren't very cool anymore. They were more like fucking wild beasts in a frenzy, and I started to lose that "cool" desired feeling and it was getting replaced with this nasty, dirty, shit-eating, trash-can feeling, and then they both shot their loads again and it was over. Just like that. And all I wanted to know was, "What about me?"

"Oh, I almost forgot," Pedro answered. "Eric, give him some money."

That wasn't what I meant! But Eric came over all guilty-looking, like a kid who got caught in the cookie jar, and he handed me a ten-dollar bill.

"Is that enough?" he asked me in his thick German accent.

"Sure, I guess so."

I heard Pedro yell from the bathroom, as I was leaving: "Eric, lock the door after he's gone, por favor!"

So what were you expecting when I said he was special? Did you think we were gonna fall in love?

MATTY LEE

Take me home...

J O H N

Am I gay? That was the question I asked myself when I woke up each day. Was I gay? It was kind of hard to deny it when I was waking up next to some old bald guy with my dried cum still stuck on his chin. Then why did I still want to be with girls so badly? How come the gay pornos didn't turn me on? A lot of guys wanted me to watch pornos with them, but I couldn't get hard watching two guys. They would try to get me into it for a while, then invariably give up with a sigh and a disgusted look and pull out the old dusty straight porn they kept around for just such an occasion. This always made me smile. I was too timid to ask for it right off, so I would just let them put in whatever movie they liked, but the whole time I would be praying to myself, *Please let this be a straight movie!*

Of course the first choice was always gay porn, and my heart would sink. But if they were the least bit perceptive and unselfish, then in a few minutes they'd get that frustrated look and throw in a straight movie.

And I loved that; watching naked women in the company of an adult just felt so dirty. Everyone knew you were supposed to hide that kind of stuff from adults, and weren't they supposed to hide it from you too? It's funny how much we hide from each other. I don't agree with hippies and talk-show hosts who go on about free love and openness. Part of the allure is the hiding, the secrets. Wouldn't you be let down if you knew there was a whole group of people doing exactly that secret and terrible thing that you thought only you did? I had this girlfriend once who liked to have her dirty panties stuffed into her mouth just before she came. I never did have the heart to tell her that she was like the third girl who'd been into that exact same thing. As far as she knew, it was our dirty little secret and that's what made it so hot.

One of my favorite dirty little acts was watching straight porno movies while a guy blew me. First off, I was too young to have access to that kind of movie by myself. Second, I didn't have to touch myself. I didn't have to do anything for that matter except concentrate, and I was good at that. I would come this way maybe three times in a night. The guys didn't seem to mind either. They just did their business like I wasn't there. I mean, part of me was there, the important part, but they were never much interested in what was going on above the waist. They never stopped, even after I came. The train just kept rolling until I came again, and again. Being thirteen, that wasn't too difficult.

So I would find myself at the bus stop hoping that Bill would come by because he had that great video with the two girls doing one guy. Or maybe John, 'cause he didn't make any noises or ask any questions. That John really knew how to treat a guy.

John would take me straight home, pop in a movie, and proceed to suck my dick for like two hours straight. He never said a word. Never asked if I liked it, and never asked me to touch him. He never even took off his clothes. We had a routine, and you know how I love routine.

We would make some small talk on the way over to his house about the weather, the news, sports, etc. Then we would go up the elevator in silence. The talking was over. When he opened the front door to his place, I would immediately get undressed and go sit on the couch in the TV room, and he would go put in the movie and unzip his fly. Then he would go to work, and I would concentrate. I caught him every once in a while reaching down shyly and touching himself, but only for a second. As a rule, he needed both hands for me. That was another good thing about John. The attention he paid to small details. Cupping my balls with both hands, tongue in my ass, taking his time, never rushing it. I used to feel guilty, and one time I even tried to touch him too, but he wasn't having any of it. When I reached for his dick, he got angry for the first time ever.

"I'm not paying you for that," he snapped.

Well, what I could I say? I just went back to concentrating. Man, did that John know how to suck a dick! Later, I would get dressed in silence and we would descend to the parking garage, only speaking after we had left his building. Then he would ask me about school a lot on the way back to my bus stop. John was extremely interested in my education. When I told him school sucked, he would get annoyed with me and explain that I would never be free to make my own choices and live a nice life unless I educated myself. He asked me once why I always sat out in front of the library. I answered that it was as good a place as any. He asked if I'd ever been inside and fearing I would give away my secrets I answered in the negative.

"Well, do you like to read?" he asked.

"I guess so."

"If I told you the names of some books, would you read them?"

"Okay."

And that's how I started reading. The classics first. *Treasure Island, The Adventures of Huckleberry Finn, The Call of the Wild, Lord of the Flies, The Time Machine,* and stuff like that. We stopped talking about the weather and sports and started talking about books. Not at his apartment of course, but in the car on the way over and back. We had a pretty tight schedule, John and I: every Tuesday night from eight o'clock to eleven thirty.

It was strange how much I knew about him and how little at the same time. I had never even seen his entire apartment. All I knew was the TV room. When we entered his apartment, the lights were always off in his living room and kitchen. In fact, all the lights were out except for a small table lamp next to the couch in the TV room. One time I asked him if I could use his bathroom, and he became pretty agitated. He said okay, but from now on he would expect me to use the bathroom before he picked me up. He said he always picked me up at eight and he didn't think it was too much to ask for me to take care of my business before then. After all, he was paying me. But only ten dollars for more than three hours I reminded him. And that's how I bumped up my price to twenty. He agreed to pay me twenty, and I agreed to use the bathroom on my own time.

With negotiations completed, he told me to wait on the couch for a minute and then I could use the bathroom this one time only. He went away for a few minutes and then came back and told me to follow him. We walked down this hallway I hadn't even seen before in the dark. There were three doors which I assumed were bedrooms but all the doors were closed. It was very dark. At the end of the hall, John opened a door and motioned for me to go into what I assumed was the bathroom.

And it was; what were you expecting, a bucket in the closet? John wasn't a freak, he just loved sucking dick. So I walked into the bathroom, but it was so dark I couldn't see. I only knew it was the bathroom because it had that bathroom smell and a fuzzy rug. I felt around on the wall and found the light switch and for an instant I was blinded by light, but then John quickly reached in and turned the light back off. Once again I was in total darkness, worse due to the temporary light. I told him I couldn't see anything, and if he didn't want me to piss all over his floor he had to turn on the light. He told me to wait and then disappeared for a minute again. When he returned, he stepped into the bathroom and plugged a small nightlight into a socket over the mirror. Then I could see, but just barely. I started pissing with John hovering over me, and I honestly couldn't tell what all the fuss was about. It looked like a normal bathroom to me, only darker. But I was beginning to get curious about John and what he was trying to hide.

The rest of that night went like normal; but from then on whenever John picked me up, I would sniff around a lot more. I asked him questions about himself, which he hated and rarely answered. I started looking over my shoulder in the car to see if there was anything suspicious on the back seats. I even started closing my eyes in the elevator so my eyes would be adjusted better to the darkness in his apartment. This actually worked too. I learned it from I book I read in the library called *The Spook Who Sat by the Door*. It's about these black militants who are planning a revolution. When they were gonna do some operation at night, they would hold the preoperational meetings in the dark so their eyes would be better adjusted when they got outside. It's like the ghetto version of night-vision goggles.

John was pretty much in his own world as we rode up in the elevator, so I would close my eyes tight and then as we walked down the well-lit corridor to his apartment I would squint my eyes into little slits. Just open enough to see where I was walking. I even tried keeping one eye closed in the corridor and then switching eyes as we entered the apartment. This worked well, and I began to notice little things I had previously missed. For one, I noticed a few odd things about the living room, previously the "dark" room I just whisked through on my way to the TV room and my couch, and my movie, and my bliss.

The first thing I noticed was that there were picture frames on the shelves and the end tables in the living room, only they were all lying down on the faces of whoever was displayed inside them. Another thing was the amount of knickknacks and stuff. By comparison, the TV room was pretty sparse. And it wasn't just the amount of stuff, it was the stuff itself. Whenever I caught a glimpse of something new, I would make a mental note of it and on the next visit I would block everything out except that object, another technique I learned from a book. Over the course of six months, I came to learn a little bit more about John, and it was pretty much his own fault for getting me started reading.

What did I discover? John was a fag! His furniture, his little knickknacks, his clever floral arrangements on the dining-room table, his never-ending tidiness, not to mention him sucking my dick like a vacuum cleaner for three and a half hours once a week. He was everything a fag was supposed to be, and I had him all figured out. In fact, I had him so pegged, I got bored and gave up my investigation. The funny thing was he didn't act like a fag. I mean except for the cock-sucking part. By that time we were talking about books a lot in the car, and he just didn't seem so "gay." He talked and walked like a normal person. He didn't swish his hips or hold his wrist at any particular angle. But what about all that girly stuff in his apartment? That was perplexing, but I just figured that John was a raging fag who wasn't *out* yet in public. At work and stuff he had to keep up his *straight* image, and even with me, he was embarrassed to let me see the feminine side of his house. Most likely the bathroom was all pink. Pink towels, pink floor mat, pink toilet paper, even a matching pink toilet seat and tank cover set. I guess I pretty much had John figured out. My first *closet case*. Actually, a lot of the guys who picked me up were closet cases, but I hadn't been to most of their homes. Did they all have girly-looking apartments? Who could tell? I lost interest.

I got back to business, the business of John sucking my dick. After all, he was my favorite one at that time. If there is one thing I learned from John, besides reading, it was to enjoy the moment. Nothing lasts, and "Nothing Gold Can Stay." Yeah, he had me reading poetry too. Whoever you're with and whatever you're doing, if it's good, then shut the fuck up and enjoy it. That's what Robert Frost meant—to me anyway. John and I had a good thing, and I learned not to question it. I just relaxed and had a good time. I was sincerely starting to like him and looked forward to our book discussions on the way to and from his apartment. I never got high or drank with him, I didn't need to. He got high on my dick, and I got high on girls in high heels inserting three inches of hot pink–painted fingernail into each other. In short, we were a happy couple every Tuesday from eight to eleven thirty.

One night, on the way back to the library, John said my reading and comprehension were improving as well as my ability to handle mature subject matter. "Next week I'm going to give you a more mature novel, no more kid stuff."

"Wow, thanks, John."

Although, at the time I was afraid he was gonna turn me onto some adult pornographic type of books. I liked the compliment, but the idea of reading porn just didn't do it for me. I mean watching it was one thing, but reading seemed like it would get a little repetitive. I didn't see the point. The phrase "mature novel" had me frightened. Did he expect me to sit there and read about some girl eating some other girl out while he blew me? I feared the worse. My good thing had come to an end.

I was a little bummed out and apprehensive as I got out of the car that night at the library. But twenty-dollars worth of sensemelia would go a long way toward cheering me up, so I scored some weed and went back to the bus stop.

I was pretty high when she pulled up and asked if I needed a ride.

That's right, she! And that was truly unexpected. I had no idea what to do or say.

"Uhm, excuse me?"

"DO...YOU...NEED...A...RIDE?" she asked, sounding out every syllable as if I was retarded or hard of hearing.

"Uh, okay."

That was so out of this world strange that I was paralyzed. But she played the same games as all the others. Once I got in the car, she asked me a lot of the same questions they all asked. Questions designed to steer a conversation toward somewhere we both wanted to go, while at the same time appearing to be just innocent questions. Did I mention she was hot? Well, she wasn't. She was pudgy and okay, I guess, but no beauty contest winner. Still, I was shaking all over. This was the moment I'd dreamed about my whole life! A girl wanted to sleep with me! A girl! A girl! I couldn't fucking believe it. I'd seen a lot of weird shit in the past nine months at the bus stop, but never a girl. I mean that just didn't happen. Or did it?

Well, there she was, and there I was in her car. Things were looking very good indeed at that moment. In the first two minutes we were driving, I fell in love. She was in her late thirties or early forties. I wondered if she had a boyfriend; obviously not. Did she live alone? I was about to find out! I imagined she was lonely and divorced and living alone in a nice apartment, like John's, only with the lights on. I moved in with her. I became her lover, her confidant, and her best friend. She became my teacher, my mother, and my devoted wife. This was all in the first fifteen minutes I was in her car. She just kept driving, and I just kept dreaming. I wasn't paying attention to where we were going; I was just savoring every minute of being with her. She had become sort of quiet, pondering. Then I knew she was about to spring the question on me.

"Would you like to come home with me? Would you like to be my son?"

That was what she was going to ask. I could tell it was on the tip of her tongue. But she had other plans.

"Get out!"

While I was daydreaming she had pulled the car over and kept repeating those words over and over again.

"Get out, get out, GET OUT!"

I was in shock; paralyzed by the impact of returning to reality.

"What?"

"Get out. I'm sorry, but I can't do this. It's just not right."

And so I mumbled the weakest and saddest okay that had ever passed though my lips. I got out. Then she sped away, almost... She stopped, threw the car in reverse, backed up to me, and rolled down the window.

"Hey, what's your name?"

"Matty."

"Don't ever be embarrassed by the scar on your face, Matty. It's beautiful."

"What?"

But she was gone.

"Thanks," I said to the empty suburban street.

Wait a minute, what empty suburban street? Holy shit. I had no idea where the fuck I was. The street was all lined with houses and trees. All the yards were neatly trimmed. I was in the suburbs!

I tried to remain calm. I didn't remember going over any bridges so I must have still been in Miami Beach. That was comforting, but not enough to take away the pain and humiliation of what had just happened. Was it the scar? I always did my best to cover it with my hand when I met new people, but I must have slipped up while I was daydreaming. Damn that fucking Frankenstein scar! So I was lost and tired and depressed. I walked around for an hour looking for somewhere to sleep, and eventually I found a house that had a boat on a trailer in the front yard. Not a huge boat, just a seventeen-foot open fisherman; a Bayliner, I think. Most kids who grow up in Miami Beach know about boats, by the way. So, I jumped up on the trailer and undid four snaps on the tarp covering the boat. Then I climbed inside, did my best to get all the snaps closed again, dug around for a lifejacket under the seats, and after finding one, laid down and cried myself to sleep on my orange pillow.

I swore that night I'd make them pay; all the women who rejected me, one day I would make them all pay. How come they didn't want me? What was wrong with me that only men could see me as desirable? I didn't know, but I swore to myself that whatever it was, I would fix it one day. One day they would want me. Sometimes I think I'm still waiting for that day, and other times, I curse the day I ever made that promise to myself.

I awoke the next day hungry and broke. I was starving. I hadn't had a thing to eat since going to the library at two o'clock the day before. I was hungry at John's but knew better than to ask him for food. Then once I got back, I had to make a tough choice, pot or food. So I was hungry. I had planned on making a little more money before I slept, but after that crazy woman dropped me in that strange suburban neighborhood it was kind of out of the question. I got out of the boat and started walking. Eventually I got to someplace I recognized. I was all the way up in San Souci. Shit. With no bus fare, it would take me like four hours to walk back down to South Beach.

When I got there I could swing by a friend's house and

probably get some food, or go to the bakery where the Cuban ladies always loved to feed me, even on my days off. But right then, I was starving! I decided to go into this fancy grocery store they have up there in San Souci and rip something small off, like a candy bar or something. Did I mention I was a thief? Well, not a very good one. In fact, I got caught. Almost the instant I put the candy bar in my pocket, I felt the large hand of the security guard on my shoulder.

What a fucking bad luck streak! First John wants me to read porno instead of watching it, then that woman dumps me all they way up in San Souci, and now I was going to jail. I hate authority. Back then, I really hated authority. As soon as he grabbed me, I started yelling.

"Get your fucking pervert hands off me, you creep!"

That slowed him down a little for sure, but he wasn't about to just let go. So I kept yelling things at him and by then a crowd was gathering and the store manager came over and I was screaming all these things about the security guard trying to touch me and stuff and if it had been 1999, that guy would have been swinging from the nearest tree. But unfortunately, it was 1982 and nobody gave a fuck. So the manager reached in my pocket and pulled out the candy bar and the crowd all *ooooooohed*. I was caught and there was no way out. I was going to jail, if I got lucky. If not...home! I didn't even want to think about that. I hadn't seen my mom and the stepdad creep in like six months.

All the possibilities were racing through my head as they dragged me toward the manager's office. The guard had found his feet again and was walking tall like a Texas Ranger, his grip tightening on my arm, and he said something about the police and how they knew how to handle punks like me. We were almost at the door to the manager's office when I heard his voice behind me.

"Excuse me, maybe I can be of some assistance."

I knew that voice.

"And who are you?" asked the manager.

"Edward Silver. I'm a teacher at North Miami Beach Junior High, and this boy is one of my students."

I turned to look and it was John, only now he was calling himself Edward, and that made perfect sense to me. He looked just like an Edward, and nothing like a John, and not very gay at all by the way. What was shocking was how different he appeared, how professional and grown-up. I must admit I hadn't really figured John out at all; or Edward either.

The manager told the security guard to keep an eye on me while he and John went into his office to talk. Five minutes later John came out and walked over to me.

"Let's get out of here," he said.

As we were walking out of the store, an older but very pretty blonde lady wearing a white summer dress walked up to us.

"Edward, is everything all right?" she asked.

"Everything is fine, dear," John/Edward answered.

"Honey, this is Matthew, one of my students who's about to run home and tell his parents to expect a call from me. Matthew, this is my wife, Mrs. Silver."

"Nice to meet you, Matthew," she said, then smiled and winked at me.

"Don't be too hard on him, Eddie. You know boys will be boys."

We all walked to John's car where Mrs. Silver climbed into *my* seat. John closed the door for her and then led me around to the back of the car. When we were behind the car, he leaned down and whispered something in my ear. I'll never forget what he said. It changed my life.

That was the last time I ever saw him: driving slowly through the supermarket parking lot with his wife, and then exiting onto 125th street. She turned and waved as they pulled out into traffic. Bye-bye now...

SECRET

Was I gay? Would I spend my whole life watching girls on videos while old men blew me? How long until someone found me out? When I got old, would I want to suck young boy's dicks too? Would my marriage be like John's? Just some elaborate cover story for my nightly perversions. Would I pay for it? Jesus Christ, would I end up paying for it too?

These were my thoughts—all day, everyday. The last one in particular would make me cry in self-pity every time I thought about it. Me, sucking young boys off in the park and paying for it! Thoughts like that appalled me. I swore I would never let that happen to me, but I knew they were only empty promises. I knew that one day that is exactly what I would end up doing: paying for it. I guess that was the greatest fear of my life, ending up like them. They were okay to give me money and suck me off, but the thought of being one of them? Suicide seemed like a better option at the time.

Oh, sorry, you want to know what John whispered in my ear that night, don't you? The words that changed my life? Okay. He whispered, "*Giovanni's Room* by James Baldwin."

That's what he whispered, but by the time I got back to the library it was closed already. So that's how I ended up at the library the next day asking for a copy of *Giorgio Armani's Room*. We couldn't find it in the fashion section or biographies, but luckily I remembered the author's name. Well, part of it anyway.

"It's by James Baldron," I said.

That made all the librarians chuckle. Then, when they realized what book I was looking for, they all started laughing like crazy.

"What's so funny?"

So the cute one, also the youngest, let me in on the joke.

"It's nothing, cutey. The book you are looking for is called *Giovanni's Room* by James Baldwin. It's over in fiction, follow me," she whispered.

And I loved to follow her. Something about women always drove me nuts. Not girls, women. Even back in grade school, I was in love with women. The first time I forgot to do my homework in the third grade, Mrs. Miller came over to my desk to write a note to my mom telling her that I had failed to turn in my assignment. That was the single greatest moment of my education. It was like I had her all to myself for the first time ever. She leaned down over my desk and wrote with such fluid movements. I was mesmerized by her smell, her handwriting, her closeness to me. I could even feel her breath on my arm. I guess I was in love. Did I mention that Mrs. Miller was hot? Well, she was.

Needless to say, I never turned in another homework assignment again. I had discovered *bad* attention and I loved it. I quickly became the class clown and screwup, but I was still careful to always be nice to Mrs. Miller and the other teachers. I was just a general fuckup, not a little prick. There is a difference. Adults always liked me, and they could never understand why I fucked up so much. Mrs. Miller used to walk over to my desk and cup my chin in her hand.

"What are we going to do with you, my little Matthew?" she would say.

She couldn't understand that the reason I was fucking up so much was because of that; the chin holding, the always prodding me to try harder, the trips to the principal's office. The principal was an older, harder lady, but after we spent a lot of time together, I won her over too. She liked to pinch my cheeks and muss my hair, which was okay, but it didn't come close to Mrs. Miller's hand on my face. If she had just ignored me, I probably would have been a good little boy.

Walking with this cute young librarian through the aisles of books toward the fiction section felt remarkably similar to when Mrs. Miller used to put her hands on my face. Something about the way she whispered "follow me" had the tone of a conspiracy. I felt like she was about to let me in on a secret. When we got to the Bs in the fiction section, she quickly scanned the shelves, picked out a book, and then handed it to me. Only she didn't let go. We were just standing there for a moment, each holding one end of the book in silence. Then she looked into my eyes, touched my face exactly the way Mrs. Miller used to, and said, "You can talk to me about this book any time you want." Then she added, "Or anything else you want to talk about."

"Okay, thanks," I said.

"My name is Robin by the way."

"Thanks, Robin. My name is Matt."

We both laughed uncomfortably. Then she smiled at me with the most sincere smile I had ever seen. I felt the warmth instantly rush down my spine. We laughed some more and it felt so good, like we really did share a secret. I felt as if Robin and I were friends. And if I have any sort of choice in what heaven is like for me, I want it to be that moment, forever. It was the first time an adult ever talked to me like that.

The kindness that has been shown to me by total strangers never ceases to amaze me. I had no idea what had just happened. I didn't know why Robin told me what she did about the book or the talking, but I did know it was different. I knew that something had happened. I had crossed some invisible border. The only problem was I had no idea where I was yet or where I was going. I wasn't even sure if this was a border I wanted to cross. I only knew that there was something special between Robin and me now, and it felt good. Better than good.

I started reading right away. I read all that day until closing. The next morning I got there early and found *Giovanni's Room* wasn't on the shelf. I never checked books out, because I had nowhere to keep them. I only read in the library. So, I went to the front and asked Robin if someone had checked it out.

"No, I have it up here. I didn't want anyone to check it out while you're reading it." She reached under the counter and handed me the book. "How do you like it so far?"

"I haven't gotten that far yet." Did I mention that I read incredibly slow?

"Well, keep me updated."

I went to my usual table and got down to business. The problem with *Giovanni's Room* was that it wasn't exactly written for thirteen-year-olds. I was having a lot of trouble with the French stuff and some of the English words too. It was a week until I understood what it was about, but I'll remember the day I finally understood it for the rest of my life. When I realized that the bar in Paris was a *gay* bar, I was in shock. First off, I had never even been to a gay bar. Second, I couldn't believe that people were actually writing about that stuff. And third, I was horrified at what the secret that Robin and I shared had turned out to be.

She thought I was gay! I wished I was dead, right there, right then.

I closed the book, left it on the table and immediately slipped out of the library. When I got outside I started running. Running and crying. I didn't know where I was going or why I was crying, but I did a lot of both. I ended up on the beach about twenty blocks from the library, under the boardwalk where I sat and cried for about thirty minutes.

"They know, they all know!"

It all made sense to me then. The guys who picked me up, the way my stepdad hated me, the way Robin treated me so kindly, the way a lot of older women treated me kindly. The softness I had always felt inside—the same softness that I had instinctively known to hide.

I was gay, and everyone knew it but me. How come none of my school or drug friends were getting hit on by older men? Because they were straight, they were normal, and everyone knew it, the same way they all knew I was different, strange, gay, a sick little faggot. I was a sick and dirty little faggot. I knew then for the first time that I had brought all this on myself. I was the criminal not the victim; I was the hunter, not the prey. So I was going to end up sucking little boys off after all. It was my destiny, and I knew it.

I knew a guy named Bob who lived in Fort Lauderdale and had been trying to get me to go up to his place for a couple of months. I had never tricked with him, but I knew what he meant by his offer. Sitting there under the boardwalk I formed a plan. I needed to get out of town. I needed to go somewhere where nobody knew about me. Somewhere I could start over, straight this time. I knew Bob was gay and all, but I thought that if I could just get away from Miami Beach, away from the library, I could some-how make things different. Maybe I could even meet a girl. I would use Bob to get out of town, and then maybe get away from him and start my new life with a girl. I spent the rest of that afternoon daydreaming about the kind of girl I would meet: slim, with dark hair and small breasts. Glasses were a plus. In short, a librarian. Preferably one who didn't think I was gay.

P A P E R   C U T
B O B

I got to the gas station where Bob worked as a mechanic at close to five o'clock and found him standing by the dumpster out back. He hadn't seen me yet, so I just stood there for a minute thinking things over. Was I sure about this? If I had a type, Bob was definitely not it. He was about five foot four and two hundred and eighty pounds; pudgy to say the least. Even in his mechanics' coveralls, he looked like a fat, messy little kid. To call him ugly would be too kind. Weird and a little scary was a better way of describing him. His curly black hair was always covered in dandruff, his skin was always greasy, and his breath always stank. He wore those athletic tube socks with red and blue stripes that only dorks and small kids wear. I would have felt sorry for him if I hadn't known he was a great big, fat, fucking pervert.

So I just stood there watching him for a couple minutes, wondering if I was making a mistake. Then Bob flicked his cigarette into the wind, which flicked it right back at him. He freaked out and started patting his chest like a baboon to put out the smoldering ashes. I started to laugh. *Why the fuck not?* I thought. *At least he's entertaining.*

"Hey, Bob. Don't get too close to the pumps while you're burning like that!" I joked.

When Bob saw me his face turned redder than usual. "Goddamn cheap cigarettes," he said. "What are you up to, kiddo?"

"Nothing, man. When are you getting off work?"

"Oh, I can get outta here in about twenty minutes. Why you asking?"

"I need a place to stay, Bob."

It was one of the most painful things I had ever said, but I tried to look enthusiastic. Bob didn't need to try. He looked like he just remembered it was his birthday, and he was hungry for cake. I waited around the station for twenty minutes, smoking and trying not to think of what was coming later that night.

"You want an ice-cold soda, champ?"

I hated when people called me names like that. The same names my stepfather used to call me: sport, champ, and kiddo.

My real father never called me names like that, even when he was drunk. He always called me Matty or Harvey Wall Banger and that was it. Harvey Wall Banger was his drink by the way: vodka, orange juice, and a splash of Galliano.

"Sure, Bob."

"Well what flavor do you want, kiddo?"

"Sprite, I guess."

"All out of Sprite, champ. Alls we got left is Coke. Is that all right?"

"Sure." Then under my breath: "Then why the fuck did you even ask me?"

It's only about a forty-minute drive from Miami Beach to Bob's house in Fort Lauderdale, but that day it seemed like the longest drive of my life. Bob didn't shut up once the entire ride. He told me all about his "connections." He knew Mick Jagger, Rod Stewart, Ozzy—all the great rock stars. And if things worked out well for us, I might get to be a stagehand for the Stones. How lovely for me. I knew he was full of shit and all, but something in me wanted to believe him anyway. It was strange how much I wanted to believe back then. So I just tuned Bob out and started daydreaming about being a roadie for the Stones, until some distraction would bring me back to reality and I'd find myself riding in fat Bob's filthy fucking car. It's no wonder I day-dreamed so much.

In my daydreams I was living with a beautiful librarian. I was always taking out the trash or fixing the leak under the kitchen sink. We would lie in bed reading every night and then discuss the books in the dark. Somehow we always ended up making passionate love. In my dreams. In reality, I had fat fucking Bob and his bad breath and dandruff. He went on talking about his famous friends for the entire ride. You know, a guy could really go far hanging out with Bob. Like right to bed; or so I thought. But Bob had other, stranger plans.

When we got to his house Bob played it cool for a couple of hours, then out came the pornos. Straight ones right off the bat. *Right on*, I was thinking, *this could work out after all*. But there was something strange about Bob's attitude toward the pornos; it was like he had a purely scientific interest. Then he got out a pad and a pencil and started taking notes.

"Damn," Bob yelled, "that's not the position I designed. This director is always screwing up my moves!"

Then, once he knew he had my attention: "Oh, sorry, kiddo. I have to get some work done. This is my second job. The one that makes me rich."

He didn't look rich to me.

"Yup," Bob said, "I invent new positions for these adult movies."

All I could say was, "What?"

"Oh yeah. They run out of new positions to do it in, and that's where I come in. I design the new ones."

Did he think I was buying this shit? "I bet that pays well," I said sarcastically.

"Oh, sure," Bob replied, "they pay me ten dollars a position and I can do about twenty positions in a night. The only problem is, I need a helper."

So here it came: the question. They all had a different way of getting there, but the question was always the same.

"Do you know anyone who wants to make some fast money?"

"I don't know. What do you have to do?"

"Just help me invent new positions for the movies is all. It's easy. You just have to pose in these new positions while I create a template."

"Okay," I said, trying not to laugh. "How much will I get paid?"

"I'll split it with you, kiddo, and that's a good deal. After all, it's me who's coming up with all the ideas. You just have to lie there."

"Okay," was all I could say; I mean I had come this far already, right?

So Bob turned off the movie and took all the dirty clothes and damp towels off his bed and then he told me to take off all my clothes. That was for realism, he explained.

And then the freak show began. It was fucking hard to believe how seriously Bob took his act. He got me to pose on all fours, and then on my back with my legs in the air, and then he covered me in these dirty old newspapers. I mean literally covering me in filthy fucking newspapers! I'd been wondering what all the newspapers were about; they were stacked everywhere. His apartment looked like someone was doing a paper drive. And all the time he was wearing these ugly bifocals with a black magic marker stuck behind his ear. To make matters worse, fat Bob got undressed too.

So picture this, if you can: a five-foot-four, fat, naked, and extremely hairy guy with bad breath and dandruff, wearing only bifocals and dirty Fruit of the Loom underwear, running around the bed making marks on newspapers that are covering my naked body. And Bob was fucking frantic. He kept yelling stuff like, "Perfecto!" and "Bravissimo!" or, "Hold that one, don't move a hair!" The only reason I could keep a straight face was that he was a little scary. Then he got this little, pathetic boner, and I was terrified that I might start laughing. I mean, this was fucking ludicrous, right?

But I didn't laugh. Actually, it wasn't really all that funny, this position I was in. Not literally. Just the fact that I was now stuck in Fort Lauderdale with Fat Bob the Freak.

"Okay," he said, "that's enough of the solo poses. Let's move on to the action couple shots!"

"Wait a minute," I said. "How many was that?"

"Ten," Bob said.

"It felt more like thirty!"

"Well it wasn't," he said. "We only did ten usable new positions. Now you're distracting me. Do you want to make more money or what?"

"Okay," I mumbled.

So then Bob climbed into the bed with me and started arranging us into all kinds of sexual positions and once we were in a suitable "new" position, he would drag the newspapers up on top of us. Then he would make little tears in the paper where our bodies were touching.

"These are the templates," he explained.

"Whatever," I said.

This went on for about half an hour and then Bob would exclaim, "I've got it," and we moved on to another so-called "new" position.

Bob achieved bliss in about the hundredth new position. He never even took his underwear off. I guess he was thinking that if he didn't come, then what we did was legit. So he shot his load into his shorts, and I wasn't supposed to notice. The filthy creep never even changed his fucking underwear. He just stood up and announced, "That's a wrap!" and then he started getting dressed.

So I didn't even get to come? This was absolutely the worst trick I'd ever done. When I finished taking a shower to get the smell of Bob off me, not to mention all the fucking black newspaper ink, Bob said he wanted to go out to eat at Morrison's Cafeteria. Well, where else would a guy like fat Bob eat?

Later on, when we'd finished our "home cooked" meal, I asked him for the cash, and he said he couldn't pay me until he got paid, which was thirty days after he submitted his work. "But the royalties," he explained, "the royalties are where we make all the money!"

Now I was fucking pissed. "What the fuck, Bob! You owe me a hundred bucks!"

"Sorry, champ, can't help you out until I get paid. We're both in the same boat."

"Like hell we are, Bob! I'm not even in the same fucking ocean with you!"

Bob handled my outburst like a patient father. "Take it easy, kiddo. We'll get paid soon enough. I'll cover your expenses until then, and you can pay me back. Besides, I haven't even told you about the best part yet!"

"Oh, I'm fucking quivering with anticipation, Bob."

"Okay," he said, "joke all you want. But you don't wanna miss out on this opportunity."

I fell for the bait. "What opportunity, Bob?"

"Well, you're great at modeling the new positions, but I think I need someone smaller than me to work with you. Besides, I can't work and pose at the same time anymore."

"So what are you trying to say, Bob," I asked.

"What I'm saying is that we need someone closer to your size that you can pose with. Don't worry, champ, I've already got a few girls in mind."

And I'll never forgive myself for falling for that one. I mean, I knew he was lying, but I wanted to believe him so badly that I just shut off my ability to reason for a little while. I suspended my disbelief. I couldn't hear Bob anymore. I was gone, starring in my very own child porn film.

Later, when we got home, he went into his bedroom for a

couple of minutes while I watched TV. When he reappeared he was carrying a large manila folder. He walked over to where I was sitting on the couch and dropped the folder down next to me.

"There you go, champ. All the girls in this folder are available for work next weekend. Take your pick."

I opened the folder and found a neat stack of photos cut right out of magazines. They were all of young girls from about twelve to sixteen. He must have cut them out of *Seventeen* or some other magazine, but I looked them over anyway. I spent hours trying to decide which girl I wanted to work with. When I finally made up my mind, I handed a picture to Bob and said, "I like her."

It was a full-length shot of a young girl sitting at a small wooden school desk, chewing on a pencil and trying to look perplexed. She had big dark eyes, and wore black plastic glasses like Elvis Costello. She had medium-length chestnut brown hair and a fair complexion. Her breasts were just starting to develop beneath her white blouse. Under the desk you could see her plaid schoolgirl skirt and just enough of her milky white thighs to make you squint and try to see a little further. My eyes kept drifting down to her white knee-high socks and black patent leather shoes. Don't get me wrong. I'm not into schoolgirls with plaid skirts and all. I mean I'm not into schoolgirls in the Japanese fetish sense or anything. But she just looked so damn smart. She was the hot sexy librarian of my dreams, and I fell in love immediately.

"Oh, nice choice," said Bob. "That's Dianne. Let me give her agent a call."

And off he went into the bedroom. I could hear him making his fake call in a voice way too loud for the phone, and couldn't help but chuckle. Bob was definitely a fucking freak. When he came back to the living room he said, "Okay, champ. She's available for next weekend on Saturday. It's all set up." He took back the folder, but I kept the picture of Dianne. Well, what else was I going call her?

I knew Bob was full of shit and all, but I couldn't help dreaming about Dianne every second for the next week. Every day, Bob got home at seven or so, and I met him at the front door. Of course he didn't let me stay in his house alone during the day. I just wandered around Fort Lauderdale daydreaming and smoking. At night we did the usual newspaper routine and pretty soon Bob was into me for like fifteen hundred bucks, minus the five he gave me every day for food and cigarettes.

The following Saturday, I was all nerves. I was at Bob's door at five, pacing up and down the corridor. Of course, Bob showed up at seven-thirty with the bad news: Dianne's agent had called him at work and they had to reschedule for the next weekend. But hey, the Stones were on tour, and Bob had made a call to his buddy Turtle, who guaranteed him that there was a job for me starting next Sunday and paying two hundred dollars a day! On tour with the Stones! Wow, maybe I could even bring Dianne. Then again, maybe not...

Like I said, Bob gave me five bucks a day for food and cigarettes. So, I didn't eat. I was squirreling away some cash for a rainy day. I would steal food while Bob took his morning shower, and then eat like a pig at night when he got home. I stayed at Bob's for over two months, every night another story, and every night the same "position game." After about ten more stories and the subsequent let-downs, I had about a hundred bucks saved up. One day I woke up and just split. I didn't think about it or plan it; I just got on a bus headed back to Miami. I never saw Bob again, but that happens a lot in my line of work.

G O I N G T O
R E H A B

When I got back to Miami Beach, I went to my friend Tommy's house to see what was happening—and because I had nowhere else to go. Tommy seemed excited to see me.

"What happened to you, Matty? We thought you were dead. You know the cops are looking for you, dude?"

"No shit? How do you know?"

Tommy told me that the police had been to his house and all my other friend's houses too. It appeared as if I was in some pretty big trouble for this little fire I started a few months before. Well, actually it was a pretty fucking huge fire. I just wanted to burn down Mr. Schneider's room, but when the rest of the school went with it, I wasn't disappointed. Tommy and I sat around and smoked a bowl or two, and we were listening to some Black Sabbath, when his mother knocked on the door.

"Tommy, can I come in?"

"Fuck you! Leave me alone!"

That's how Tommy always spoke to his mom; go figure. She was always so nice too, always giving him money and shit. Maybe if I talked to my mom that way, she'd be nicer too. But this time Tommy's mom was pissed. The door flew open like someone had kicked it in. It was just like on one of those cop shows. And then there were two guys in ugly suits with gold badges on their belts standing in the doorway. Just like a fucking cop show.

"That's no way to talk to your mother, Tommy," one of the guys said,

"...and you must be Matthew."

"Yeah, that's me."

"We've been looking for you, Matthew. My name is Detective Miller and this is Detective Whitley, and you are under arrest."

Just like that, and I was on my way to jail. Tommy's mom was a rat, Bob was full of shit, and I was going to jail.

But what about the Stones, I was thinking. *What about Dianne?*

And what about Dianne? Don't be daft, there never was a

Dianne; not for me anyway.

I'd like to tell you I played hardball with those cops, but that would be another lie. The truth is I was a big pussy. That was the first time I really got busted good, and I was scared. So mostly I just sat in the back of their car and cried. They took me to the station, where we filled out some paperwork, and then they called my mom and asked if she wanted to keep me until the trial. My mom declined; tough love, I guess. So Detective Miller, who really wasn't all that bad, called for a transport van to take me to the Dade County Juvenile Detention Center. Before I left, he took me aside and told me he thought I was a good kid. He said he'd spent a lot of time interviewing my parents, and he thought they were more screwed up than me. He said if I ever needed anything to give him a call and he handed me his card.

"Are you married?" I asked.

"No," he answered.

Then I knew where he was coming from.

"No thanks," I told him. Bob was still too fresh in my mind.

I spent some time there in the DJDC, and some interesting things happened. Mostly I read: The Old Testament, The New Testament, then the old one again. I even got saved. But anyone who's spent time in jail can tell you that promises made on the inside are just that. I wasn't out for more than thirty minutes before I was born-again bad and forgot all about my Christian rebirth. In fact, that dusty old Holy Bible couldn't really even hold my attention while I was locked up. One day I found a neglected stack of Harlequin Romance novels on the book cart, and that was it for the good book. I studied the romance novels like test books. They were my guides into the secret world of women's desires. And that didn't turn out to be too mysterious after all. What women wanted was to be rescued by a dangerous criminal with a soft heart and a bushy mustache. So, I would lie in my prison cell at night and imagine that my facial hair was growing. Okay, so maybe it wasn't real prison, but it was close enough for me.

The Juvenile Courts thought that all the bad things I was doing were related to drugs, and so they offered me a deal. If I went to a drug rehab, then they would knock time off my sentence and let me out early. That sounded good to me. I took the deal. With less than a year served, one day they told me to pack my shit.

"What for?" I asked.

"You're going to rehab."

And to rehab I went, and it wasn't all that bad either. The counselors there were nice to me. I made some friends, I didn't get high, and I got to read a lot. They even put me on a special diet so I would gain weight. All in all, things were better than they had ever been in my life. I felt comfortable there. Of course I still got into trouble, but they knew how to deal with me there. Mostly we resolved our problems by talking them out, but occasionally, when I would get beyond talking, they knew how to deal with that too. Every once in a while I would go fucking crazy ape shit. Then they would put me onto a bed facedown, restrain all my limbs, and shoot me in the ass with something that made me sleepy. The next day they would let me off of the bed, and we'd be a happy family again. They never got violent and never said mean things to me. They never got drunk. They were perfect parents, all thirty of them.

One night when all the kids were asleep, I went to ask the night nurse, Marsha, if I could watch TV for a little while until I got sleepy. She grabbed me by the face, in a nice way, like a mother.

"How come you never look me in the eyes?"

"I don't know."

"Are you afraid of girls?"

"No!"

"Well, you have no reason to be. You're a gorgeous boy, and one day you'll be a gorgeous man."

She proceeded to describe all the good things about me. I was so embarrassed! I felt like I had a fever. As soon as she let my face go I ran back to bed yelling "good night" over my shoulder. But I never forgot what she said. It was the nicest thing any adult had ever told me. Thanks, Marsha.

And so things went. Nice things. Tom, the teacher at the rehab, told me that I was smart and that he didn't think I even had a drug problem. He said I would be fine as soon as I turned eighteen and got my own place. James, the ex-professional football player who was the muscle of the joint, gave me some good advice too.

"What you need, little Matthew, are two VCRs and a girl. That'll keep you out of trouble."

The girl I understood, but the two VCRs was a mystery to me. So I asked him about it.

"That way you don't have to get out of bed to change the tape!"

Still some of the best advice I've ever gotten.

Nigel was a surfer from California, and he gave me someone to look up to. He was my first adult male role model. He was definitely straight but also sensitive. He wasn't talking about girls and their tits all the time. He had respect for women. Nigel had a sort of visible calm, and I liked that. He told me it came from surfing. I always remembered that.

Murray was a gay counselor. He was the first adult to treat me like an equal. He never talked to me like a child and when he touched me, it made me feel like being gay didn't have to be so bad. It didn't have to be some stranger sucking your dick in an alley. Murray never touched me in a sexual way; there was just something about they way he'd put his arm around me. He was strong yet gentle, and I felt protected. When I looked at him, I could imagine *being* with him, and that didn't seem like such a bad or dirty thing.

My favorite was Lee, the ex-professional wrestler. Lee would come into my room just before lights-out, and if I wasn't in bed, he'd throw some wrestling move on me and end up body-slamming me into the bed. This was the first real physical contact I'd ever had with an adult male that didn't make me nervous. Lee was just a big overgrown kid. Every night he'd give me the "Claw," the "Boston Crab," or some other new wrestling move. It got so I had trouble sleeping on Lee's nights off.

Mark was a night guard who let me stay up late and smoke. He taught me how to play poker. Jim, a male nurse and a huge queen, pierced my ears for me with a hypodermic syringe. Big Richard, who looked and talked like Sidney Poitier, taught me how to play basketball. In short, I had a dad. A dad with all the qualities one looks for in a dad: gentle, strong, smart, and funny. I had one dad with ten different personalities and ten different names. And all this time, not another human being knew what I had done except me and the men I did it with. At rehab, I was just a normal-though-somewhat-fucked-up kid. I was happy there, until...

T H E
P H O N E   C A L L

One night at rehab I got a phone call. I had gone to bed early so
I was still sleepy when I picked up the phone.

"Hello?"

"Don't worry, Matty. I'm coming to get you out of there!
That bitch can't lock you up!"

In the background I could hear the jukebox and the clinking
of glassware. He was in a bar, and it sounded like he'd been there
all day.

"Do you know who this is, Matty?"

"Is it Underdog?" That was what I called my real father
when I was little and he used to call home from the bars.

"That's right, Matty, and I'm coming to get you out of there!
I'm leaving tonight, as soon as I get off work."

So, he had a job now.

"Are you at work now?"

"Sure, where else would I be?"

"At the bar."

"Oh come on, Matty, you sound like your mother. I'm at
work and I'm coming to get you tonight. Pack your stuff and get
ready to go. I'll see you first thing in the morning."

"Okay."

Then only silence and more barroom noise. I heard my dad
telling someone that those were his quarters on the pool table.

"That's right, it's my game! Give me a minute. I'm talking to
my son!"

He pronounced *son* with all the pride he could muster.

"Dad?"

"Yeah, Matty."

"I love you."

"Well tell me that in person when I see you tomorrow. Okay,
sport?"

"What did you call me?"

"Sport. It's just an expression."

"I know."

"I've gotta get back to work now. I'll see you in the morning."

The line went dead before I could say okay. I hadn't spoken to him since that day on the stairs at my grandma's house when he cried so much. That was ten years earlier.

One Christmas morning, a couple of years before we moved to Florida, we got a phone call. My sister Kristin answered the phone; she was ten.

"Hello?"

Her face lit up.

"Merry Christmas, Daddy," she yelled.

That got my mom's attention. He had never called on Christmas before. I don't remember him calling at all. My mom smiled, and tears welled up in her eyes. Kristin was glowing.

"No, Daddy, I didn't get your presents yet... All right Daddy... Mom, he wants to talk to you."

My mother looked a little frightened as she took the phone from my sister.

"Hey, Charlie, thanks for calling. It means so much to the kids."

All of a sudden, she looked deathly ill.

"Oh, I understand. It's all right. There's no need to apologize... Don't be embarrassed, it's okay... She'll understand... Merry Christmas to you too."

When she hung up the phone she was already crying. She went into the bedroom and closed the door. All I wanted to know was why she didn't let him talk to me and Stephanie. When she came out of the room a few minutes later I wouldn't let up.

"Why did you hang up on him? Why didn't you let me talk to him?"

She didn't answer. She looked as if she were going to cry again.

"Mom, why didn't you let me talk to him? Mom! Why?"

"It was a wrong number, Matthew!" she screamed.

As I hung up the phone I remembered that call on Christmas, and I never did pack up my stuff. I just sat up all night thinking about Dianne. I had recently taken to cutting pictures of girls out of magazines. I covered all the walls of my room with them. I would lie awake in bed at night and conjure up all the details of my relationships with those girls. That night it was back to old faithful Dianne. Well, it wasn't the real Dianne, but another model who looked sort of like her. I never whacked off to the girls in the pictures. Well, maybe once or twice, but mostly I just imagined our lives together, every detail. I had *Better Homes and Gardens* to pick a house from, *Road & Track* for a car, and *National Geographic* to plan our vacations. It was all pretty elaborate. One time I even picked up a *New Mother* magazine in the hospital lobby and looked for a baby that looked like Dianne and me. I would arrange the pictures on the wall together: the girl, the house, the baby, the vacation, the whole deal. The girl I would never have, the car I would never drive, the house I would never live in, the life I would never lead.

Morning came and went. No Dad, no Dianne, no Rolling Stones. Nada.

I did get another call the next night though. This time I was wide awake when I answered.

"Dad, where are you?"

"Who? Matthew, this is Françoise. Do you remember me?"

"No. I'm sorry, who are you?"

"I met you at Tommy's house about a year ago, at the party. We kissed, don't you remember?"

"Oh, Françoise. Sorry. I was expecting another call."

And I did remember. She was a petite girl about nineteen or twenty, with short dark hair. She was from France, and her name was Françoise. I didn't remember kissing her though. I was pretty drunk at that party. Just like me to miss the best part of my life.

"That's all right," she said. "So how are you doing?"

"I'm doing great, if I could only get out of this place."

"That's what I'm calling about, Matt. Can you...get out?"

"I don't know, I could try I guess. What for?"

"Matt, are you still a virgin?"

What kind of a question was that? How did she know I was a virgin? I couldn't answer. We just sat there for a few moments. All I could hear was the static on the line. In the mideighties most phone calls became digital, and the static noise was all but eliminated. A lot of people got worried when neither party was speaking and the lines were completely silent; so the engineers created a digitally simulated static to play in the background of calls. They called it "Comfort Noise."

"Matt, are you still there?"

"Yeah, I'm here."
"Matt, I want to take your virginity."
Comfort noise.
"Did you hear me?"
"I heard you."
More comfort noise.
"Well, what do you think?"
"Okay."
Two days later I was gone.

F R A N Ç O I S E

They took us to the park next to the hospital every day to exercise. The problem was that the day after Françoise's call, Nigel and Murray were working. Nigel was a surfer, and he was in pretty good shape. Murray was a former high-school track star. So splitting with them around was not an option. The next day, however, Richard and James were on duty. James had been a tight end for the San Diego Chargers, but that was over ten years ago, and considering the advice he'd given me about the two VCRs, I think he was slightly out-of-shape. Richard had been a great basketball player when he was in high school, but that was over twenty years ago. That was the day to run. So I made a plan.

At fourteen, I was the youngest at rehab. Yeah, my birthday came and went while I was in the detention center. In any case, when the older kids heard that I had the chance to get laid, they were more than willing to help out. So when James and Richard brought out the basketballs, we all screamed that we wanted to play football instead. Eventually they agreed. David had a great arm; he always played quarterback. That day, I was the wide receiver. I went deep. Over and over again, until one time I was very deep, near the gates to the park. I just kept on going and didn't look back. I ran for ten or twelve blocks, and then jumped on a bus. In an hour I was back in Miami Beach.

Back at Tommy's, no cars were in the driveway, so I went up to his door and knocked. He was there of course, listening to Black Sabbath and getting high as usual.

"So Matty's gonna get laid!"

"How do you know?"

"Everyone knows," he said. "And by a twenty-three-year-old no less!"

"She's twenty-three?"

"Fuck yeah, she is. Are you gonna call her now?"

"I guess so."

And I did. Two hours later I was alone with Françoise in Tommy's room. She said hello, took off her clothes, and climbed into Tommy's bed. I was just standing there, fully clothed, with hands in my pockets, staring at her.

79

"You need to lose those."

"What?"

"Your clothes."

I did as instructed. Then I was standing there naked.

"Come here."

And I did, shaking violently. Then she showed me how to kiss her, how to touch her breasts, how to eat her out, and finally how to fuck her. She wanted me to come inside, which I did. Afterward, she explained birth control to me. She was on the pill. We took a shower and fucked again, and again, and again. We fucked all day long. It was pretty good too, but not what I was expecting. Not love, just sex. Well, it wasn't love on her part anyway, but I was a little smitten. We agreed to meet back at Tommy's the next day. Françoise didn't show.

I saw her a few nights later at a party. She was making out with some guy who looked like he was thirty. I got upset and ran out of the party. Françoise followed me. She said she wanted to take my virginity, not be my girlfriend. I was no longer a virgin, so her obligation to me was over. I cried and cried and eventually got drunk and vomited all over the thirty-year-old guy's car. He was actually pretty cool, and he let me crash at his place for the next few days.

But I wished I was back at rehab. I wasn't doing too well on the outside. I had no money, nobody to talk to, and nowhere to go. The only way out I could see was the bus stop, and so that's where I went. For the next nine months, I went to the old bus stop in front of the library every night. Sometimes I would spend the night with a guy; other times I slept on the catamarans behind the Fountainbleu Hilton. During the day I swam in the hotel pool or just walked on the beach. Sometimes I'd get to the library early and hide in the bushes watching Robin and the other librarians get into their cars and head home for the night. I fantasized that I was going with her, that we were discussing *Giovanni's Room* on the way back to her house.

Nine more months of tricking, nine more months of anonymous sex; another birthday gone by, another birthday, another Thanksgiving, another Christmas. Just days going by, and with each passing day I got a little harder, asking for a little more money each time, doing something else I never thought I'd do and with someone I'd never imagined doing it with. The dirty old man, the tweaked-out gak head, the guy with the armpit fetish, the crack fiend, and even sometimes the cops too. Those were the people in my neighborhood.

One wanted me to touch his balls lightly while he jerked off. Another wanted to take me to a hotel where I'd play dead for an hour while he did his thing. The next wanted me to piss in his mouth.

"That'll cost extra."

Slowly, I was losing that feeling of power I once had. It just wasn't the same anymore. I started feeling like they didn't like me so much. I was just a trick to them, nothing more. What I had mistaken for real desire and passion was only perversity run amok. They were just big, fucked-up, perverted kids indulging every sick thought they had. I was just a small part of their fantasies, someone they could get to do the things other adults would laugh at them for. Someone they could forget about right after they dropped me off.

Things were going downhill fast. I was doing any drug I could get my hands on: pot, LSD, speed, cocaine—a lot of cocaine. Night after night, I would get into cars with strange men. Night after night we would act out their fantasies together. They gave me whatever drugs or money it took to make me pliant, to mold me into what they wanted. Sometimes it took quite a bit of both.

One night in particular, I met this guy named Ray. When we got to the hotel he started laying out lines of coke and I started snorting them. Then he pulled out all these girl clothes from a brown paper bag and told me he wanted me to put them on. I just couldn't get my head around it, no way, no how!

"No fucking way, man!"

But he insisted. He told me he'd give me the rest of the coke (an eight ball) and a hundred bucks.

"Okay."

Ray had everything too: little girl cotton panties with cherries on them and a matching training bra; a little pink sundress; a pair of white stockings; and patent leather shoes. I put them on—everything but the shoes, which didn't fit. And then Ray was gone, gone to somewhere where guys who like little boys dressed in little girls clothing go. He just got this crazy glassed-over look. I started snorting coke like a fiend, line after line. Ray told me to bend over and let him see my panties from behind. So I stood up and turned around, bent over and snorted another line.

"Don't move!" Ray screamed. "I see Paris, I see France, I see Dorothy's underpants!"

Who the fuck was Dorothy? I didn't give a shit; I was gone too. Gone to somewhere where little boys who dress up like little girls and snort coke go. I just kept snorting lines and bending over, oblivious to what he was doing behind me. All I was thinking was that I wished he'd hurry up and come so I could get the fuck out of those clothes.

"Here!" he screamed.

"What?" I turned around. Ray was sitting on the bed with his dick in one hand and a jump rope in the other.

"Take this!" he yelled. "Take this and start jumping!"

I put down the straw and started to jump rope. Actually, I was pretty good at jumping rope. Did I ever tell you about the time I won the jump-rope competition in third grade? Well, if I did, I was lying. I could have won it, but I took a dive in the final round. It was just me and this little girl, Tyrecia, in the finals. Her parents, Tyrone and Alecia, were there and they were just so proud and so encouraging that I kinda wanted her to win too. I mean it didn't mean that much to me anyway and my parents weren't there. So I took a dive and she won. The first of many dives I'd take; the beginning of a long string of losses.

So I took the rope and started jumping; nothing special at first, just jumping rope. Then I started throwing in some double jumps, cross-overs and fancier stuff, not that Ray could even appreciate it in the condition he was in.

"Make your dress fly up so I can see your panties when you jump!"

That was difficult, but I got the hang of it. I just had to thrust my pelvis a little.

"That's fucking good! Don't stop, don't you fucking stop!"

But that is exactly what I felt like doing. In fact I wasn't feeling all that good. I got dizzy. I fell down. The last thing I remembered was Ray standing on top of me shouting for me to get up and start jumping again.

G O I N G   B A C K
T O   R E H A B

I woke up in the hospital. I always hear about people waking up in the hospital and not knowing where they are, but I didn't have that problem. I knew exactly where I was. I mean I didn't know which hospital or how I had gotten there, but I knew I was in a hospital. It felt familiar, like rehab. Judging by the cross over my bed, I guessed St. Francis in midtown. I just lay there for a long time staring at the ceiling, thinking about nothing in particular. I was at peace for the first time in a while. Hours later, a pretty little nurse walked in.

"Oh, you're awake. Good morning. Do you know where you are?"

"St. Francis."

"Do you remember how you got here?"

"No."

"Well, I won't go into that now. How are you feeling, Matthew?"

"How do you know my name?"

"Your library card. It was stuck into your panties."

She turned a little red when she said that.

"Oh." That was all I could say. I remembered Ray and the dress and felt like going back to sleep forever.

"What's gonna happen to me now?"

"I'm going to take your vitals now, and then we'll let Doctor Kouri know you're awake and she'll handle the rest."

Doctor Kouri showed up a little while later. She was an elderly Cuban woman with a gentle manner and nice eyes. She introduced herself.

"Hello, Matthew. I'm Doctor Kouri. How are you feeling?"

"Fine, I guess. Am I all right? I mean is there something wrong with me physically?"

"I'm not that kind of a doctor, Matthew. I'm a psychiatrist. But the other doctors tell me you'll be fine. You just need some nourishment. Do you remember what happened?"

"No," I lied.

"Well, when you got here last night you were unconscious.

83

You were suffering from dehydration, exhaustion, and malnourishment. I'm sure the drugs didn't help much either. Would you like to talk about what happened?"

"Not particularly. Do I have too?"

"Well, not if you don't want to, but the police may not be as patient as me. Where did you get that dress, Matthew? Did a grown-up give it to you?"

"No." And that was the truth.

"Do you wear girls clothes often?"

"No!" And that was the truth.

"Do you remember who dropped you off in front of the hospital?"

"No." And that was the truth.

"Matthew, that's a beautiful name," she said. "It's Mateo in Spanish."

"I know." And that was the truth too.

"Well, Mateo, you're going to have to start telling me the truth. When you arrived here last night you had enough cocaine in your system to kill you. We also found male semen on your stomach. Do you know what that is?"

"Of course I know what that is!"

"Was it yours, Matthew?"

I couldn't speak. I was paralyzed. I didn't talk much about sex to anyone, much less an elderly woman. Telling her about Ray was out of the question. We sat in silence for a few moments.

"How do you feel about returning to the drug rehabilitation center again, Matthew?"

"I would like that." And that was definitely the truth.

"The police have called your parents and informed them of the situation. They said they don't want to get involved."

"What else is new?"

"The police don't know what to do with you. You weren't carrying any drugs when they found you and dressing like a girl is not a crime, so they are reluctant to arrest you. We found out from your parents that you used to be in rehab until you escaped nine months ago. Legally you're a runaway and a ward of the state, but I've talked to the police and we agreed that the detention center might not be the best place for you now. We think rehab might be best. How do you feel about that?"

"Great. When can I leave?"

"Well, the doctors want to observe you for a few more days because of the malnutrition, and then we'll see. Oh, and we've got to get you some new clothes, right?" We both chuckled uncomfortably.

A few days later I was on my way back to rehab again. Because of my previous escape, I was transported back in a police van, same as my first visit. I stepped out of the van as the other kids were in the parking lot getting ready to go to the park. James and Nigel were there.

"Welcome back, Matthew," said James. "I guess you got a touchdown, huh?" We both laughed. "Next time you can stop after you cross the goal line, all right?"

The other kids were staring. I could tell they were impressed. Not many kids got brought to rehab in leg and wrist shackles. Nigel signed the release papers for the cops, and they took off my restraints. He gave me a hug.

"Welcome home, Matty. Wanna play some football?"

"Don't you think I should sign in first?"

"That's up to you, but we're going to play some football, and if you wanna play you'd better hustle."

I was home again. After football, I signed some papers at the front desk, and that was that. The kids were all different, but the staff was the same, and they honestly seemed happy to see me. I can't tell you how relieved I was to sleep in my old bed again. I felt safe and protected. Just before lights-out on my first night back, I went to the bathroom to brush my teeth. When I came out of the bathroom I felt a huge hand on my forehead.

"Did you miss the claw? We've got a lot of catching up to do, little sissy!"

"Ouch! Come on Lee that hurts!"

"That's right it hurts, baby girl. You've gotten soft after nine months away from the claw!"

We wrestled around for half an hour or so, and then Lee had to make his rounds. He turned off the lights on his way out of the room. I called after him.

"Hey, Lee. Uhm... I missed you."

"I missed you too, Matty. Now go to bed!"

Now I'm not the sharpest tool in the box, but either they were all very good actors, or they really did miss me. I decided to stay awhile, just to find out if they were faking it. And after two months back there I started to believe they really did miss me. I mean, sure, they were getting paid and all, but I could tell they honestly liked me too. I became the undisputed favorite patient of 99 percent of the staff. This was mostly due to me being there the longest, but at least part of it must have had something to do with me. That second time in rehab had to be one of the happiest times of my life, but of course it couldn't last.

It turns out that some of the doctors had gotten together to discuss my case, and the results weren't good. They believed I was a little too comfortable there. They thought that most of the staff and I were too close and that I was not getting the discipline that I required. This all came about because Dorothy, the new night nurse, complained that I was being spoiled. The fat cow!

Dorothy was an old, overweight spinster, the kind of person that would take a job working with kids even though she hated kids—maybe because she hated kids. I used to imagine her jumping rope in Ray's little pink dress. This always made me laugh when she was talking to me. That drove her mad, which would only make me laugh more. She was in her fifties, the same age as Ray, so you never know...

Dorothy made a lot of notes in the night log about me, and then one morning I was summoned. Murray walked me down to a meeting room on the first floor near the cafeteria. Before I went in, he told me not to worry.

"Just answer their questions honestly," he told me. Then he hugged me and told me he loved me. I don't know why, but that made me cry. Murray hugged me until I stopped crying and then ushered me into the room and made a hasty exit. There were four doctors in the room waiting for me—all the big guns. They asked me questions about my treatment and how I thought it was going. They asked me about the staff. One at a time, they read off the names of the staff, and asked me to describe our relationships. Me being me, I thought they were suspecting some sexual foul play on the part of the staff. So, I went off on a tirade about how great each staff member was, all except Dorothy. I spoke for thirty minutes about Murray alone, then James, Nigel, Mark, Richard, Patty, Lee, Tom, and all the rest. I was selling hard, but then again it was the truth. I loved them all; they were my folks.

So right when I thought I had them convinced that they had

the greatest staff in the world, I noticed them all shaking their heads in dismay. They had that look that said, "It's much worse than we thought."

Doctor Gonzalez cleared his throat. "Matthew, there is no question that we all feel a certain warmth for you here. You were one of our first patients when we opened the Adolescent Treatment Wing, and over time we have all grown to like you very much, myself included. And therein lies the problem. Matthew, we feel that you are not getting the treatment you deserve here anymore. The staff has way too much invested in you on a personal level, and we feel this it not beneficial to you or the other patients. We think it's time for you to move on."

Well, at least he didn't say this was going to hurt him more than me.

"Matthew, believe me when I say, this is probably more difficult for us than it is for you."

"Yeah, right!" I screamed. "I guess you'll all be missing the state's money!"

"This isn't about money, Matthew. It's about what's best for you."

"Fuck you! Fuck all of you!" I started bawling again.

"You just want to get rid of me. Why don't you just tell me the truth?"

That night, I thought it over but it didn't make sense to me. If they loved me, then why were they sending me away? I had the feeling that they knew I had manipulated them into liking me and that wasn't good. Now they were on to me. They knew who I really was and they wanted to get rid of me. No matter how much I tried to get people to like me, they always found out I was a shit in the end. Then they always sent me away. I wasn't mad at them; I knew it was my own fault. I had let them in, and they had seen the truth. The morning after my meeting with all the doctors, James and Nigel drove me to the airport. They let Angie come along for the ride.

Did I ever tell you about Angie?

A N G I E

It started out innocent enough. I was sitting across from her in the lunchroom. She was eating her grilled cheese, and I was eating a high-protein meal and drinking a Sustacal, a special weight-gain drink that I had to have four times a day. I was still a little malnourished, I guess. I saw her staring at my drink, and I made a dumb joke.

"Breakfast of champions!"

She giggled.

"Knock, knock," I said.

"Who's there?"

"Joe."

"Joe who?"

"Joe Mama!"

We both giggled.

"Knock, knock."

"Who's there?"

"Jeff."

"Jeff who?"

"Jeff Father!"

And by then we were both laughing.

"Knock, knock!"

"Who's there?"

"Angie."

"Angie who?"

"Angie grand mammy too!"

It wasn't all that funny, but we thought it was hysterical.

"That's my name," she said. "Angie."

"I know," I told her.

"What do you call a paraplegic on your porch?" she asked.

"I don't know."

"Matt!"

Then we were both crying with laughter. Maybe we were just nervous, but everything we said seemed so fucking funny.

"That's my name," I laughed.

"I know," she said.

After that, we rarely parted.

Angie was seventeen. She was more the victim of sexual abuse than drugs. Her father, her brothers, her doctor, the list went on and on. Rehab was no exception. The only way Angie knew how to relate to people was through sex. Almost every guy there had slept with her—every guy but me. At least that's what they all said. We were inseparable except when she would do her thing. The older boys would sneak into her room at night, but during the day she was all mine. She told me everything about her, and I told her nothing. I was in love with her. There was no way I was going to let her know what a perverted freak I was. There was nobody I would allow to know that side of me.

It's funny, but they all thought I was still a virgin. I told them about Françoise, but nobody believed me. I was just too shy with girls. I still couldn't even look them in the eye. So I would just listen to her talk all day long, and I think she told me more than she ever told her therapist. I learned then that if you just listened to girls, they would eventually tell you everything. This is a skill that evaporated the more familiar I became with women. The more I had sex with them, the less I listened. But back then, with Angie, I was all ears.

One day we were at the park sitting in the shade of a banyan tree, in between two of its giant roots. I tried not to think of the crying guy.

"Did you know that fruit bats like to live in these trees?" I asked her. "There are probably some up there sleeping in the branches now."

"Gross," she said.

She reached over and took my hand, studying it for a while, and then just holding it. I was frozen with terror and my palms started to sweat, but she didn't mind, I guess, because she never let go. We sat like that in silence for half an hour, until it was time to go back upstairs.

We sat like that every day for the next few weeks. The counselors never asked why I had lost interest in sports; they knew. Everybody knew I was in love with Angie. All the other kids teased us. They told her that she was wasting her time, that I was a pussy when it came to girls and I probably didn't even know how to kiss. They told me that Angie was a whore. I got mad and got into some fights, but she would always calm me down. She told me that they didn't understand; she told me that they were jealous.

Then a couple of weeks after we started holding hands in the park, she told me she wanted me to come into her room after lights-out.

"Tonight," she said. "Wait an hour after lights-out. Then when you hear Dorothy turn on the TV, come to my room. Don't knock, just come in."

"I'm not that stupid. I wasn't planning on knocking!" But of course, I was. That night after lights-out, I waited nervously. Like clockwork, I heard the TV in the rec room go on at eleven sharp. I got out of bed and peeked into the hallway—just the TV's blue glow coming from the rec room and nothing else. The hallway was clear. I silently thanked the interior decorator or whoever had decided to put the couch and TV around the corner. You couldn't watch TV and the hallway at the same time. But then again, the TV was for us, not the night nurse. I crept into the hallway and slid down the wall to Angie's room. Then I froze outside her door.

When I was very young, maybe five or six, my mother and I shared a room. She worked all night, so I was mostly alone. My sisters shared another room down the hall. I had a lot of nightmares that would end with me pissing the bed. When I woke up, I would be terrified and drenched in piss. The walls of the room always looked distorted and menacing in the dark. I imagined something bad under the bed, in the closet, peering into the window. I would get so frightened that I would get out of bed and slowly feel my way to the door. Then, hugging the walls, I'd slowly feel my way to my sisters' door. Then I would freeze. I wanted so badly to go in and wake them up, but I was afraid they'd be mad at me. My pee-soaked pajamas didn't help much either.

Once I realized I couldn't go in their room, the terror would take over. I got so fucking scared I became paralyzed—with help so close, yet so far away. I imagined I would die right there in front of my sisters' door. My mom would find me this way when she got home in the morning; asleep in front of my sisters' room, curled up in a ball and smelling of piss.

I sat like that, frozen in front of Angie's door, for twenty minutes. Well, at least I wasn't covered in piss. I just couldn't move. I had the feeling that Angie was going to be mad at me.

And what if she wasn't? What if she expected me to come in and make love to her? With all the guys she'd been with, I would look like an inexperienced little boy, which I was. I remembered Françoise and what a mess I had made of that. Then I heard Dorothy get up from the couch and I had no choice. I opened the door, slipped inside, and closed the door silently.

"You sure took your time," Angie whispered. "I almost fell asleep."

"Sorry, Dorothy was moving around."

"Shhhh! Shut up and come here."

I went over to her bed.

"I can't believe you still wear pajamas," she whispered in my ear, laughing.

"Take them off."

This was beginning to remind me of Françoise, but I did as I was told. I climbed into bed wearing only my underwear. Angie kissed me on my neck and ears and lips.

"We can do anything you want," she whispered in my ear.

"I'm cold. I just want to get warm first, okay?"

Angie didn't answer; she just pulled me down on top of her and wrapped her arms around me. She was so warm; warm and soft. I could feel her breathing and her breasts moving under my chest. I could smell her girl smell and feel her long curly black hair all over my face. I kissed her just a little on the neck. She groaned quietly and ran her fingers through my hair. I looked into her eyes and then kissed her softly on the mouth. She returned the kiss and slipped her tongue into my mouth. We kissed for a while. The best kiss of my life. Her lips and tongue were so soft. She was so gentle with me. *Girl* was the only word I could think of. *Girl, girl, girl, this is a fucking real girl!*

I reached down and cupped her left breast in my hand. She pushed my head down until my lips were even with her nipple.

"Kiss me there," she said.

I kissed, and then sucked on her nipple softly. I was in heaven. This was what I had always dreamed it would be like to be with a girl. Then I heard her sniffling, which I ignored. I was already forgetting how to listen. Then she was sobbing. I looked up and her face was covered in tears. Then, I was crying too. Why does someone crying always make me cry? It's like she was saying "life sucks," and I was just agreeing.

I woke up with the sun in my eyes. I reached over to close the curtains and felt Angie beside me.

"Holy shit," I yelled. "Angie wake up, I've got to get out of here!"

"What?" she said. "What time is it?"

"How the fuck should I know? It's fucking morning, I guess!"

We formed a plan. Angie put on some sweatpants and a T-shirt, then threw her bathrobe on over them. She walked out the door into the hall and then opened her robe, pretending to adjust it, only holding it wide open for too long—just long enough for me to sneak down the hallway back to my room. Behind me, I heard Marsha.

"Good morning, Angie dear. You're up early."

Then I was back in my room. All was well. Around noon Murray came for me and told me that the doctors wanted to talk to me.

"Which one?" I asked.

"All of them," he answered.

DESTINATION UNKNOWN

The next morning I was on the road again. Nigel and James drove me to the airport, and like I said, they let Angie come along for the ride. That was one of those days you remember for your whole life but can't explain why. Something just felt different. The way James and Nigel spoke to me, the way Angie held my hand, it all felt different. James and Nigel treated me like a friend that day, not a patient. For the first time in my life I felt the isolation of being an adult. It was sad, but it gave me a strange sense of freedom. I knew that James, Nigel, and Angie couldn't come with me, couldn't hold my hand anymore. Whatever happened next, it was going to be up to me. For the first time in my life I felt as if I might have some influence over my own future.

Although Angie and I never did have sex, I felt as if I had crossed some invisible line with girls. I mean, shit, it was almost like I had a girlfriend. I felt I was on the verge of a great discovery. Maybe I didn't have to end up as an old man chasing little boys through the city with a ten-dollar bill in my hand. I had hope. I felt like a normal life was almost within my reach. Maybe I could work everything out and leave all that other shit behind me. At the airport Angie and I made plans to call each other, and then Nigel and James took an extra long time getting my bags out of the back, giving us time to kiss. And we kissed like adults. Not little kids hiding in the woods or behind the schoolhouse, but like all the other adults saying their goodbyes at the airport. Then Nigel walked me down to the gate and gave me a hug.

"Make us proud," he said.

I told him I'd give it my best shot, and then I got on the plane. As soon as I took my seat I started to cry. I knew I wouldn't be seeing any of them again.

That plane took me to Philadelphia, where another two counselors picked me up at the gate and drove me to another rehab. Angie never called, but then again I never called her either. What we had was what we had, and that was all. In Philadelphia I met a girl named Janice. She was sweet and she liked me. We had sex

93

several times and got caught several times. So much so, that they kicked me out of that rehab too. I was only there a month, and the last week I had to spend down in the adult psychiatric ward. They sent me on to Boston, where I lasted six weeks, and then on to Baltimore. I wasn't the favorite anymore. I mostly caused a lot of trouble wherever I went.

The cat was out of the bag, so to speak. It appeared as if my records now contained the *dress* incident and my reputation preceded me wherever I went. That began to cause a lot of problems for me. Everyone just treated me differently. If a girl liked me or thought I was cute, then the local boys would get extremely pissed and that resulted in a lot of name-calling and a lot of fights. The most common insults were about cross-dressing. Then there was *fag, fairy, homo, pussy,* and all the rest. I wasn't prepared for that. I had always been athletic and masculine, and nobody knew about that other side of me. But somehow at each new rehab, the kids found out about the dress, and after that I was labeled a fag.

The staff members didn't seem to like me much either. They treated me like some disease that would spread if not quarantined. I got the feeling that most places didn't even want me there. They just held on to me long enough to find somewhere else to put me. An all-boys *boot camp* in Ohio was considered, but they rejected me; probably due also to the *dress* incident. They didn't want me coming in there, turning their wholesome military-style camp into some Genet-style penal colony. You know how one bad apple can spoil the bunch.

And spoil the bunch I did. Wherever they sent me, usually in just over a month, I would be driven back to the airport. The place would be in turmoil when I left. They were expecting trouble when I arrived, and I never failed to deliver. It seemed like everything I did was laced with some dirty, sexually deviant behavior. In Boston I was playing football and I tackled some boy. I was proud; I had single-handedly stopped him from scoring. We were both struggling to get up when this male mental health technician came running up and yanked me off the kid by my shirt.

"Just what in the hell do you think you're doing?"

"Playing football."

"Well that's not how we play football around here!"

That night someone wrote FAG on my door. I was gone by the end of the week.

In Baltimore a male staff member who obviously hadn't been briefed on my perverted nature was doing his night rounds. He shined his flashlight through my window and right into my face. Then the flashlight went out and the door opened.

"Having trouble sleeping?"

"It's not really trouble, I just don't sleep that much."

"Do you want to talk a little?"

"Okay."

His name was Robert and he was nice. Nice and gay. Nothing noticeable though; he wasn't swishy or anything. I don't think anyone else there knew he was gay, but I did. The same way I knew he never had any sexual intentions with me. But try explaining that to a born-again Christian night nurse.

Robert was black as night and extremely handsome. He was tall, muscular and yet gentle. He had a quiet manner and soft voice which was in complete contrast to the lean, hard lines of his body. He reminded me of Mr. Davis. We talked for a while, and then I started feeling homesick for my first rehab and began to cry. I was embarrassed so I turned over on my stomach and buried my face in the pillow. Robert put his hand on my head. He started stroking my hair and then rubbing my neck. He was the first person to be nice to me in a few months and that made me cry more. Robert just sat there rubbing my head and my back. Don't ask me to explain this, but I knew what he was thinking, and it wasn't about sex. I knew this like I knew my own name. It was a fact. Sex was something I had become highly tuned to. They could have used me in a courtroom as a sexual lie detector. Again, I can't explain this, but by the age of fourteen, I just knew what people's intentions were sexually. But try explaining that to some dried-up old cunt of a night nurse who hasn't been laid in decades. Who doesn't even remember she has a cunt much less what it's used for.

I never even heard the door open. All I heard was the flashlight hit the floor and then, the voice of the night nurse.

"Oh my God," she gasped.

Robert jumped up; I sat bolt upright in the bed. The nurse picked up her flashlight and ran out of the room. Robert cursed under his breath and then ran after her. He stopped at the door and came back to me. He knelt next to my bed and took my face in his strong black hands, just like Marsha, just like Mrs. Miller, just like Robin the librarian. He looked into my eyes and whispered:

"This isn't your fault. Whatever happens is not your fault. Do you understand?"

"I understand," I said. "They see what they want."

Robert left the room. I heard him down the hall arguing with the night nurse.

"It's not your fault."

I kept hearing his words in my head, seeing the incredible whiteness of his teeth and eyes in the dark as he spoke to me. My back still tingled where his hands had been. I felt warm and tired. He was wrong, you know; it was my fault. They were all looking for a trick, and that's what I was. The men on the street, the doctors, all the night nurses and gym teachers: they all wanted to believe I was some freaked-out, perverted kid, and so did I. I let them believe, and I became what they wanted.

In the morning I was transferred to the adult psychiatric ward. By eleven I was meeting with more doctors. More questions. Why was I sleeping without a shirt? Didn't I have pajamas? Was I wearing any underwear under the covers? Had Robert removed my shirt or did I? I knew what they wanted to ask, but for some reason that's the only question they left out.

"Was Robert trying to have sex with you?"

That's all they needed to ask, but they never did. Would they have believed me anyway? Would they have trusted my hustler's intuition? By the end of the week I was gone. I never saw Robert again.

Eventually I ended up back in Florida; Fort Lauderdale this time. My stay there was brief. They picked me up at the airport and drove me to the hospital. When we got there I had an interview with this crazy-looking doctor named Drew. He asked a female nurse to accompany us into his office, and she just stood there the whole time observing. What was she supposed to do, intervene if I made a grab for his dick? He looked very worried the whole time he was talking to me, like he couldn't wait to get away from me. He asked me a lot of questions about why I was kicked out of so many rehabs. I answered as best I could, but I knew he didn't like me. I knew he didn't want me there. He asked me about how I got arrested and if I still liked to burn things. He asked a lot of embarrassing sexual questions too. I lied a lot. Then the interview was abruptly over. He asked me to wait out in the lobby.

I sat there alone in the lobby for about forty minutes. Just sitting on this orange pleather couch and staring at one of those posters with the kitten hanging from a tree. It said, "Hang in there, baby!"

But I couldn't. I just got up and walked out. I left my bags in the lobby with the kitten. I don't know why I left, I just did. Maybe I was tired of being passed from place to place, or maybe I felt bad for the young Doctor Drew. He looked as if he had enough problems of his own. In any case, I just said fuck it, and walked right out of there. Nobody even came after me. I think that might have been their plan all along.

P O O L   B O Y

I walked all day and got to Sunrise Boulevard just as the sun was setting. Always the right place at the wrong time. I walked down Sunrise to A1A and then went north. I walked a couple more blocks before I noticed I was being followed. A guy in a new white Cadillac kept driving slowly by me and then circling around the block again. I was taking my time, thinking things over. By the time I decided to get in his car I think he must have been pretty tired. He had circled the block at least ten times. He looked so frustrated and desperate by then that I felt sorry for him. I made my decision. When he came back around the next time I walked slowly, timing it so I reached the corner just before he did. When I got to the corner I turned around to face him, grabbed my dick, and then walked quickly around the corner to where it was dark. I was a hustler after all, right?

That was the first time I had ever been so aggressive, and it felt good to be so bad. After that, my hand was practically glued to my dick. I walked around Fort Lauderdale grabbing my dick every time a guy in a car went by me slowly. I let them all know who I was. I just didn't give a fuck anymore. The guy in the Cadillac was Frank. He was a retired real-estate agent, but he reminded me of an aged movie star like Rock Hudson. Frank was not in the closet. He dressed in clothes that were gay, mostly white suits with black turtlenecks and a lot of jewelry. He combed his thinning white hair to one side like Hugh Hefner. His movements and gesticulations were all overtly feminine. He had a sort of feline elegance. Overall, Frank was actually a pretty handsome old queen.

One night he showed me some old photos from when he was young. They were mostly beach photos taken in Cuba in the late 1940s. He didn't have to point himself out, he was the only gringo. There was this young and extremely attractive Frank in khakis and white cotton shirts surrounded by hot young Cuban boys in bathing suits. His shirts were always unbuttoned and I was amazed at how great he looked. I was amazed at how great they all looked and how much fun they seemed to be having. Frank knew what I was thinking.

"What, did you think I was born an old dried-up troll? I was once a young chicken like you, the belle of the ball. And if you're lucky, you might look as good as me when you're my age."

I just laughed. I liked it when Frank would get back some of his former dignity. I never had much respect for most of the guys I tricked with, but Frank was an exception. He wasn't trying to hide anything. He knew what he was, and he knew who I was. We didn't play a lot of games.

I liked Frank and I think he liked me too. At first he would just pick me up and blow me in the car behind the mall on Sunrise Boulevard. Once a week, then twice, and then he started taking me home. The night he showed me the pictures he also showed me his pool house. It was a nice little cabana out behind the pool. It looked like a room out of some 1950s beach movie. It had terrazzo floors and a matching rattan couch and love seat with some blue Hawaiian-patterned cushions. There was a small desk with a ship-in-a-bottle lamp on top and a bar with a matching lamp. Behind the bar were shelves with all sorts of tropical stuff like coconut drinking cups and hula girl statues.

"Wow, Frank. I feel like I'm in Hawaii!"

"There's a bathroom with a shower in there too."

"That's great."

"So you like it?"

"Yeah, it's a pretty cool little pad."

Frank got all serious.

"Where do you sleep, Matthew?"

I still hadn't caught on to that alias stuff.

"Around," I said. "Different places."

"Well, you've been wearing the same clothes since I met you and to be honest you're beginning to stink a bit."

That pissed me off.

"Fuck you, Frank. You're not my father. You're not any-body's father!"

Nobody ever told me I stank before and I was a little embarrassed, but all I could do was get angrier. I felt like I was going to cry.

"I'm sorry. I didn't mean to offend you. I just think maybe you'd be happier having your own place with a shower and a decent bed. I thought maybe you'd like to stay out here for a while."

I was trying hard not to cry, and I screamed at him.

"Well, you thought wrong. You're not my father, so stop trying to be!"

"I'm not trying to be your father. I'm just trying to be your friend."

"Fuck you, Frank. You just want me to live here so you can keep me all to yourself! Fuck that! Fuck that and fuck you!"

After I ran out of Frank's house I got some old wino to buy me some beer and proceeded to get drunk.

He's not my fucking father. He's not my fucking father!

That was the thought that kept running through my head until I got drunk and started to laugh. The whole fucking scene was hysterical to me: moving into his house, cleaning his pool, being his houseboy. Who the fuck did he think I was? I pictured myself in those low-cut bikini briefs the Cuban guys were wearing in Frank's old photos, and I laughed like crazy. I would clean the pool while Frank lounged in a recliner wearing a panama hat and sipping lemonade. Maybe we could get a little fucking poodle too!

I was sitting on a bus bench still laughing when the Jag went by real slow. Inside were two middle-aged men. Well, maybe late-middle-age. They looked like twins. Both had short gray hair cut military-style, both had a single diamond earring in their right ears, and both were wearing expensive white jogging suits. I saw them staring and immediately jumped up and grabbed my dick. They looked a little shocked, but not enough to stop them from pulling up to the curb. The power window on the driver side went down, but nothing happened to me that time. I was just standing there holding my dick in one hand and my beer in the other. I wasn't all nervous or excited like in the past. My heart wasn't beating like crazy. I was just there, really in the present for once. Thinking and planning. Sizing them up to see what I could score and how I should play it.

"You're a feisty little one," the driver said. "You wanna party?"

"Sounds great," I said, already making for the back door.

They drove me to a house near the beach in the richer section south of Sunrise. The house was fucking unreal. They had everything: a huge TV, a pool, a hot tub, and that wasn't all. They had coke, and lots of it. As soon as we got in the door, David started cutting up some lines and Chris got me a beer. Or was it David who got me the beer and Chris who laid out the coke? I couldn't tell them apart. When I asked if they were brothers they both laughed.

"Worse, honey. Lovers," David or Chris said.

They were in the business of selling cocaine and from the looks of it, business was good. I hadn't done any coke since that night with Ray, so I was all over it. Is that strange?

The very first time I tried heroin I overdosed. My friends had to put me into a tub of ice water for hours. Even in the ice I kept nodding out. I just couldn't stay awake. They were all yelling at me and slapping my face so I knew they were upset at me for something; I just didn't care. Eventually I came around and they were all screaming.

"Jesus Christ you fucking idiot, you almost died!"

"Really," was all I could say. The next day I woke up and tried to get them to shoot me up again but nobody would. I was pretty afraid of needles, and I definitely couldn't hit my own vein without fainting. So I just cooked some up and shot it into my asscheek. My friends were all laughing. They thought it was pretty funny that I almost died and woke up the next morning wanting more. I didn't think it was all that funny. I didn't think at all.

So I was diving right into that coke with David and Chris when one of them stopped me.

"No more for you until you've had a shower."

I guess I really was starting to smell.

"Okay. Where's the shower?"

Did I say *shower*? It was more like a sauna or something you'd see at a health club. It was about the same size as the showers in the juvenile detention center, but those were for eight guys at a time. This was made for two, and occasionally three. So they got all into washing me, and I got all into how good the hot water felt. There were six shower nozzles and I had never seen anything like that in my life. They had really nice soaps and stuff too. Did all rich people have that many products?

I was feeling pretty good. I thought Frank was rich, but these guys were beyond rich. They were fucking rich! I guess I was a little drunk too, 'cause I hadn't really noticed how the looks in their eyes had changed from lamb to wolf so fast. By the time I did notice, it was too late. It was Pedro and Eric all over again, only this time they were Chris and David. But the crazy look of desire was the same, the groaning sounds were the same, and I was the same too. I couldn't utter a single word of protest, not even a whisper. I was thinking to myself, *Hold on a minute here, guys — let's just slow down.*

But my lips weren't moving. On the contrary, theirs were. They were all over the place, like two octopi if that's not too cliché. Then we got out of the shower and started doing more coke. All three of us were wearing these incredibly soft white bathrobes. I was swimming in mine. My sleeves kept falling down over my hands and landing in all the coke. I must have wasted at least a gram on that robe, but they didn't seem to mind. They just kept putting out more lines and smiling at each other. Then there were more drinks and a little yellow pill, or was it blue? And then I was really fucking high.

We were in the bedroom, and I couldn't get hard which was pissing them off to no end. They put in a straight porno, but it didn't help. They were both all over me. I felt one trying to put his finger up my ass, and I tried to tell him to stop but no words would come out. The other one held a little brown bottle up in front of my nose and told me to inhale. I thought it was some type of smelling salt and that he was trying to wake me up. I was really starting to lose it. I inhaled deeply. Things went from bad to worse. A ringing started in my ears that was coming in waves and kept getting louder and louder. My vision was starting to get wavy too. Even my thoughts were coming in waves. The only thing I was sure of was that there was definitely now a finger in my ass and it was extremely uncomfortable. I wasn't really feeling the least bit sexy or turned on. The brown bottle appeared before my nose again. I thought or said or screamed, "Nooooo!"

I must have just thought it because the bottle didn't go away. In my ears I heard the ringing and a voice saying, "Inhale, inhale, inhale, inhale."

I tried to push the bottle away but my coordination was all screwed up. Then the bottle was gone so maybe they did get my point after all. Thank God.

"The little bitch spilled the Rush on the fucking bed!"

"Calm down!"

"No, I won't calm down. Look what you did, bitch. Look at me!"

I felt a sharp pain on my face. It was hard to concentrate, but I felt like David or Chris was mad at me for some reason. I tried to concentrate. David or Chris was standing in front of me. A finger was still in my ass. I saw his hand come up in front of me and felt a sharp stinging on my face again. I felt sick — really sick.

"Oh shit, bitch. He's going to vomit on the bed!"

My scalp hurt like shit. Why was someone pulling my hair? My sister used to pull my hair a lot. Fuck, it hurt. I was sliding on my back. Why? I felt the burning vomit coming up my throat and into my mouth. Instinctively I tried to hold it in, but this only created more pressure and it finally burst out.

"Holy shit! Turn him over or he's gonna choke on his own vomit!"

"Not on the fucking carpet!"

"Just shut up and turn him over quick!"

I felt the carpet on my face and someone was still pulling my hair, but to my great relief, there was no longer a finger up my ass. With the relief came more vomit. And vomiting felt so good. I surrendered myself to it. It kept coming and coming and the more I vomited the better I felt. I started to get happy again, I felt so relieved. That was exactly what I needed.

David and Chris were still arguing loudly but I couldn't tell what about. Then I was sliding again but this time on my stomach and the hair-pulling had stopped. They were dragging me by my feet. I felt the cool grass against my face, and then they turned me over and I could see the stars. It was a nice night. Cool and crystal clear. I sat up and looked around. I was in the grass next to the pool. It was a really a nice pool too. I could see David and Chris through the sliding-glass doors. They were in the Florida room and still arguing. They needed to relax. One of them came out and stood in front of me with his hands on his hips.

"Are you happy now, bitch?"

"Yeah, I feel a lot better. Do you think I could have a glass of water, please?"

"Oh, the bitch who just ruined my carpet and duvet wants some water now. I'll give you some water!"

He stormed off. He seemed pretty tense. He came back a minute later and stood in front of me with a garden hose in his hands.

"Here's your water, bitch!"

He started spraying me with the hose. What the fuck was his problem? What was with these guys? The water was freezing, and he kept spraying me in the face. I couldn't see and I started yelling for him to stop, but he didn't stop. I was getting madder and madder. Then suddenly it just came out.

"Stop it, you faggot!"

The water stopped.

"What did you call me?"

"Nothing, I just wanted you to turn off the hose."

"Oh, I'll show you who the faggot is, bitch!"

He got on of me and started hitting me. He looked so mad. I couldn't understand how he had gotten that mad. His face was all red and his fists were moving so fast. I couldn't really feel anything except that I was gonna be sick again. I tried to turn over on my side and cover my face, but he kept rolling me back onto my back and pulling my hands back from my face. It was like a game. I put both hands in front of my face, then he would peel one back and hit me in the face. Then he would go for the other hand, and I would put the first one back again. We repeated this game a lot. I didn't like it so much and I suspected that I was losing. He was starting to scare me. My face was sore and my head was beginning to throb.

"David, stop it!"

"This is between me and him. He called me a faggot!"

"David, you're going too far, stop it!"

They were wrestling on top of me and screaming at each other.

"Let me go!"

"Go back in the house!"

"No, you go back in the house!"

I turned over on my side in the grass and vomited some more. I was really cold. I was shivering and this got me to thinking about my clothes. Where were they? Where was that white bathrobe?

"Here, get dressed."

"What?"

Turning over I could see one of them standing over me with my clothes in his hand.

"Get dressed."

He tossed my clothes down in the yard next to me. I wanted to ask for a towel to dry off with first, but I remembered what happened when I asked for water, and decided to do as I was told.

"Hurry up! We haven't got all night."

I just left my socks and underwear in the grass and put on my jeans and T-shirt. He picked up my shoes, underwear, and socks and took me by the arm.

"Come on."

He led me around the side of the house, through a gate, and into the driveway. He opened the back door to the Jag and pushed me in, throwing my stuff in behind me. I spent the next few minutes trying to get my shoes on and then he told me to get out.

"Where are we?"

"Where we found you."

"Do you think you could let me have twenty bucks?"

"You've got to be kidding."

I sat on the bus bench for a while. I was cold and wet, and somehow being a pool boy didn't seem so funny anymore.

ANONYMOUS

I got up from the bench and walked the twenty or so blocks to Frank's house. It must have been close to four or five in the morning when I knocked on the door. No answer. I tried the doorbell. After a few minutes I saw a light go on inside. The door opened. There was Frank in his pink kimono-style bathrobe. He looked like shit, but then again so did I.

"Oh my God, what happened to you? Never mind, just come inside."

"Okay."

Frank had dignity, and he allowed others to maintain theirs as well. He never made me say I was sorry or that I was wrong. He never asked me what happened again. He just cleaned me up, gave me a pill, and put me to sleep in his bed.

I woke up in the evening but I was still tired. I climbed out of Frank's big girly canopy bed and went into his bathroom to look at my face, which now hurt like shit. Looking at my face in the mirror was a bit disturbing. I never really liked the way I looked so much, but this was awful. Both my eyes were swollen and discolored badly; I had cuts all over my face; my lips looked like I had stuck them in a blender; and my nose was covered with dried blood. I got a little panicky and ran back to the bed. Shit! The pillow was covered in dried blood. Frank was going to kill me! I started to take the pillowcase off—I was planning on hiding it under the mattress like I did with the sheets when I was little and I pissed the bed. I heard footsteps behind me and turned around with the bloody pillowcase still in my hand.

"Don't worry about that. I was planning on getting new sheets soon anyway. Those are a bit too girly, don't you think?"

"Yeah," I agreed.

"Sorry for all the mess, Frank."

"It's nothing. How are you feeling?"

"Better, I guess."

"Are you hungry?"

"Yes."

"Well, let's get you something to eat, and then we'll see about getting that old pool house ready to be lived in."

And being a pool boy wasn't that bad after all. Frank didn't do any drugs—except for the occasional Cuba Libre—and he was a great cook. He was retired, so we ate all our meals together, but most of the time we spent in our own houses. Well, technically they were both his, but the pool house started to feel like mine. Two or three times a week we did our thing. Mostly he would come out to the pool house in the morning while I was still asleep and I would wake up with him sucking my dick. That was all. The rest of the time we lived like father and son. Well, more like mother and son, I suppose. He bought me some clothes and took me to get a haircut. Every so often we would go out to dinner and sometimes a movie too. Most nights I would just lie in bed, reading. Frank had a lot of books. *Giovanni's Room* was one of them, but I couldn't bring myself to read it.

A couple of months went by and then Frank started getting pissy.

"That pool is filthy! Don't you ever clean it? And your room...don't even get me started on your room."

One night I found Frank eating dinner all by himself. I just stood behind him and stared. I didn't know what to say, but I felt like I had lost my best friend.

"Well don't just stand there looking like a sad puppy. Fix yourself something to eat. You can't expect me to always cook for you."

I went and got a bowl and poured some cereal and milk into it; I didn't know how to cook. I sat down at the table and started eating my cereal.

"Now that's a nice healthy dinner," Frank said sarcastically.

"Well, I don't know how to cook."

"Don't you think it's time you start learning?"

"I guess so."

"I think it's time you start learning to take care of yourself a little better. I'm going out tonight. Don't wait up."

He finished his dinner and I finished my cereal, and then Frank took a shower and started dressing. I went to the pool house and read for a while. When I came back to the main house he was already gone. I watched a little television and fell asleep on the couch. When I woke up the next morning I went to the kitchen to get a bowl of cereal. Frank was there in his pink bathrobe, cooking eggs.

"Good morning, princess. How'd you sleep?"

"Don't call me that, Frank." I heard laughter and turned toward the table.

"Princess, this is Johnny. Johnny, Princess." More laughter from Johnny.

"Don't call me that, Frank!" Johnny was a lot older than me, maybe eighteen or nineteen, with sandy blond hair that fell in his face. He was sitting at the kitchen table, eating eggs and wearing only a pair of old blue jeans.

"My name is Matt," I told him.

"What's up, Matt?"

"Nothing," I said and went out to the pool house.

About an hour later Frank came in and sat down on the couch. He told me Johnny might be moving in. He said he didn't think it was working out with us. He wasn't throwing me out right away, but if I would start looking for somewhere else to stay he would appreciate it. Two weeks should be enough time, he said. I knew when I was no longer wanted—and I didn't like that feeling at all—so less than an hour later I was gone.

I really didn't have a place to go. I only knew that I had had enough of Fort Lauderdale. I took the twenty bucks Frank had given me and went to the Greyhound station near US1 and Broward Boulevard. I bought a one-way ticket to Miami on a bus that left later that day. I roamed the streets around the bus station looking to score a few bucks before I left. A car with an old bald guy driving pulled up to me.

"Need a lift?"

"No."

I walked away quickly. Wait a minute! What did I just say? I could not believe I just said no. I went back to the bus station and waited on a bench until the bus for Miami was loading. On the bus I started thinking about what had just happened, but I couldn't really figure it out. Maybe I had gotten a bad vibe from him. Maybe I was just tired. I didn't know, but that was the first time I had ever said no to anyone. Well, you know what I mean. Anyone asking me if I needed a ride or if I wanted to watch movies or party or make some money; anyone asking me for sex.

I thought about this a lot on the way back to Miami. I thought about rehab and Nigel and Murray. I wished I could go back there again. I wondered if they were playing football right now. And then I got an idea. In rehab they used to take us to some Narcotics Anonymous meetings at night. I had never really paid attention to them, and I wasn't much interested in anything but looking at the girls, but at least it was somewhere to go. Tonight was Saturday. They had a meeting at South Miami Hospital. Maybe the kids from rehab would be there. Maybe I would see Murray!

I got to North Miami Beach around five. I caught a city bus from out in front of the Greyhound station downtown to the OMNI, then transferred to a southbound bus that took US1 through Coconut Grove and then onto South Miami. I arrived at the hospital just after six and went straight to the meeting room. When I opened the door I saw the meeting had already started. It was not the huge crowd I had seen here on other Saturday nights, just like ten people sitting in a circle. In the front was a blackboard with writing on it.

BEGINNERS MEETING
POWERLESSNESS

I sat down in an empty chair and everyone smiled at me. I just listened for a while. All right, so I wasn't actually listening, I was thinking about my own problems, like where I was going to sleep. Besides, they were just reciting all the usual crap.

"Let go and let God."

"It works if you work it."

"Easy does it."

"Keep it simple, stupid."

That last one really got on my nerves. So I just sat there thinking about me, as some guy told the incredible-but-true story of his addiction. It sounded like a bunch of crap to me. If his addiction was so great, then what was he doing at an NA meeting? If he was such a big coke dealer, what happened to all his money? When he was finished everyone was looking at me. The lady leading the group told me to go ahead. I hadn't even noticed I had raised my hand! I swallowed, took a deep breath, and out it came.

"Hi, my name is Matty, and I don't have a place to sleep. Oh,

and I'm a drug addict."
    "Hello, Matty!"

T H I R T E E N T H
S T E P

Yeah, I know that AA and NA are Twelve Step programs, but it was the mysterious thirteenth step that got my attention. That was what they called it when some more-experienced person in the program would take advantage of a newcomer. In short the thirteenth step was using your experience and alleged recovery to get a newcomer into bed. That was the only step I planned on working. On the bus to Miami, I thought that if I presented myself at an NA meeting and made it known that I had nowhere to stay, some old queen couldn't resist trying to help me out, if you know what I mean. After my brief introduction, they all just looked at me in silence. Finally the lady leading the group asked me if I had anything more to say.

"Nope."

"Well, thanks for sharing, Matty."

The meeting continued as normal. I fell asleep. The meeting ended at seven, and we all made a circle and said the Lord's Prayer. Afterward, I kind of skulked around the parking lot waiting to see if anyone took the bait; nothing, not a single person talked to me. Nobody there was going to help me. I was upset and about to leave when I saw my friend Jorge from rehab pull into the parking lot. Jorge had been a good friend in rehab, but I hadn't kept in touch with him since I'd split. I ran over to his car and called his name as he was climbing out. We had the regular reunion scene and it was nice. I could tell Jorge was happy to see me. He told me there was another bigger meeting at eight, and later I could crash at his house. I was saved, for the night at least.

We went back into the hospital and sat through another boring meeting. Mostly I drank coffee and stepped outside for a cigarette every ten minutes. When the meeting was over, we hung out with some of Jorge's NA friends. We went to Denny's and had coffee and desserts. It was pretty cool, too. I mean, I was a little shy back then, but nobody seemed to mind. People were nice to me and they seemed genuine. I had a good time, but I was still a little preoccupied with my need to find a more permanent place to live. Every time Jorge would introduce me to an older guy, I couldn't help sizing him up to see if I could maybe hook up. Unfortunately, they were all pretty straight-looking. I got a lot of phone numbers though.

"If you ever need a ride to a meeting, don't hesitate to call," they all told me. But I was thinking, *What about a blow job and twenty bucks?*

We went back to Jorge's, and I slept on the floor in his room. The next day Jorge had to go to work at this sub shop down by Dadeland mall. I didn't have anywhere else to go, so I went along. The owner of the sub shop was an Italian guy named Silvio. He was in his early forties, about five eight and slim with salt-and-pepper hair and a heavy Boston accent. He was pretty cool too. He let me hang out in the shop behind the counter with them, and even taught me how to make subs. I had a lot of fun that day, mostly listening to Silvio rag on Jorge or Judge as he called him. After work, he and Jorge went out back to smoke and when they came back in Silvio asked me if I wanted a job.

"Here at the shop?" I asked.

"No," he said, "painting my house. I'll give you two hundred bucks a week and a place to stay until you're finished. What do you think, Matty?"

First off, I loved it when people would call me Matty. And second, I just had a good feeling about Silvio.

"Sounds good to me," I said.

After we closed up the shop I rode home with Silvio. He lived up in Morningside, a couple of blocks off Biscayne Boulevard. He had a nice house too. We went inside and he showed me around. Then we went out to the backyard. He lived on a canal and had a nice Donzi ski boat parked outback.

"Wow, nice boat!"

"You like boats, Matty?"

"Shit, yeah. I love boats, especially Italian boats."

"You wanna take her out for a spin?"

"Fuck, yeah. Right now?"

"Why not?"

And we did, right fucking then. And let me tell you, nothing is prettier than cruising though Biscayne Bay and down the Miami River at night with all the lights of the city reflecting in the black water. It was great, and Silvio was great too. He really treated me like an adult. He let me drive the whole time and didn't panic once, not even when I almost rammed the dock on the way back in. We washed down the boat together, smoked a cigarette, and went inside.

In the living room there were a lot of pictures over the mantel.

"Who are those kids?"

"They're mine. That's little Sil, he's my youngest, and that's Tommy, his older brother. Sil is nine and Tommy is thirteen. They live with their mother."

"How long have you been divorced?"

"About five years. Wanna see your place?"

"Sure."

He took me back outside and around to the front of the house. We stopped in front of a door that led into the garage.

"This is your entrance, Matty. I'll get a key made in the in the morning. There's another door that connects the apartment to the house, but you'll probably want to use this one."

We went inside. It wasn't the shitty garage with a mattress on the floor that I had been expecting. It was fucking great. Not just a room, but a separate apartment. It had its own kitchen and bathroom, a bedroom, and a living room. It had a waterbed, and the kitchen was fully stocked with pots and pans and stuff. There was even a washer and dryer in the closet. No TV or radio, but I wasn't into TV anyway. Silvio told me to get some sleep and left me alone.

That night I thought that my life was finally changing. I had a job, I had an apartment of my own; things were really looking up. I lay in the waterbed, laughing to myself and thinking how things could be so different from one moment to the next, and how fucking strange my life had been so far. Now, I had everything but the girl.

The next day Silvio went to work at the sub shop and I started painting his house. He paid me two hundred bucks in advance and told me that I would owe him two hundred on the first of every month for the rent on the apartment. I did the math. Two hundred a week times four weeks was eight hundred dollars a month, minus two for rent. That left six hundred dollars a month just for me! When Silvio left for work, I fucking lost it. I ran around his yard laughing like a psychopath for twenty minutes. Then I started thinking about Frank and that kind of sobered me up a bit. *All this can't be free*, I kept telling myself.

But Silvio didn't act gay at all; and what about the kids and the ex-wife? Still, something was fishy. I guess two and a half years of steady hustling had left me a little suspicious of adults bearing gifts. But I wanted to believe. Just like with Paper Cut Bob, I wanted to believe that everything wasn't just about getting in my pants. My innocence was my ability to suspend my disbelief — to trust them and keep chasing that dangling carrot. Now I call it innocence; back then I thought I was just fucking stupid.

So I got down to painting the house. All day I painted and wondered about Silvio. What was his deal? Why was he being so nice to me? Was it possible that he was just some incredibly cool straight guy? And if he was gay, did that really matter? This line of thought frightened me. It led somewhere I didn't want to go. Was I secretly hoping he was gay? Was that what I really wanted? I blocked those thoughts from my mind and resigned myself to wait and see.

At six thirty I was out front cleaning the brushes when this silver El Camino hot rod pulled up in the driveway. Behind the wheel was a beautiful girl with long red hair. She gunned the engine a couple of times and then cut it off. Cut to slow motion! The driver's door opened and she stepped out of the car. She was tall and thin like a model and that's about all I can say, like a model!

From the ground up, the first thing I saw were her shoes. Cork platform-type sandals with leather laces that wrapped around her ankles and calves. What incredible legs! Above them, she wore a denim miniskirt that was much too short. For the first time in my life I understood the phrase "legs right up to her neck." Above the skirt was her smooth flat belly and above that she wore a yellow T-shirt that said, $1.69 SUBS, MORE MEAT THAN YOU CAN EAT!

I think it said more underneath but it was tied in a knot right over her navel. She had such beautiful pale skin, and like I said, long red hair that just barely touched her waist. I was completely paralyzed. She aimed her blue eyes right at me. She was stunning, about twenty-four-years old, and just absolutely perfect.

"You must be Matty. I'm Trish, Silvio's girlfriend. I live here too."

I was still paralyzed.

"Matty, you're getting your shoes all wet."

"Oh shit, sorry!"

"They're not my shoes, but maybe you should turn off the hose."

"Oh, right."

Movement slowly returned and I managed to turn off the hose.

"Do you have a cigarette, Matty?"

"Sure."

I handed her my pack; like I had any choice. If she would have asked for my liver I would have carved it right out on the spot for her.

"Wow, you're doing a nice job on the house, but don't work too hard or you'll push yourself right out of a job." We both laughed, not real laughter, but an uncomfortable sort of chuckle. I wondered if she knew about my situation and that made me embarrassed. I started picking up my brushes and pretending to be busy.

"I'm going in to take a shower, Matty. Silvio will be home in an hour or so. Are you going to have dinner with us?"

I was just a fumbling ball of nerves.

"Uh, okay, I guess, if you don't mind."

"I'll see you at dinner then." She started walking toward the house.

"Silvio was right," she said at the door. "You *are* cute." Then she went inside—and thank God for that; I could barely breathe.

That night the three of us ate dinner together, and the rest of the week too. By Friday night I was getting so I could actually speak around Trish and sometimes even make jokes. Of course later on, I would lie in my bed and abuse myself thinking of her long hair and long legs. I couldn't believe that I had thought Silvio was a fag! I had to learn to start trusting people again. I mean, some people were just nice, right? Everything didn't always have to be about sex. That first week we were like a happy family, only my mom was incredibly hot and my dad was incredibly cool.

And I was a good boy too. I worked hard all day painting. If I finished early or needed to let the paint dry, I would find some other chores to do. I mowed the lawn, cleaned the boat, and trimmed the hedges. At night I would always do the dishes and take out the trash. Silvio started to trust me; he thought I was a good kid. At dinner on Friday night, after being there less than a week, I felt warm and comfortable, like I belonged. I felt like I was at home. We would talk a lot and they would actually listen to me. I would make jokes and they would laugh—not the patronizing laughter of adults either; they really thought I was funny. After dinner on Friday, Silvio told me to get some sleep.

"Judge is coming over in the morning, and we're all going waterskiing."

I was up at seven and out back getting the boat ready by seven thirty. At eight I made a pot of coffee. Silvio came out of the bedroom about ten minutes later.

"Matty, you made coffee," then to himself, "I love this kid."

He got two cups and poured coffee into them, and then he looked at me with a glint of trouble in his eye.

"Hey, Matty, take this in to Trish and wake her up."

"Fuck that," I said blushing.

"Come on, she's pretty bitchy in the morning. I think it's my face that scares her, but who could get angry at your pretty face?"

"Forget about it, Silvio. She's your girlfriend, you wake her up!"

"Come on, Matty, don't be like that. She's naked..."

The last part he said with a teasing voice. I turned red.

"Really, no way, Silvio. Forget about it!"

"Come on, Matty, be a man. She won't mind. Maybe she'll like it!"

"Maybe I would. At least he's got more manners than you, Sil."

Shit! I turned bright red. Trish was standing in the doorway wearing only baby blue cotton panties and a cutoff T-shirt.

"Now look what you did to Matty, Trish. I think he's going to hyperventilate! Breathe, Matty, breathe!"

We were all laughing, only I didn't think it was that funny. They drank their coffee and I went out and lowered the boat into the water. Silvio came out and told me to go get some gas.

"Where?"

"Follow this canal to the bay and then right before you reach the intercoastal. There's a marine gas station on your right."

He handed me his credit card. Silvio just blew my mind when he did stuff like that. No adult had ever trusted me to do anything before. There he was handing me his credit card, not to mention his forty-thousand-dollar boat, and telling me to go get gas. I think it was at that moment that I fell in love with Silvio, real love. All I wanted to do was live up to the respect he had just given me so freely. It was impossible for me to ever betray him after that. I just wanted to make him proud of me. Is that so strange? After only one week? There was nothing he could ask for that I wouldn't give him if I had it. Like I said, I was in love.

When I got back, Jorge was there with his new girlfriend, Amy. Don't even get me started on her. Of course, I was in love with her too. I was in love with everybody. We all went skiing. Silvio let me drive the boat and said he was impressed with my nautical abilities. I grew up in Miami Beach, what else? Jorge might have been better with the ladies, but he grew up in Kendall and didn't know the bow from the stern, so this was my moment to shine. Silvio went first. He skied well and I was impressed a little bit more. Jorge went next and we all laughed like crazy. He couldn't get up on one ski, so we gave him two. That didn't help much either. He must have tried like fifty times before he stood up.

Amy went next. She was a rich girl who had also grown up in Miami Beach. She jumped right up on one ski and started carving all over the place. I could have towed her around forever. The water was like glass. It was a perfect day. I felt so masculine driving the boat and towing this pretty girl behind me. It was all pretty erotic, I guess. I felt like a man. Trish went next. And if I felt like a man with Amy back there, then I felt like a superman towing Trish.

Biscayne Bay is full of large sightseeing boats. On any given day there are at least ten boats with fifty to a hundred tourists on each, taking pictures and stuff. I started towing Trish right up alongside them. Can I get a witness?

Hey, look at me! I'm not gay! I'm not gay! This is Matty Lee towing around this hot girl over here!

Every once in a while I would catch Silvio staring at me and smiling. I thought that he knew what I was feeling. I felt like he was happy for me and that made me love him even more. When we got Trish back in the boat, Silvio told me to put on a vest and get in the water.

"Come on, Matty. Show us what you can do."

And I did. Did I mention I knew how to ski? I didn't. There was this moment, right as they were pulling me out of the water, when all eyes were on me. They were all looking back expectantly to see if I could get up on one ski. I was so nervous. Then the boat picked up speed and all of a sudden I was standing. And that was it. I don't know if it was beginner's luck or what, but I just did it. I was so fucking proud of myself. I couldn't believe it. I looked up and they were all smiling and cheering for me. The wake on either side of me was terrifying, so I just tried to stay in the middle. Silvio went straight for a while and then started gradually turning the boat. This made me swing out over the wake. I held on tight and leaned back and then I was over it and outside where all the water was glassy. And that felt amazing! One of the best feelings I've ever had. Like a bird. I remembered Nigel, the surfer, and promised myself to try surfing one day too.

I was getting into it and trying to impress the girls by making little turns and stuff. I'm sure I was much worse than I remember, but that day I felt like a pro. After ten minutes or so, Silvio stopped the boat and ended my high. They circled around and came back to me; Silvio cut the engine and drifted the last few feet.

"Hey," I yelled. "What happened?"

"I got tired of you showing off," Silvio yelled.

Then the boat was right next to me.

"I got a bet for you, Matty. I'll give you twenty bucks to ski past that tourist boat naked."

Everyone was laughing, except for me and Silvio. We both knew this was serious. More than just twenty bucks was at stake here.

"I'm serious, Matty."

"Okay, but keep the twenty and you go next!"

We were all laughing hysterically.

"You've got a deal, Matty. Anyone who doesn't want to swim home has to ski naked first!"

I reached down and took off my trunks and handed them to Jorge. Jorge looked shocked.

"Holy shit, he's gonna do it!"

"Give me the vest," said Silvio, upping the stakes.

"That's not safe," I told him.

"Oh, come on. A hot skier like you needs a vest?"

And that was what I liked so much about Silvio: he was fun.
So I handed him the vest and treaded water while the boat pulled
away. The next thing I knew I was up and skiing naked. We
circled the tourist boats like ten times and I was laughing so hard
I could barely ski. Their flashbulbs were all going off and all the
tourists were running to whichever side of the boat we were
passing. Silvio was screaming things at the tourists; and Jorge,
Amy, and Trish were rolling on the deck laughing. I had never
felt so free before in my life. It was the best time and the most fun
I had ever had. I'm still in love with all of them: Silvio, Jorge,
Trish, and Amy. I can't think of any of them without remembering that day.

And nobody backed out either. Silvio went next, and then
Amy, who I think was dying to get naked; and why not? She had
every reason to be proud. She was seventeen and gorgeous. Then
Trish, who actually had red pubic hair, skied naked too! I saw
nothing else but that patch of red hair the entire time she skied.
The funny thing was that I didn't really get turned on. I mean
yeah, they were hot and naked, but I felt like we were a gang or
something—like we had separated ourselves from the normal
people, from the tourists. Sex never even crossed my mind. I
don't think any of us thought about sex that day. We were just
like kids having innocent fun. And I never knew you could do
that: get naked with other people and not have sex. It was pretty
cool. But I never could get my eyes above Trish's waist.

Afterward, we went to a dockside restaurant where Silvio
bought us all dinner. Then we cruised down the Miami River at
night. Both couples were snuggling up and kissing and stuff
while I drove the boat. But I didn't feel like an outsider. I wasn't
lonely. I mean, sure, I wished I had a girl too, but I felt like they
were trusting me to drive the boat. They were depending on me.
And the day had been so good that I didn't want to let all those
poor me lonely feelings fuck things up. It was truly the happiest I
had ever been in my life.

The next morning I woke up with a strange feeling. Had I been
dreaming of sex? I was still a little groggy, and wasn't sure if it
was real. But then yes, it was real all right. Could it be Trish? No,

I could feel the razor stubble. Silvio was definitely sucking my dick. I just thought, *Oh, well, I guess he deserves it.*

Then I closed my eyes and pretended it was Trish.

Later, he told me I had a great dick and we talked about sex a little. Silvio was different. He wasn't ashamed, and he didn't treat me any different after. For the next six months he came into my room a lot of mornings. I guess nights were reserved for Trish. We had a lot of fun, and the sex wasn't that bad either. Silvio, Trish, and I became pretty good friends too. After I finished painting the house, I got a job up in North Miami Beach where Trish's sub shop was. Silvio had given her one of his shops. In the morning, after Silvio and I did our thing, Trish would give me a ride to work. At night they would do their thing, and I would go to NA meetings with Jorge and Amy.

This got a little confusing, and I couldn't help but wonder what was wrong with me. I mean Silvio had a girl and Jorge had a girl, so where was mine? I had slept with that girl in rehab in Boston, and there was Françoise, but I couldn't seem to make my moves on any pretty girls that I liked. When I liked a girl, I would tell Jorge. Then he would sleep with her. Amy would get mad and cry on my shoulder; I would get mad and cry on her shoulder; then we would both forgive him and things would go back to normal. Even though I was dying to, I couldn't tell Amy I was in love with her. Even though I fantasized about Trish every night, I could never let her know. Silvio even tried to set us up a few times.

Once we were all sitting around watching TV and Silvio just popped in a porno and left the room. I fled immediately to my waterbed without a word. A few weeks later after dinner, Silvio and I were smoking in the backyard. Then, out of nowhere, he said, "Trish is waiting for you, Matty."

"What?"

"You heard me, Matty. She's in the bedroom waiting for you."

"Fuck you, Sil. Don't screw with me!"

"I'm not screwing with you. She's waiting for you. We discussed it before dinner, and it's what we both want."

"What about what I want?"

He started laughing. "We all know what you want, Matty! Now just go and get it."

And I did, sort of. The house was all dark when I got inside. Only candles burning in the dining room. Their bedroom door was all the way open and candles were burning in there too. I crept slowly up to the door and looked inside. What I saw terrified me! Trish was lying on her stomach, on the bed, completely naked. Her long red hair was pulled to one side, leaving her back exposed. And what a magnificent back! The most amazing back I had ever seen. Her ass was angelic. I would have gladly given up the rest of my life to lay my head on the small of her back just once. My arm wrapped around her legs, my chest next to that perfect ass. All I had to do was the impossible: walk into the room and lie down next to her. I pictured this in my mind — kissing her ass lightly, her back, her neck, her shoulders. How could I ever have questioned my sexuality? The fairer sex was the only one for me. No razor stubble and coarse body hair, just the downy blond baby hairs on her ass that I saw glistening in the candlelight. But like I said, it was impossible.

I thought she was probably waiting for Silvio and he was trying to set me up. If I went in there, she would freak out when she realized it was me. *I'm not that stupid*, I thought.

But I was. She turned on her side to face me, exposing her small round breasts with pink nipples and the aforementioned red pubic hair. She was the most beautiful woman I had ever seen, and she was staring right at me. Our eye contact lasted only a few seconds but that was long enough. I turned and ran out of the house. I ran all the way to Biscayne Boulevard, where I stopped to catch my breath.

They're perverts! At least that's what I told myself. Some kind of weird swingers or something, and that was not my scene! Just who the fuck did they think I was? I wasn't a freak! But that wasn't working. No matter how much I tried to close my eyes, it was there staring me in the face — her eyes, her soft blue eyes. The truth was in her eyes. I was terrified of women! That was it. That was it all along. That's why I couldn't go into the room and that's why I let Jorge fuck all the girls I liked. I was too scared to do anything; too scared of the rejection. If I never made a move, then I would never be rejected. And they would never find out that I was gay.

"You need a ride?"

It was a businessman in a rental car.

"Yeah."

I jumped in the car. Twenty minutes later we were parked behind the old Playboy Club near 79th Street and Biscayne Boulevard and he was sucking my dick. I was safe again. Safe with what I knew. I always felt comfortable with a stranger sucking my dick. I started to cry, but he didn't notice. I was still crying when I came in his mouth. I didn't let my emotions get in the way of the physical act; I was a professional.

I didn't go back to Silvio's that night. I didn't go to work the next day either. I was back up to my old tricks again.

R O C K   S T A R

It didn't take me long to get back in the swing of things. The next night I found myself in a cheap hotel on 56th and Biscayne with some guy named Walter. There was a lot of dick-sucking going on. Walter sucked mine, I sucked his, and we both sucked the "glass dick." I had tried smoking crack a few times before, but with Walter it was a bit extreme. He wasn't a crack addict, he was a Rock Star!

We smoked all that night and into the next day. Around noon, we took a sleeping pill each and slept for three or four hours. When we woke up, we went right back to the pipe. I liked smoking crack too. It wasn't like getting *high*, it was more like getting *low*. Crackheads don't want to feel better, they want to feel worse. As soon as I took my first hit, I felt like the devil himself. There was nothing too dirty or too bad that I wouldn't do. The only problem was getting Walter to do it to me. He would get all excited after his hit and tell me all these things he was going to do to me. I would get all excited and take a hit and get ready, but then Walter would want another hit to keep his high going and then me again and then...

It was a vicious circle with no end. We spent three days in a sleazy hotel naked and hard but accomplishing very little. I came on the first night, about fifteen minutes after he picked me up, but after I started smoking it was all talk. Crack really opened up the door to my darker side, and I was into everything he said, we just never got around to doing it. He told me he wanted to film me jerking off and I got into it. Then he got out the video camera and checked the battery and of course took another hit. Then I took a hit and started jerking off but instead of filming, Walter just took another hit. I was into the camera, though, and eventually I got it hooked up to the TV so whatever I pointed the camera at would show up on the hotel TV. I liked that. Maybe I was a bit narcissistic or maybe it was the crack, but if Walter was too high to film me, then filming myself was the next best thing.

In the end, Walter was good for nothing except producing an endless stream of twenty-dollar rocks. As far as sex was concerned, I was on my own. I got his camera all set up and watched myself jack off on TV. I watched myself smoking crack naked, "sucking the glass dick." That turned me on immensely. Everything dirty turned me on. I spit on myself and watched it on TV. I pissed on myself and watched it on TV. I came on myself and watched it on TV too. I was fascinated. It was like my very own television channel; performance art where I was the performer and the audience.

"This next piece is something I like to call 'Trashy Kid Puts on a Cockring for the First Time.'"

Did I mention that Walter had toys? Not that they did him any good, but I tried them all—on TV of course. If it wasn't for the crack and the TV, I don't think I would have, but everything I saw on TV seemed so unreal. I tried them all: the cockrings, the nipple clamps, the seven balls on a string. What the fuck do you call those things, by the way? For a while there, my show turned into the Home Shopping Network for sex toys.

I've always watched television in spurts. I get really excited about all the stuff I've been missing and I can't turn it off for the first couple of days. After about three days I reach my threshold and get sick of it again. Watching me naked on TV was no exception.

"Shit, I've seen this one before."

I turned the channel. There was a new show on. It was called "Later Walter." I had a hard time leaving the video recorder and the TV, but Walter was easy. That last day he just sat in the bathroom smoking on the toilet. I couldn't even get him to open the door and give me a hit. I had to piss in the sink. This got old fast and the more I came down, the less I liked Walter. So I got dressed and recorded a goodbye video for Walter. I told him he might want to check out some NA meetings sometime. I told him he was a drag and if he saw me on the street again to keep driving. Then I showed him my dick and told him that was what he missed out on. Like he cared...

It was hard to leave that camera—my audience, my beloved fans—but the curtain fell and I split. I turned off the camera and took all the money I could find lying around, which was about fifteen bucks. Then I took this nice silver cockring, shoved it in my pocket, and left.

It was dark outside the hotel, and I felt like shit. Some guy picked me up after about fifteen minutes of walking. He blew me

in the car and gave me twenty bucks, but couldn't offer me a
place to sleep. I took my thirty-five dollars and got a skanky
motel room for the night. I spent the next day walking north on
Biscayne and stopping at all the adult bookstores. By nightfall, I
had reached 125th Street and sixty bucks. Things weren't all that
bad. I felt much improved compared to my three days with
Walter. I grabbed a Whopper at BK and then walked up a few
miles to where Biscayne is less full of shops and lights and stuff.
I found a bus stop near the FIU campus that was secluded
enough and sat down to wait.

About thirty minutes later a royal blue Audi 5000 drove by
doing about sixty-five. Right after passing me, the driver
slammed on the brakes and popped a U-turn right in the middle
of Biscayne. He drove right past me again, this time at about fifty.
Then he made another U-turn and pulled right up to the bus
stop. Oh fuck! It was Jorge and Amy. Amy put down the power
window and Jorge told me to get in.

"I'm waiting for the bus."

"Yeah, right," Jorge said sarcastically. "Get in!"

"So what are you guys up to?" I asked as if nothing were
wrong.

"Where the fuck have you been!" Jorge screamed.

"I've been around."

"We've been looking for you for three days."

"Silvio told us what happened. He's been looking for you
too. He feels bad and he wants you to go back."

"Whatever. It's no big deal. I just needed some time alone."

Jorge said my time alone was over for now. They took me to
an NA meeting in North Miami Beach and afterward I told them
I didn't want to go to Silvio's house. Amy said we could all crash
at her place as her parents were out of town. So we did.

When we got there I jumped in the shower. As soon as I was
alone under the shower I started to cry. Sometimes I'm such a
pussy! But I was embarrassed by where they found me and how
Jorge had said "Yeah, right" when I told him I was just waiting
for a bus. What was that supposed to mean? Did they know? Did
everyone know? And what did Silvio tell them? Did he tell them
that I was afraid of Trish?

That line of thought was getting me nowhere. I couldn't stop
crying, and I really wished I was dead. Then I heard the bath-

room door open, and I was a little embarrassed as Amy's shower had one of those glass doors instead of a curtain. Not even a frosted glass door. If it wasn't for all the steam I would have died. So I stopped crying and tried to look like a casual person just taking a shower.

Then the door slid open behind me and I was too terrified to look back.

"Can I come in?"

It was Amy.

"Okay."

But it was not fucking okay! I was shaking like a leaf and wondering what the hell was going on. You'd think after three days of watching myself naked on TV and two and a half years of sleeping with anyone who happened to ask, I would be comfortable with my body. Wrong. I was terrified that she would think I was ugly, or my dick was too small, or I was too skinny. And what about my pitiful little patch of pubes? I was almost sixteen, and I still had less than one hundred pubic hairs. Seventy-three to be exact, but who was counting?

"I'm cold," she said and stepped a little closer to me. She was right behind me. I felt her closeness and it was killing me. She stepped closer still and put her arms around me. I felt her naked body on my back. I got hard immediately.

"You're shaking like a leaf," she said.

"Sorry," was all I could come up with.

She reached down and grabbed my dick. She squeezed it hard, then started slowly stroking it. I turned around and then we were kissing. My shaking subsided a little. I pulled her toward me and kissed her deeply, forcing my tongue into her mouth. I cupped her breasts in my hands and squeezed them softly. She let out a little moan. I got down on my knees and buried my face between her thighs. She moaned some more, louder this time. I was licking her slowly and trying to keep from drowning. I must have swallowed a gallon of water. I looked down to keep from swallowing more water and saw six feet. Two were mine. The two with red nail polish were Amy's and the two behind her belonged unmistakably to Jorge.

I looked up and saw him standing behind her kissing her neck and holding her breasts. When were they planning on telling me? Maybe I was supposed to notice his dick sticking between her legs while I was eating her out. Maybe I would have mistaken Amy for a hermaphrodite.

Either way, it was a bit shocking. Was everybody a fucking freak? I knew Jorge and Silvio were trying to help me in their own weird ways, but it was getting ridiculous. I got out of the shower and left them to it. I sat on Amy's bed in a towel for ten minutes or so, trying to make sense of it all. They came into the bedroom and sat next to me on the bed. Amy reached down and opened my towel. She started stroking me, then licking me. Jorge moved around behind her and entered her that way. I couldn't get hard. All the time I kept thinking that if Jorge wasn't there I would have come three times already, but it just wasn't happening this way.

"Look," I said, "I know you guys are trying to help me, but this isn't working."

Jorge was a little annoyed, but Amy seemed pleased. We went to Denny's and had some coffee and talked until four in the morning. It was nice. I mean, at least I hadn't gotten scared and run away like a little kid. We talked things over and worked it out. They said I was too serious about sex. I guess they had missed the jumping rope while dressed up like a schoolgirl scene, but they were right, of course. I was too serious about sex with girls. They told me that Silvio and Trish were really upset and that they blamed themselves for my leaving. Jorge said that he had never seen Silvio so depressed. I was a little touched. Jorge told me that Silvio was only trying to help get me over my fear of women.

"What fear of women?" I said defensively, but I got the point.

The next day Amy and Jorge drove me back to Silvio's and we made up, so to speak.

T A K E M E
H O M E

Things went back to normal at Silvio's with only two noticeable differences. First, Silvio's morning visits to my room slowed down to about once a week at most, and second, Trish and I were a little uncomfortable when left alone. This lasted about two months. We mostly made small talk and laughed uncomfortably a lot. Then one day we were out back in the yard together while Silvio was at work. Trish was sunbathing and I was cleaning the boat. I sat down next to her to smoke a cigarette and she bummed one off me. Then, out of nowhere, she said, "I'm sorry, Matty."

"For what?"

"For what happened that night."

Silence.

"I know things got a little weird. How could they not be weird with Silvio involved?" We both laughed.

"But I just wanted you to know that it wasn't all him. I mean, I wasn't doing anybody any favors. It's what I wanted."

More silence.

"I just wanted you to know that."

Extended silence. She leaned over and kissed my forehead.

"Okay?"

"Okay."

And it was; we really were okay after that.

One month turned into six, and life went on as usual. We were all friends again, and we had a great time. Silvio treated me more and more like an equal. One time he even asked me to take Little Silvio out skiing while he was at work. I couldn't believe that he trusted me to look after his son. I felt grown up and the truth was that I was growing up. I went to work, I paid the rent and the bills, and I went to my NA and AA meetings at night. I was becoming a responsible member of society. At the meetings I made a lot of friends and even got a sponsor.

After a while people started trusting me there too. Whenever a young kid would show up, the adults would introduce us and tell them to hang out with me. I was sort of a role model for young people. Jorge and Amy were too. Most of the young people who went to those meetings would only last a few weeks at best before they would disappear again. Jorge, Amy, and I had like six months clean. They even started taking us to high schools to speak to the kids about the woes of drug addiction. That was a little disturbing to me.

When I sat in some classroom talking to kids about drug addiction, I couldn't help but think that I was supposed to be one of them. Our message was for them not to end up like us, but I couldn't help wanting to be like them. They had little brown bags or Tupperware containers under their desks. I imagined they were stuffed full of sandwiches and treats like snack-packs and stuff. I imagined their mothers packing their lunches and mussing their hair on the way out the door, and I was jealous. Deep down I knew they all had their problems and some were even worse off than me, but I couldn't stop wanting to be one of them.

On the night of June 20, 1985, I came home to find the house completely dark. That was strange; Silvio and Trish were both at home when I had left for my NA meeting and they hadn't mentioned going out. Another strange thing was that Amy and Jorge weren't at the meeting that night. I got an uncomfortable feeling that something as wrong. Call it a premonition, but when I went to open my door I was feeling a little nauseous. I had a bad feeling. I opened the door and reached inside for the light. It didn't turn on. I guessed that the fuse had blown. I cursed to myself and stumbled through the living room. When I got to the couch I reached down to turn on the table lamp but before I could get there, all the lights went on.

"Happy Birthday!"

I almost jumped right the fuck out of my skin. Silvio and Jorge were rolling on the floor laughing. "Did you see his fucking face, Jorge? I think he pissed himself!"

And I almost had. Once I recovered from the shock I was so embarrassed. I had forgotten about my birthday, and that was the first time I had ever had a party, much less a surprise party. Well, nobody ever really forgets their birthday; I just felt sorry for myself all day thinking that everyone else had forgotten. But they hadn't. It was a real party too. There were about ten people from NA there, as well as Silvio, Jorge, Trish, and Amy. Jorge got me a journal to write in, Silvio got me an antique typewriter,

Trish got me a great shirt, and Amy got me a book. The rest of the presents from the NA people were *Recovery* literature and stuff, but it's the thought that counts, right? It was a great night. We drank nonalcoholic champagne and ate cake. My first-ever personalized cake.

The next day two strange things happened. First, my NA sponsor called and started asking a lot of funny questions about Silvio and my living situation. Second, and strangest of all, my mother called me. She said she had heard that I was living near downtown, and she and her new husband would be up there tomorrow and would like to drop by and see me for my birthday.

"Okay," I said, "but my birthday was yesterday."

I gave her the address anyway and as I hung up the phone I couldn't help thinking, *What does she want from me?*

I hardly slept that night. I was confused. I just couldn't get my mind around her motives. Why now? Was she jealous? Why, when I was doing so well? Why not before, when I needed her?

They showed up around four the next day, and I could tell immediately that they had been caught off guard. They were perhaps expecting some rat's nest with a week's worth of garbage piled up on the floor. They were expecting to find me just waking up from another long night of partying. The way they looked when they got out of the car was guarded, like they expected me to try hitting them up for money first thing. What they found instead was me cooking some breakfast and listening to my new stereo. I had been trying to learn to cook, if you could call it that.

We exchanged polite greetings, and I offered them some coffee. They walked around my apartment with this amazed look on their faces. My new stepfather picked up my AA Big Book and scoffed. My mom, who looked so much older than I remembered her, fidgeted nervously with her coffee cup. Then they got down to business.

"We want you to come and live with us again," my mom said.

"And go back to school," my new stepfather added.

"Okay," I said, and that was that.

I'd like to explain that to you, but I still can't explain it to myself. I knew it was a stupid move, but I guess I just wanted to believe.

After they left I cried and cursed myself for giving in to them, but then I started imagining myself as one of those little rich kids in the schools. Maybe I would have bagged lunches too, maybe I would meet a normal girl, and maybe I would even go to college. Later that night I told Silvio and Trish about my decision. Silvio seemed disappointed, but he tried to keep it to himself. He told me that if it didn't work out, my apartment would still be there. The next day my stepdad came and got me and drove me down to Homestead, where they had bought a house. The house was way out in the country, in the middle of nowhere, and I felt trapped immediately.

The rules started right away. No smoking or coffee, lights-out at ten thirty, no music, no phone calls longer than ten minutes. If I had to go to my NA meetings during the week then I would have to be back in the house by nine. Most of the meetings ended at nine so I was fucked except for the weekends. My stereo and TV went out in the garage with anything else that remotely resembled freedom. After the rules came the nagging.

"Stop using so much toilet paper."

"Close the refrigerator door."

"Turn those lights out." The Juvenile Detention Center had fewer rules.

By far the worst part was the taunting my stepfather did.

"If you had stayed in school and done well we would have bought you a car," or "If you weren't so screwed up we would have paid for your college."

That killed me. I knew he was full of shit, but like always, I wanted to believe. Okay, so it was all my fault, I was a bad kid. If I had only tried harder then they would have treated me better too. Bag lunches, a car, yearly vacations, even a trip to the dentist. Did I mention I had bad teeth?

The second day I was there, my mom took me down to the local high school to register. The next morning, I found myself standing with six other kids waiting for the school bus on a deserted country road.

"Do you like the Ninja Turtles?" some skinny, freckly kid asked me.

"Are they a band?"

"No, it's a cartoon. Do you watch *Miami Vice*?"

"I saw it once at the rehab."

"Where?"

"Never mind."

Luckily the bus pulled up and saved me from any further conversation. Being the new kid, I got on last. The bus was full. There was only one seat left next to this tiny little Spanish kid with a bandanna on. I asked him to move over so I could sit down.

"Fuck off," he told me and everybody laughed.

"That's funny," I said. "Move over."

"You deaf motherfucker?"

I couldn't fucking believe it. I've never been big, but this kid was tiny.

"Come on man, I'm not playing with you. Please move over."

"I'm not playing with you either, bitch!"

Silence... He just sat there with this shit-eating grin on his face. I glared at him. The bus started moving; the driver was obviously unaware of our situation. I looked at the kid again then back at the driver. I felt like crying.

"She ain't gonna help you, pussy. If you want me to move, then make me."

I've never been very tough. I hate violence. I don't even like to watch other people fight. In fact, I'm the biggest pussy I know. But one thing I learned at the detention center was that if you let one person fuck with you, then everyone will fuck with you, and you'll end up like some fucking whipping boy or something. Another thing I learned at the detention center is that anyone who talks about fighting with their hands down by their waist doesn't really want to fight. Guys who fight a lot stay out of your reach, and if you get too close then their hands come up instinctively. So like I said, I was feeling like crying, but I just hit the little prick in the face instead. It wasn't much, just a little peck on the nose, but he started bleeding right away and curled up like a ball in the seat. All the kids started yelling, "Fight, fight, fight!"

The bus driver pulled over and came back to us. I was still standing over him with my fists balled up in front of my face. She put some girl next to him and me in the girl's old seat and then she quieted the rest of the kids down and off we went to school. Some nerdy kid leaned over and told me I just beat up a Latin King and that now I was dead for sure.

"What's a Latin King?"

"It's a gang, stupid."

When we got to the school, the bus driver told the little "Latin King" to go and see the nurse and then took me to the principal's office. I got an extremely long lecture on "my type of kid" and how they dealt with us down there in Homestead. The principal never even asked me what happened; he just gave me a week of outdoor suspension and called my mom to come pick me up. Nobody answered at my house, so I had to take the city bus back home. When I got there my stepdad's car was parked crooked in the driveway with the driver's side door wide open. I went inside. All I was thinking about was how I was going to explain to him what had happened, but I never got the chance. He was so drunk he didn't even notice that I was home early.

"How was school, kiddo?"

"Not so hot. It's difficult to fit in with the kids there. They all act so young."

Then I was lying on the floor with my face stinging like shit. He was standing over me screaming. His face was bright red and he looked so fucking ugly; all swollen and porous.

What a fucking craterface, I thought to myself.

"You ungrateful little spoiled brat! You prima donna! Your mother and I worked hard to set this up for you, and now you're gonna fuck it up on the first day. Don't you tell her what you just told me, it'll break her heart."

He picked me up by the ears and started swinging me around the kitchen. He was like a fucking madman, and I hadn't even mentioned the fight. So, I was swinging around the house and he was in some kind of rage. He was kicking and punching a lot, but luckily most of his blows were missing. And then it was over, as quickly as it began. I picked myself up off the floor and looked around. He was gone. The back door was wide open, so I crept over to it and looked out. I saw him sitting under a tree in the backyard talking to himself. His face was still red. I went back into the kitchen and called my NA sponsor. I told him what had happened, and he told me to wait by the phone. Ten minutes later he called back.

"I'm stuck up in North Miami Beach, but I called some friends and they are coming to get you now. Their names are Tammy and Phil and they'll be there in fifteen minutes. Stay out of your father's way until they get there."

"Stepfather," I reminded him.

Like clockwork, fifteen minutes later a gold seventies Mustang Mach 1 pulled into the driveway. I went out and walked up to the car. The lady on the passenger side opened the door and told me to get in. Like I said, they were Tammy and Phil and they were great people. They were a married couple in their fifties who had been through hell together. They got high together, got clean together, had kids together, and I got the feeling they would always be together. Phil offered me a cigarette right away. Tammy asked if I had eaten. They took me to lunch and then to dinner and an NA meeting in Coconut Grove later that night. They dropped me off at nine thirty in front of my house.

"Are you sure you're going to be okay?" asked Tammy.

"Yeah, he's probably calmed down now."

Phil told me to call him if anything happened and he'd be there in fifteen minutes.

"Thanks, Phil. Goodnight."

"Goodnight," in chorus.

They hadn't given me a key yet, so I had to knock on the front door. My mom answered wearing her usual nothing-but-a-worried-face. Why was she always naked? And why didn't she ever shave that damn bush?

"Well now you did it," she said.

"Did what?"

"Terry is very upset with you, and so am I. He told me what happened."

"So what now?"

"Now you have to leave. You can come back in the morning to get your stuff."

"All right, can I use the phone?"

"I don't think that would be a good idea."

"Okay, goodnight."

"Goodnight."

She closed the door. So in the end I never did have to explain about that fight.

Now I don't know about you, but I'm fucking scared of the woods. It was so dark out there and walking down the road to South Dixie Highway I could hear all these animal sounds and shit. I was getting a little freaked out, and I still had like two miles to go before I even reached the bus stop on the corner. Another bus stop, my home away from home. But two miles was a long way, and like I said, I'm a little scared of the woods, so when the first car drove by I stuck out my thumb. This nice church lady in a station wagon picked me up and drove me the rest of the way to the bus stop on Dixie Highway.

"Where are you headed to this late at night?" she asked.

"Band practice," I lied.

"That's funny, I thought you were a musician when I saw you, because of your white hair. You look like Billy Idol."

"Thanks." But I wasn't quite sure if she meant it as a compliment.

"Are you into that Punk Rock?" she asked.

"A little I guess. Here's my stop, I can catch the bus from here."

"Okay. Be careful."

"Thank you. Goodnight."

"Goodnight."

Needless to say, I never caught a bus that night. But I did catch a ride with a taxi driver who blew me on the way to Coconut Grove but refused to pay me for my time.

"I give you free fare! That's like money to me."

"Fuck that, man. You said twenty dollars!"

"This ride would have cost you thirty!" He drove away.

That's the first and last time I ever tricked with a cabby; damn cheap bastards, and dirty too. He dropped me off in the center of Coconut Grove. It was close to the holidays and I knew that Narcotics Anonymous had this twenty-four-hour "help room" open down by Mercy Hospital. I started to walk and I got to the room close to midnight. It was just a little meeting room behind the hospital.

As I walked up I could see all the addicts out front, smoking and talking. There was a lot of laughter and camaraderie. I got a warm feeling inside as I got closer and began to make out the faces in the dark. There was Julio, my sponsor, talking with Jim the sailor. There was Lance, the nicest guy I had ever met, and of course there were Tammy and Phil. Jorge and Amy weren't visible on the porch, but I knew they were either inside or on their way. I knew at that moment that I would never go back to that other family again; my so-called *real* family. My family was going to be one of my own choosing from now on.

S I L V I O

My sponsor thought it would be better if I did not go back to live at Silvio's house. I agreed with him simply to avoid any suspicion, but it wasn't what I wanted. I wanted to go right back to my little apartment with Silvio and Trish. I missed them both so much, and I missed my life there. Silvio was different from all the other men that came before him. I wasn't just a trick to him, I was a friend. I told him stuff about me — the real me — and he did the same. We talked openly about our sexuality and the confusion we both shared about sleeping with boys. Silvio had his pick when it came to sex. He had this boyish charm that made him irresistible to girls and boys alike. What I couldn't understand was why he wanted to sleep with me when a girl like Trish was waiting in his bed.

But Silvio had been with many women. He had been married and divorced and still he preferred boys. I think the only reason he kept Trish around was to avoid coming out of the closet publicly. Don't get me wrong, he wasn't ashamed. I mean I'm sure he had his battles with facing the possible rejection of his family and friends when he did come out, but that wasn't all there was to it. With Silvio, I saw for the first time that someone could be unsure of their sexual preference. It didn't always have to be, and seldom was, a black-and-white issue. To put it simply, he was confused, and so was I. The only difference being that I had slept with more men by the time I was fourteen then Silvio had in his entire life and Silvio had slept with more girls than I probably ever would. We used to laugh about that a lot. What if I was straight and he was gay? We both sure had a fucked-up way of expressing it — me sleeping with boys and dreaming of girls and Silvio sleeping with girls while dreaming of boys.

In the end, though, I think Silvio was much closer to working out his sexual identity than I was. I still had a few years to go, and I wasn't ready to give up on girls just yet. On the other hand, I think Silvio was ready to do just that. I often thought that if I told him how much I loved him and that I wanted to be with him exclusively, he would have gone for it. But like I said, I wasn't exactly ready for that yet.

So Silvio was a turning point for me. I began to consider a life as a homosexual, and it didn't seem all that bad. It would make my life so much easier if I could just accept it and forget about girls altogether. Men were so much easier to deal with. I didn't have to find them; they would find me. I didn't have to take any risks because they were the ones putting it on the line. I just had to sit back and be myself and occasionally let them know I was open to "possibilities."

It all seemed so ridiculously simple if I could just accept what I was. If I could just accept that I was gay. But life always seems simple when viewed from the outside. On the inside, where I was, it was impossible. There was just something missing. I felt love for Silvio and I enjoyed the sex, but I never initiated it. I just went along with it like always. I never had an uncontrollable urge to suck his dick or kiss him on the mouth or anything. On the contrary, I was lusting after every woman I saw. I couldn't even look women in the eyes because I thought they would see through me. I thought they all knew I was fantasizing about them. When I would see a girl I liked at an NA meeting or on the street, I would immediately begin fantasizing about her. Not just perverted shit, but like true-love romantic stuff too. I would long to kiss her and to hold her and to walk on the beach holding hands. I never thought about boys like that.

The contradiction was hard for me to understand. I thought that maybe society had tricked me into fantasizing about girls due to the stigma associated with being gay. Maybe I had even tricked myself into believing I was straight too. Then why did I sleep with men almost exclusively? This was always on my mind, twenty-four hours a day, seven days a week. I had no answers.

So when my sponsor, also gay, by the way, told me moving back to Silvio's wasn't such a great idea, I went along with him. He thought Silvio was taking advantage of me and that he secretly wanted to sleep with me. I couldn't bring myself to tell him that Silvio and I were already sleeping together, much less that it might have been a little more than just sex, so I just agreed with him and looked for another place to stay.

S T R A I G H T
& N A R R O W

For the next year I bounced around Miami staying with different people from the NA meetings. They were all nice people, but none of them were gay and that created a huge problem. I had no way to support myself. If I was going to lead a so-called "straight life," then I was going to have to find a job. I asked around the meetings and found plenty of work. The first job I got was working for another recovering addict named John. He was a tree climber. I had no idea what that was, but he told me he'd give me ten bucks an hour so I said, "Okay."

The next day John picked me up at five in the morning. As I climbed into his pickup truck he handed me a coffee and I felt all grown up. Here I was headed to work, smoking a butt and sipping a cup-a-joe just like any other normal guy. We drove down to this church in Coconut Grove and started unloading the gear from the back of the truck. John got me set up in this cool harness like a mountain climber and then started teaching me how to operate a chainsaw. We walked around to the back of the church and John pointed to a huge old banyan tree. "That's the one we're cutting down," he said.

"What?"

"That tree...we're going to cut it down."

"Shit, man, you're kidding me, right?"

"I shit you not."

"Dude, that tree must be like four hundred years old!"

"Well it ain't gonna see four hundred and one."

"Seriously?"

"That's what we get paid for."

"Who's paying us?"

"The church."

"But that tree is older than the fucking church, man. That's just wrong."

"Were your parents hippies?"

"Come on, dude, be serious. We're not really gonna cut that fucking tree down, right?"

"That's what I get paid for, man. If it was on my property, I'd leave it alone. But it's on the church's property, and they want to put more parking back here. It's their property, their tree, and more importantly, their money."

"Dude, that's fucked."

"Dude, that's life."

It didn't seem like life to me, it seemed more like death. For the next week we slowly killed that fucking tree from the top down. You can't just chop down a banyan tree and yell timber like in a cartoon or something. You have to start at the top on the edges and slowly cut it away piece by piece. It was horrible watching that tree come down. I kept thinking of the Buddha, and I felt so guilty. I mean this was the tree under which he achieved enlightenment, right? In the East they build great temples around banyan trees, and here we were chopping one down for more church parking. I think that was the worst job I ever had.

By Saturday, John was ready to dynamite the stump out of the ground and I was ready to quit. The whole church showed up to watch the explosion and they all cheered when it went off. *Hooray, now we have somewhere to park all our fucking stupid minivans!* The whole scene made me sick. On Sunday night I met this carpenter named Frank at an AA meeting in South Miami. He told me he needed a helper and that he'd pay me eight bucks an hour. "As long as I don't have to chop down any trees," I told him.

So on Monday morning I started working for Frank. He was rebuilding an old farmhouse in the woods down on Old Cutler Road. Even though it was extremely hard work, I liked it. I felt good doing honest work and not destroying anything. Frank was cool. He had respect for the past and the carpenters that came before him. He wanted to restore the house to its former glory. All day long I would catch him staring at some old woodwork and shaking his head. "What's up, Frank?"

"Do you see the details in that molding? They don't make it like that anymore. Whoever made that was a true craftsman."

I loved when Frank would say shit like that. Through him I learned to appreciate the amount of work that went into everyday things. I learned to have respect for those who came before me and those who took pride in their work and through that I learned to take pride in my own work too. Other times I would see him shaking his head in dismay. "I can't believe this."

"What?"

"You see here where this joint is uneven?"

"Yeah."

"Okay, there's a brick wall behind there."

"Really?"

"Yeah man, some joker just drywalled right over it."

"So we're gonna bust it out, right?"

"Absolutely, man. Right after lunch."

And that's exactly what we did; we came back from lunch and tore that drywall right down. Underneath was a brick wall just like Frank had said, but it was painted like four hundred colors. I got the great job of taking all the paint off, and what a shitty job that was too. I covered the whole wall with chemical stripper and then scrubbed it with a wire brush for a week. Not once, but like twenty times. Each time I thought we would see bricks, but it would only be one more layer of ugly paint. I cursed all the fuckers who painted that wall a million times a day. But finally one night, close to quitting time, my little wire brush hit red bricks and that was truly a great feeling of accomplishment. The next day I put more stripper on and started scrubbing with renewed enthusiasm. By the end of a week that wall was looking as good as new, and I was proud as hell.

Frank wasn't impressed. I mean, he said I did a good job and all, but he was preoccupied with something else. He had been acting grumpy for a few days so I guessed that something was seriously bothering him. The day I finished the wall I asked him what was wrong.

"The owners, man. They are what's wrong."

"Why?"

"Goddamn yuppies, man. They want this wall down. I'm sorry, man, but they want the whole fucking thing torn down. They basically want to change my whole design. I know I went over budget a bit, but now they want to change the whole fucking thing. They got some idiot contractor friend who told them he could've done the whole thing for a quarter of what I charged them. So now they want me to start cutting corners and slapping up drywall. I mean we might as well go to Home Fucking Depot and get the fucking doors there!"

Frank had spent the last three weeks ordering wood for these french doors he was going to make himself. I don't know much about wood, but I can tell you that the stuff he ordered was something special. The guys who delivered it looked more like art handlers than truck drivers. We had to stack it in the master bedroom with a drop cloth in between each piece.

"So what are you going to do?"

"Well, I'm gonna cut costs and send back that wood and tear this fucking wall down is what I'm gonna do."

"Really."

"I need the money, kid. I can't afford to lose this job."

"That sucks."

"You know what really sucks?"

"What?"

"That's a cavity wall."

"What's that?"

"A double wall. So we gotta tear them both down."

And tear them down we did; well sort of. First we went to work with sledgehammers. When that wasn't going too well, Frank went and got a small hand-held jackhammer type of thing, and then he went and got a bigger one. Finally, he left one morning and came back with three day laborers, three huge fucking sledgehammers, and all kinds of assorted picks and pry bars and stuff. I never heard so much cursing in all my life. I felt like I was in an old prison movie. All day the five of us swung those picks and hammers and that fucking wall barely budged. The three laborers worked on the outside one and Frank and I worked on the inside. Frank said it was the most solid wall he had ever seen.

It took us five days of the hardest work I've ever done in my life to get that wall down. One Saturday morning when there was only about a foot or two of the wall left, the three laborers walked up to Frank. One of them had this old-looking bottle in his hand. He held it up to Frank.

"What's that?" Frank asked.

"Encontré dentro de la pared."

"What?"

"En la pared."

"What the fuck is he saying?" asked Frank.

"I think he's saying he found that in the wall."

"Si, en la pared."

"Let me see that."

Frank took the bottle and examined it. It was most definitely old; very old. It looked like an old whiskey bottle from the Civil War or something. It was clear glass but covered in dust and grime and it had an old cork stuck in the top. Inside was an old yellow folded-up piece of paper. Frank just stared at it and then looked up with this confused look.

"What the fuck?" he said.

He uncorked the bottle and using his needle-nose pliers, he carefully pulled out the piece of paper and gingerly unfolded it.

"It's a note," he said more to himself than anybody.

He read silently to himself and then burst out laughing.

"What's it say?" I asked.

Frank just kept on laughing like crazy.

"What's it say?"

He thrust the note into my hand and walked away laughing. He walked all the way to his truck still laughing out loud. He got in his truck and sped away. He didn't show up to work the next day, or the next, or the next. Eventually the owners did show up wondering where the fuck Frank was. When I said I hadn't seen him for three days they flipped out. They asked me what the hell I had been doing for the last three days, and I told them I had been waiting. What was I going to say, that I had been studying an antique note that we found in a bottle?

I guess they had had enough, because they fired me right then and there. That was okay, because I didn't want to work without Frank anyway. In fact I was getting pretty tired of construction all together. I walked away, but then I turned around and went back to them. I reached into my pocket and took out the folded-up note and handed it to the owner.

"What's this?" he asked.

"It's for you," I said and walked away.

This is what he saw:

Better men built this house
than them that are tearing it down!

Frank didn't come to the meetings anymore either. I guess he had just had enough of the straight life. I wasn't that far behind. For my next job, I became a human guinea pig, testing stomach-ulcer medicine. The drawback there was that they wanted to take a lot of blood samples, and I already told you I was deathly afraid of needles. I fainted the first time they took my blood and woke up with holes all over my arm. I struggled to the pay phone and called my sponsor to rescue me. Then I got a job at McDonald's. I flipped McBurgers, mopped McFloors, swept McParking Lot, and took out McTrash for two weeks. The manager told me to color my hair normal and take out my earrings, and I told him to go McFuck himself! There goes another lie. That's what I wanted to tell him, but I could never tell adults to fuck off without Cheevie. The truth is I just said okay and never showed up to work again.

The problem was that I already had a profession that I was good at. Not only was I good at it, but I liked it too. My heart wasn't really in any of those other jobs. I kept thinking that I could make more money doing what I did best—and I didn't have to punch a clock or listen to some uptight, undereducated manager bitching at me all the time. Even if I could go to work for Silvio at the sub shop, it would be better than all these dead-end square jobs. Trust me, when you're sleeping with the boss it makes all the difference in the world.

Without sex, I just couldn't seem to get it together in the real world. It's like I only had one way to relate to people. There were guys who wanted to sleep with me, and there were girls who I wanted to sleep with, and the rest were just background noise; elevator music in my world of rock and roll.

In the meetings they called what I was going through "self discovery." I called it depressing. In fact, I was starting to find the whole so-called straight life depressing. As far as I was concerned, reality sucked. I didn't have a place of my own after I moved out of Silvio's, and that sucked too. I would lie up at night on some stranger's couch or floor and think about the only thing I was really any good at.

Sometimes I would think about how fucked up it was that I was only a good-for-nothing hustler, but most times I would fantasize about going out and doing it again. The most common result of that type of thinking would be to get up and go wander the streets all night. Sometimes I would hook up with a guy and sometimes not, but it just gave me an excited feeling to be back on the streets again. One strange thing is that I stopped taking money. I've never been able to explain that, but for some reason I just wouldn't take their cash anymore. They would always offer and I would always refuse, even when I was flat broke. Stranger things have happened, right?

That was how I lived for that whole year: going to NA meetings, having normal friends, sometimes even a job, and sleeping on peoples couches. Nice people's couches, people who wanted to help me and who weren't interested in sleeping with me. Some I suspect even loved me, but I didn't feel loved or wanted unless they wanted to sleep with me. At night, I would go out secretly and do my thing with whoever happened to be driving by.

It's funny how there was at least one in every neighborhood. I had no control of where I'd be sleeping back then, but there was always someone driving around looking for sex. You just had to keep your eyes open and occasionally grab your dick at an opportune moment. In the suburbs you don't want to do an outright grab; save that for the city. In the suburbs, try a more discreet approach, like you have an itch or something. That way it looks innocent enough to save you from getting beat up by some homophobic rednecks, but the ones who are looking will get the point.

I think that was the closest I've ever come to having multiple personalities. Monday morning I would be speaking at some high school about the woes of drug addiction and Monday night I would be parked behind the school with some frustrated suburban PTA dad. I had some close calls too. A couple of times people I had met in the NA meetings would see me on the street late at night and ask me if I was okay. Usually I would tell them I was up late working on my fourth step and couldn't sleep, so I had just stepped outside for some air. This would usually result in me getting driven to Denny's for coffee and fourth step advice. Nothing like recovery talk to put me off sex for the night.

What I couldn't really understand was why all these strangers wanted to help me when I wasn't all that interested in helping myself. I felt good being off of drugs and all, but I didn't want to stop the other stuff. After Silvio, things were just different. I started to sleep with men because that's what I wanted to do. I still fantasized about girls, but they were just too difficult to sleep with. And although I hadn't given up on them yet, I had put them on the back burner for a while. The thing was that I liked sex and I had a sure thing almost every night, so why fuck it up?

Just after my seventeenth birthday I had one year clean and sober. How lovely for me! I was now a fixture at all the meetings, and I even became a sponsor myself. Some younger kids started showing up at the meetings and one kid named Rusty asked me to be his sponsor. In retrospect, I don't know if that was such a good idea. Talk about the blind leading the blind. I did have a year off drugs, but that was about all I had. I was still leading this double life that nobody knew about. My first instinct was to tell Rusty to forget about it, but when I looked into his eyes I knew that he was coming from where I had already been. We had walked the same streets, and we were both still walking them. He was still actively hustling. He didn't say so, but I could tell. I was still doing the same only I don't know if you could still call it hustling when no money was involved. Was I hustling for love? Don't ask me.

I became Rusty's sponsor. It turned out that it didn't entail much on my part. After he asked me to sponsor him, he called me a couple of times and asked me for advice and then a week later he disappeared. I never spoke to him again. Meanwhile, my own sponsor got the "package." He got really sick and was admitted to South Miami Hospital. They told him he had pneumonia due to a weakened immune system. A week later they told him he had full-blown AIDS. That was not good. My sponsor's name was Julio and I loved him.

J U L E S

Julio, or Jules as he was known in the NA meetings, was probably the closest friend I had at that time. I used to cry on his shoulder a lot. When I finally got around to telling him about the hustling, he wasn't surprised; he had suspected for a while and had been waiting a year for me to come out with it. After I told him, he thought it might be a good idea for me to share my story at an NA meeting to get over my fears. So that's what I did. It didn't go over too well though. I was shaking when I raised my hand that night. I don't remember the exact words I used but I basically confessed all my sins: the hustling, the fear of women, the great tragedy that was me. I don't know if you've ever been to an NA or AA meeting, but after you're done sharing, they all share back with you.

Thanks for sharing Matty. I really related to your story and it made me think of blah, blah, blah...

But that time, there was only dead silence after I finished sharing. We all just sat there and looked at each other for a minute or two, and then finally some lady raised her hand and started talking about her dilemma with insulin. She was diabetic and the insulin needles reminded her of shooting up. How fucking stupid was that? Well, not too stupid, I guess, because the rest of the meeting was about her and her stupid fear of relapsing due to insulin. After the meeting, I felt like I had leprosy. Nobody talked to me. Even my friends there were shying away. This older straight guy named Wayne felt sorry for me, I guess, because he walked right up to me and said, "That was pretty deep, kiddo. But we've all done shit we're not proud of, even me."

"You mean you've done that too?"

"Shit, yeah, when some beautiful woman comes up to you and offers you money for sex, who could say no?"

Maybe he wasn't listening to me when I spoke in the meeting or maybe he was sitting too far away to hear, so I reminded him.

"I wasn't talking about girls, though."

"Yeah, whatever," he mumbled and then he saw his friends and walked away.

The next person to talk to me was this really old guy named Don. He asked if he could speak to me in private and then led me back into the now-empty meeting room. I thought he was going to open up to me and confide that he was a hustler too, back in the day of course. I thought wrong.

"Matthew, I hate to be the one to tell you this, but what you shared tonight was completely inappropriate. That's just not the sort of thing we discuss here. Maybe you should go to see a private therapist."

"Whatever," I said and walked away.

I'm not trying to rag on self-help programs. I met a lot of good people there. It just so happens that none of them were present when I dropped my bomb. The fact is that the only reason people go to those types of meetings is because they are fucked up, so you have to expect to run into a lot of fucked-up people there. I knew this, but it didn't help me much that night. I was totally pissed off and pretty much decided that the "A" meetings weren't for me anymore.

On the way out, some lady ran up to me in the parking lot. She was out of breath when she introduced herself.

"Hi, Matthew. I'm Karen."

"Hi."

"Wow, I'm glad I found you. I thought you had already left. I just wanted to tell you that what you said in there tonight was the most interesting and honest thing I've ever heard at one of these meetings."

Something about the way she said "one of these meetings" sounded suspicious to me.

"Are you an addict?" I asked.

"No, I'm a writer. I'm just doing a story on Twelve Step programs for the *Herald*, and that's what I wanted to talk to you about. Can I include some of what you said tonight in my piece? No names, of course."

"Okay."

"Thanks. Seriously, Matthew. I think you have a really nice way of putting things. Maybe you should consider writing."

"Thanks," I said.

By the time I got to the hospital I was depressed again, but when I walked into Jules' room I immediately forgot all my problems. I had last seen him just three days before, but he had changed so much. He looked like a ghost. He was so thin and gray. He had on an oxygen mask that got all fogged up with his breathing. He was asleep, and thank God for that. I was glad he didn't get to see my initial reaction. I sat down and started to read. After a couple of hours, the nurse brought me a cot and I fell asleep. When I woke up Jules was still sleeping. I took a shower in his room and then went down to get some coffee. I drank coffee and smoked on the hospital's patio for an hour or so. I had never seen anyone die before, and I knew that was what I was seeing now. Somehow I could just tell that Jules wasn't gonna come out of that room alive. I've heard people say, "The room smelled like death."

I didn't know about all that—it smelled like a hospital to me—but something was different. More than him looking like shit and all, it was like things just seemed final—like an ending was hovering in the air, his ending. Everything we did or said had to be measured out carefully. I didn't want to waste any time or use too many words.

When I got back to the room Jules was awake. We hugged, and then I kissed him on the forehead. I climbed into the bed with him and we just lay there in silence for a while. I combed his hair back from his eyes with my fingers and held his hand. His Cuban grandmother walked in and found us like that and crossed herself immediately. I didn't get up. I guess I had had enough with the straight world. I mean, fuck her anyway. Did she think that the sign of the cross would save her from gay exposure? Eventually I did get up and leave them alone, but not before she got my point. Not before she understood that I was not ashamed.

For the next week I stayed at the hospital twenty-four hours a day. Some of Jules' friends from NA brought me money and cigarettes and stuff. They were all very grateful that I was staying there and that most of the time Jules seemed pretty content. I wasn't really being so kind and all; I liked the hospital. It was safe and clean, and Jules and I became closer than I've ever been with another person. We talked a lot and ragged on all his family members and how they were dressed. They kept wearing very bright colors—to cheer him up, I guess; but the men ended up looking like they had just walked off the set of *Miami Vice* and the women...don't get me started.

Our friends from NA would visit at night. They would always bring pizza or subs, and we would all eat and tell funny stories about the losers at the meetings. It was fun, everyone left all their troubles at the door. They kept telling me how much it meant to Jules that I was there for him and how much it helped them that I was there while they were at work and taking care of their kids and stuff. I felt important, and I liked that. Later, after all our visitors left, Jules and I would watch bad television and complain about it a lot. Then he would start crying, and I would hold him and that was all. I didn't know what to say to make him feel better so I just didn't say anything at all.

One week turned into two, and every day Jules was thinner and thinner. Every day the doctors brought more bad news, and every night the NA people would bring more food and good cheer. And still every night after lights-out, Jules would cry and I would hold him. I stopped using the cot and slept with Jules most nights. One night I dozed off and when I woke up his hand was on my dick. He was lightly, weakly squeezing it. I opened my eyes and turned to face him. His oxygen mask was all fogged up. There were tears welling in his eyes. I reached down and took his hand off my dick. We lay there in silence for a while just holding hands, then I told him I was gonna go down the hall and get a Coke. I grabbed my shoes and shirt and walked out of the room. I never went back again.

I'm so sorry, Jules...

I left the hospital and walked down US-1 for a while. I got to the South Miami Cinema and saw on the billboard that they were doing a midnight double feature of *Sid & Nancy* and *Dogs in Space*. I paid and went inside. *Dogs in Space* was okay, but nothing special. *Sid & Nancy* was something totally different. In case you haven't seen it, it's about two extremely fucked-up junkies. During the film, I was thinking about how fucked up they were and how sad it all was, but still, I was captivated. When the film ended, I wanted to be just like them. Don't ask me why, but I wanted to ruin my life just like Sid and Nancy. When I left the theater I was feeling bad and looking for trouble.

I made a collect call to a drug dealer named Jamie. He lived in Coconut Grove, about twenty minutes from the theater. Jamie told me to come right over. By the time I got to his house it was close to five in the morning. By five fifteen, my year of recovery had come to an end. I guess I snorted my first line at about ten after five. A week later I found out that Julio died that night at exactly eleven minutes after five. I'm so sorry still. This is one of the few things in my life that I am still truly sorry for. Considering all the fucked-up things I've done, I guess that's saying a lot.

But cocaine had a way of improving my mood, and I didn't find out he had died until a week later, so that night I wasn't sorry at all. On the contrary, I was still pretty mad at Jules for putting the moves on me in his deathbed. I didn't understand back then this great need we all share to be touched and loved, and how sometimes this need is expressed in the most peculiar ways. I didn't know that the reason why I did what I did and why Jules did what he did was the same. We both just wanted to be loved so badly. To be desired, to be touched. It might sound weird, but I'm sorry I rejected Jules. I told myself it was because I loved him and that was not what he needed, but that was probably exactly what he needed. And if I loved him I would have given it to him without question.

Is that odd? Does that sound sick to you? That was what had gotten him into his situation, wasn't it — sex, right? But was that really so bad? Was it so sick and perverted that we both wanted to be touched? Did he deserve to die because of his longing? Did I? Did anyone? What's so sick about wanting to be loved and desired? Is it really so much different from Romeo and Juliet just because it happens in a car or in some sleazy motel or even in a hospital bed?

I can't answer that. I only know that some sex is considered beautiful and uplifting and some is considered ugly and sick. To be honest with you, sometimes it's hard for me to tell the difference. I once felt the most exquisite intimacy with an old guy who blew me in the restroom at some high school. I was there as usual, speaking about the horrors of teenage addiction. Actually, I was glamorizing my addiction as usual and leaving out anything that might even slightly resemble the truth. I noticed this older teacher who couldn't take his eyes off of me the entire time I spoke. When I was finished speaking, there were two other addicts who were going on after me. I got up and walked to the back of the room where this older teacher was standing and went right up to him.

"Can you tell me where the bathroom is?"

"Oh, it's through this door and up the stairs, then down the hall on the right."

I looked straight into his eyes and sort of adjusted my pants a little.

"Will you show me?"

And he did.

He definitely was not the type to cruise hustlers or pick up young boys on the street. In fact, I think this might have been his first time, even though he was in his late fifties. He was so shy and nervous which I thought was adorable. When we got to the bathroom he made the excuse that he had to pee also, *pee* being his choice of words, not mine. Then he made a big show of going to the urinal farthest away from me, but I could hear he was not peeing. I asked him if he was a teacher there and what classes he taught and so on. I made sure to stand a bit too far back from the urinal so he could see me perfectly, but when he still didn't look, I had to get a little more aggressive.

I kept him engaged in meaningless conversation, which by the way is the hottest foreplay ever, and slowly I turned to face him. When he saw me standing there, now completely facing him with my dick in my hand and making no effort to cover it up or put it away, he sort of lost his train of thought and got all quiet. I said I couldn't hear him and walked over to the urinal next to him. To hear better, of course! He looked away and tried to concentrate on his peeing which was a nonevent. I moved even closer, now right next to him, my dick inches from his cheap gray teacher's slacks. I just stood there rubbing my dick slowly.

Hot is not the word to describe the situation. What fucking incredible tension! He just stood there trying not to look at me for five minutes. He was shaking and so was I. I couldn't believe my own audacity. In all my years of hustling I had never seduced anyone before. I can't begin to explain how intense and erotic it was. I knew he had never done this before, but I also knew he wanted to more than he had ever wanted anything in his life. I didn't know what was holding him back, but I didn't care. I was only sure that he did not want me to leave. He wasn't rejecting me; he was just fighting his own internal battle. Once I was certain that he wanted me, I felt surer of myself and got hard immediately. His breathing became labored and his dick started to swell too. He wouldn't stroke it though; he just kept up his act, pretending he was trying to pee, which had become ridiculous by that point. If he had peed then, he would have ruined his cheap suit for sure.

I kept rubbing my dick and staring at him. He wouldn't take his eyes off the urinal. His shyness was turning me on to no end and I was about to come when he suddenly got down on his knees and took me into his mouth. He didn't really suck my dick; he just sat there with it in his mouth and started to rub himself. We came simultaneously, me in his mouth and him on the tile floor. He got up and started pulling himself together immediately. Then he hugged me and whispered "thank you" into my ear and walked out of the bathroom.

I sat down on the floor and smoked a cigarette, something I always wanted to do in high school but never got the chance. I felt extraordinary, like I had just taken part in something very special. It's hard to explain so I won't. Try it some time if you like. Sometimes being a whore can be the most uplifting and freeing experience. Sometimes being dirty leaves you feeling so clean.

T O I L E T

So where was I? Snorting lines with Jamie I believe, Jamie and the others. Did I mention the others? Jamie was never alone — few coke dealers ever are. That night, or morning rather, there were about seven or eight people hanging out in his house. Actually there were exactly eight. Seventy-two hours later I had slept with four of them plus two more who had wondered in off the streets. The only two I missed were lesbians, and it wasn't because I wasn't willing. Don't ask me how this all happened, I forget. Well, there I go lying again, I remember it all. It went like this: I said okay and okay and okay some more.

When I got there, like I said, there were eight people. They were all doing lines, talking and listening to music. But just after I arrived they decided to go out to get some breakfast. Jamie introduced me to his friend Paul who was visiting from New York. He told me that Paul didn't want to go out with them and asked if I would stay behind and keep him company. When he saw the worried look on my face, he said, "Don't worry, Matty. I'll leave some candy behind for you!"

"Okay."

A few minutes later I was alone with Paul, and Jamie was definitely going to owe me for this one. Paul was a real leper. As soon as we were alone I started doing lines and Paul started working his way into my pants. The problem being that, besides being incredibly unsavory-looking and a drooling pervert, Paul had the social skills of a doorknob.

"So what brings you down here from New York?" I asked.

"Uhm, does coke make you horny?" Paul replied.

"Yeah, sure sometimes. Are you on vacation?"

"Do you like porno?"

I could see that this wasn't going anywhere and Paul wasn't even going to pretend to be civil, so I just unzipped my jeans and pulled out my dick.

"Do you like that, Paul?"

That would be right about the time that Jules was pronounced dead.

Paul and I were now speaking the same language. Lowest

common denominator is my strategy. So Paul, who's about fifty years old and still had the worst case of acne I'd ever seen, mumbled, "Yeah, I really like that." And he just sat there like a big dumb bore staring at my dick with this look I've seen so many times before.

Just a couple of years ago, I went to a strip club for the first time in my life. Not my cup of tea, really, but fascinating. The guys at the bar all had the same look as Paul. This one guy in particular was getting like twenty lap dances in a row from the same girl. Only she wasn't on his lap, she was just standing on this small platform in front of him dancing. The height of the platform was perfect to put her crotch right at his eye level. Probably it was designed that way, but I don't know; I'm naïve about that sort of thing. Anyway, he just sat there with his stupid face inches from her pussy, holding his longneck Budweiser between his legs. I honestly don't think he moved or even blinked the entire time I was there. I had the incredible urge to walk up and tap him on the shoulder and say, "Hey, man, that's a vagina. All girls have them. You should really try to get out more."

I never understood this intense fascination. I mean, sure, if you're into dicks then I guess dicks look good, and if you're into big tits, then I guess big tits look good too. But the look I'm talking about is an entirely different thing. It's like sexual hypnotism or something. And that's the look Paul had. He was frozen, hypnotized.

But I knew what Jamie wanted me to do, and I knew he'd be upset if I didn't do it. And if Jamie got upset then I would get no more coke, and the way Paul looked at my dick was the way I looked at coke: frozen like a deer in the headlights. I knew I had to do something as Paul was just sitting there frozen. I walked over and started hitting him in the face with my cock. Don't ask me why; coke just makes me a little sleazy sometimes, I guess. In any case, this turned out to be the right thing to do. Paul went nuts for it. He started cringing and telling me not to do that again, which is, of course, exactly what I did, only harder this time. Then he had his hand in his pants and he was begging me not to get rough with him, but I knew what he was really saying. I just kept slapping his face with my dick harder and harder until my dick was starting to hurt.

I started calling him names and raising my hand back like I

was going to hit him. That really got to him, and his hand was going like crazy in his pants. So I just fucking slapped him right in the face. I don't know, it just came to me, I guess. Call it divine inspiration. Was I a born dominatrix? I doubt it—back then I honestly didn't even know what the word meant. I definitely got off on it, though. The more he begged me to stop, the more I hit him. Paul would guide me to what he wanted by begging me not to do it. "Please don't piss on me," while he was taking off his clothes and moving into the kitchen so it would be easy to clean up. So I pissed all over that motherfucker.

"Please don't shit on me," but I had to draw the line somewhere, right? So I just hit him some more and told him what a sick fuck he was. And that did the trick for Paul; one down.

Next up was Peter. Paul immediately retired to Jamie's guest bedroom after he came, and I was left alone with my coke. I did some lines and thought about how ridiculous what had just happened was. I mean, Paul might have been old, but he was at least six foot two and in pretty good shape. I was stuck at about five foot four and weighing in at just over one hundred pounds. What was I doing hitting him? He could have kicked my ass easily if he wanted. While I was thinking about that and cleaning up the kitchen, Jamie and the rest of his friends returned from breakfast and Paul emerged from the bedroom. He didn't talk, but he kept staring at me intensely, which was making me uncomfortable. I whispered to Jamie that Paul gave me the creeps, and he laughed and told me he'd take care of Paul.

"By the way," Jamie said, "my friend Peter thinks you're cute."

That made me blush. Peter was by far the most attractive and alive person in the room. He was about twenty-five or twenty-six and way better looking than I was. I mean, I had youth and I think that was about 90 percent of my appeal, the other 10 percent being that I was straight. Yeah, I know that's hard to believe, but everyone still thought I was a straight boy. Well, everyone but me. Peter's appeal was that he was fucking beautiful. It really hurt to look at him. He had brown hair that was short in the back but fell to his chin in the front. He was constantly running his hands through his bangs and combing the hair back out of his eyes. Every time he did, that I got the feeling he was lifting a veil and I was seeing him for the first time. Five minutes after I met him, I decided to grow my hair long in front like his. Ten minutes after I met him, I decided I wanted to be him.

The only way I knew to be him was to be *with* him, and that was my plan. After Jamie told me that he liked me, I found a spot on the couch between Peter and two young lesbians named Gina and Sam. They were much more social than Paul. We all did coke and talked for hours. We got pretty friendly, and soon the four of us were a little clique. The girls were young, too—early twenties, I think. We all had a lot in common. We were all into what was then referred to as *underground* music: independent music that wasn't played on the radio. This underground attitude gave our conversation the tone of a conspiracy. We were all excited about being young and different from the masses, whatever that meant.

Pretty soon we were as thick as thieves, all touchy-feely and stuff. Paul was watching us from across the room. In fact all the older people there were watching us. One of the girls made some joke about Paul's acne, and we all laughed. Youth can be so cruel. I whispered to Peter that I had just pissed in his mouth while they were at breakfast and he screamed, "Oh my God, you didn't." His laughter was uncontrollable. The girls wanted to know what was so funny, so I told them too. Then we are all laughing uncontrollably.

The funny thing was, that was the first time I remember talking about my sex life with anyone in such a casual way. Well, my secret sex life anyway. I was not ashamed. Maybe it was the coke; I only know that it felt pretty good to be talking about something so bad in such a casual way. It felt like waterskiing naked with Silvio. Jamie walked over to us.

"All right, youngsters, what's so funny?"

"Matty pissed on Paul," answered Peter.

We were all laughing again hysterically. I was hitting Peter and telling him to shut up.

"Be careful. One day that might be you across the room smelling of urine," Jamie warned us.

Peter and the girls laughed at this too, but I just sort of chuckled as my old fears resurfaced. I knew he was right. I knew that one day I would be the one begging people not to piss on me, begging people not to love me.

"Listen, children," Jamie said, "playtime's over. We grown-ups want to watch a movie now. You kids can go into my bedroom and listen to music or just keep laughing at us old folks."

"All right, Dad," we said in chorus and vacated the couch.

We grabbed the small mirror and Peter got another gram from Jamie, and the four of us went into Jamie's bedroom. Peter locked the door behind us. I turned on Jamie's stereo and tuned in a local underground radio station, and we all sprawled on Jamie's enormous bed and did some more lines. It felt like a really fun sleepover party, only with drugs. I was lying on my back and Peter rolled over and put his head on my chest. I started playing with his hair. The girls started making out and we were off to the races. The next thing I knew, I was still playing with Peter's hair but he had my jeans unzipped and he was taking my dick out. The girls were in their own world. Gina was lying on top of Sam and they were kissing wearing only their panties. What happened to their clothes? The whole situation was turning me on immensely and then Peter had my dick in his mouth. Gina went down on Sam and Sam turned her head toward me. We made eye contact and she smiled at me. Then she closed her eyes and tilted her head back.

Okay, at that point I was freaking the fuck out. I mean, I knew there was a guy sucking my dick and all, but so what! I was in the same room, just inches away from two girls making love. It was just like the Playboy Channel only I was there! Well, not exactly like the Playboy Channel. First off the girls weren't wearing high heels and no pink nail polish either. Shit, they weren't wearing any makeup at all. Second, they weren't moaning and groaning like all the girls do in the porno movies; nobody was. The whole scene took place in something close to silence. Another thing missing was the toys. Don't lesbians always carry toys with them? Gina and Sam didn't. Actually, the more I thought about it, the less it resembled the Playboy Channel.

It was fascinating to watch them anyway, and it turned me on, but in a different way. They appeared to be in love. You could tell it wasn't so much about the actual act as it was about the bond they felt together. Peter and I were now completely naked and he was sitting on top of me, straddling my hips. We were masturbating together. Peter looking at me and me watching the girls. The girls did the same. Gina straddling Sam and both of them masturbating, only they were looking intently into each other's eyes and kissing a lot. I had never seen such intensity.

Completely opposite from the look Paul had given me hours before, but just as intense; maybe more intense. I felt guilty watching them, like I was invading their privacy. Also, I felt bad for Peter. I looked up at him and sort of helped him along. With my hands and my eyes, telling him it was okay and that I wanted him to come on me. He did; they did; everyone did but me. I blamed it on the coke, but something was gnawing at me. We all took some Xanax that Peter had and crashed out. Peter with his head on my chest and Gina and Sam in each other's arms. Two down. Or does that count as four?

When I woke up later that evening, the girls were gone, but Peter was still lying next to me. He was awake and watching me.

"Good morning, or evening, rather," he said, laughing.

"Did you have a good time last night?"

"Part of it," I answered.

"Which part was that, then?"

"The part where I got to piss on that guy!"

We both laughed, and Peter put his head on my stomach.

"And what about the part with me, did you enjoy that?" he asked quietly.

"Of course I did. I wouldn't have done it if I didn't enjoy it."

And then I closed my eyes. They say that sometimes when people are lying they close their eyes. It's an instinctual reaction, shutting your eyes on the truth, on reality. Is that what I was doing? How much truth was there in what I had said? I liked sex, I still do. But did I enjoy the sex with Peter? Wouldn't I have rather been with Gina or Sam or both? It's hard to explain. The answer is no to both. I would have just preferred to lie there with Peter's head on my chest and the girls lying next to us. I would have preferred not to have sex with anyone.

To be totally honest, I would have chosen the sex with Paul over all three of them. Is that strange? It is to me. Something about dirty anonymous sex with older men turned me on. It was comfortable, and I knew my role.

"How old are you, Matty?" Peter asked, interrupting my train of thought.

"Sixteen. I'll be seventeen next week."

"I think I'm falling in love with you," Peter said.

"What?" I screamed. "You just met me!"

"I know, but it's true. At least I could fall in love with you."

He looked up at me and pushed his bangs back off his face.

"Could you fall in love with me?"

He looked so innocent and fragile then. I forgot which one of us was under the legal drinking age.

"Of course I could. You're beautiful."

And that was the truth. I could have fallen in love with Peter, and I already had, just not in the way he wanted. I wanted to be near to him, I wanted to touch him, and I wanted to see where he lived and what kind of car he drove and what music he listened to. I wanted to watch him shave, and I wanted to know what kind of toothpaste he used. But after I answered he smiled and kissed me on the mouth, and did I want that? Well, not exactly, but I wanted to make him happy.

"Let's go see what Jamie's up to," I said and jumped out of bed.

Jamie was up to no good, of course. Jamie, Gina, and Sam were on the couch with a mirror in front of them.

"Good morning, lovers," Jamie said. "Breakfast is ready."

I didn't hesitate, I never did.

"What time is it?" I asked after snorting my first line of the day.

"Time to go and get a drink," Jamie said.

Everyone agreed except me.

"I can't get into any bars," I complained.

"Don't worry. I'll tell them you're my son," answered Jamie.

We all laughed. And he did too. After rounding up everyone in his apartment, we all walked over to a local disco in Coconut Grove where Jamie told the doorman I was his son and it was my eighteenth birthday. The doorman smiled a mischievous smile and let me in. He let me into a world I had never known: my first gay bar. It was fascinating and everyone was gay! Girls were dancing with girls, boys were dancing with boys, and everyone was having such a good time. I had never seen a happier group of adults before. I started thinking that maybe that's where the term *gay* evolved from. It was fantastic. Jamie gave me a hundred-dollar bill and told me to go buy them all drinks, which I did, and the bartender actually served me! I brought the drinks back to the table and everyone was laughing.

"Did he even card you?" Gina asked.

"Of course not," I said, and we all laughed some more.

It's always been a little scary to me how fast I adapt to new environments. Peter grabbed my hand and led me to the bathroom. We walked into what I thought was the men's room, but there were three girls standing in a stall right in front of us. The stalls had no doors. I thought we had walked into the ladies' room by mistake and I turned around to go, but Peter grabbed my wrist and pulled me back in.

"Where are you going?" he asked.

"Nowhere," I said.

We went into the stall next to the girls, and Peter dipped his key into a bag of coke and offered it to me. I accepted. Then he did some too.

"Got anything for us?" It was Gina and Sam. Peter handed them the bag and started kissing me.

"Do you like it here?" he asked.

"Yeah," I said. "It's great."

"It's your first time, right?"

"Yes."

"Let's go dance," he said.

Gina and Sam followed us to the dance floor. We all danced and did coke for hours. It was fantastic! The music sounded so good and everyone was so free. I had never really been to a nightclub before and I wondered if they were all like this. Were straight clubs like this too? I had been getting groped all night. Not that I minded, but I kept wondering if I could do the same at a straight club. Could I just walk up to some girl I thought was cute and grab her ass? Right on! I couldn't wait to try. But for some reason that night, straight thoughts just kind of floated through my mind but refused to take root. It was a gay club, you know, and when in Rome...

So we danced and we drank and somehow made it back to Jamie's by about one thirty. Peter said he had to go because he had work in the morning. He asked me if I wanted to go with him, but I refused. I liked him and all, but it was Jamie who was holding all the cards, if you know what I mean. So Peter left and so did Gina and Sam, which left the crowd a little thin at Jamie's. There was Jamie, myself, some guy named Roberto, another guy named Edward, an old dried-up troll named Hector, and a young girl named Felicia.

Just after Peter and the girls left, Jamie took me into his

bedroom and asked if I had ever been filmed having sex with anyone.

"Nope," I answered.

"Well, would you like to?"

"Depends on who it is and what's in it for me."

"What's in it for you is one hundred dollars and all the coke you can do, and who I film you with doesn't matter."

"Not a problem," I said.

So Jamie got all excited and went and got his video camera and a tripod and started setting it up in front of the bed. All I was thinking was that it was finally going to happen. I was about to be in my very own child porn movie! Well, teen porn movie at least. That must be what the girl Felicia was there for. She had shown up at the club and had come home with us. She and Jamie had been talking a lot at the club and going to the bathroom a lot too. Maybe he was setting things up for me and her to do a movie together. This line of thought was getting me pretty excited. If that's what Jamie had in mind, it was fine by me. I had my eyes on her all night. She wasn't the hottest girl I had ever seen, but she wasn't all that bad either. She was about twenty-two or twenty-three, with long hair and dark eyes. I think she was from South America because she had the most beautiful bronze skin. While Jamie was busy setting things up, my palms were getting sweaty with anticipation.

Then Jamie left and returned with Roberto and Edward and my heart sunk. It all made perfect sense to me though. I wasn't made to sleep with girls; it just wasn't in the stars for me. Some things are predetermined. It doesn't matter what you want if you've been chosen for something else. I had been chosen to sleep with men. There was nobody to blame, that's just the way it worked out. Dreaming about sleeping with girls was just dragging me down. A few years later I remember someone telling me, "Hope keeps the misery in place." No truer words...

So under Jamie's direction, Roberto and Edward slowly undressed me in front of the camera. Then we got busy. I wasn't really there; I was far away, in the other room with Felicia, in another room with Trish and Amy, on another planet with my first love, Dianne. If only I could have cut my life out of a magazine. If only we could all cut our lives out of magazines.

Mine was right out of a magazine all right: a gay porn maga-

zine. I can't remember the details of the sex with Roberto and
Edward. I guess you can watch the film if you can find it. I
remember it wasn't good. I remember I felt used and dirty
afterward. I remember I thought of Jules and considered going
back to the hospital and granting him his dying wish. I mean if I
was going to sleep with Roberto and Edward, two men I didn't
even know or care to know, not to mention Paul, then why not
sleep with Jules whom I knew and loved? Was it just because he
had AIDS? Was that all I was afraid of?

I decided to go back to the hospital that night and sleep with
Jules. But right then, I had some unfinished business to take care
of with Jamie. I asked for the hundred bucks and some coke for
the road, but he told me he had to go to an ATM. He had to take
Paul to the airport so he would stop at an ATM on the way home
and settle up with me when he got back. Roberto and Edward
left with Jamie and Paul, so that left me alone with you know
who...

Hector. I guess Felicia had left while we were in the bedroom
making our video. Well, Hector wasn't so bad. He must have
been in his late seventies. He told me stories about when he was
a young man growing up in Cuba. Not gay stories, just kid
stories. He had such charm and a gentle manner of speaking. I
was in love with him after like twenty minutes. I wanted to do
something to make him happy, to make him like me. If I had that
hundred dollars Jamie owed me, I might have bought him a
cigar, but I didn't. So I gave Hector the only gift I could give. In
the middle of one of his stories about playing baseball in Cuba
with other boys, I got down off the couch and kneeled in front of
him. Hector looked at me like I was crazy.

"That's not necessary, Mateo."

"I know it's not necessary, I want to."

"You don't know what you're getting into. It could take days
and maybe I can't come at all anymore!"

We both laughed.

"Let me just give it a try?"

It really didn't take that long at all, and I have to say that it
was an extremely rewarding experience for both of us. Something about having sex with someone you had assumed was
retired from sexual practices was extremely enjoyable. For him
this was just icing on the cake of his sexual life. He really didn't

163

seem to have too much invested in the outcome. Whatever happened, he was happy. He wasn't interested in getting anywhere; he was someone who truly enjoyed the journey. This was nice and relieved a lot of the pressure and tension I usually associated with sex. I didn't have to perform for him. The result was that I think we both felt a lot of relief and he came faster than either of us expected. Afterward, I got a towel soaked in hot water and cleaned him up. Through the whole affair he never once lost his dignity. He maintained this aristocratic air, as if I had just shined his shoes. I never felt once that he was a dirty old pervert. In fact, I felt pangs of guilt for seducing him.

Hector asked me to walk him home, which turned out to be next door. When we got to his door he told me to go back to school. He told me to date girls. He told me to stop doing drugs so much. He told me that this was no life for me. As he closed the door, I felt like I had just blown my grandfather. I went back to Jamie's and did more coke. I waited for hours. I got bored and tried to call Jorge. I got an answering machine. I left a short message, probably not making much sense. Finally Jamie got home and gave me my hundred bucks. He said he was proud of me and that all of his friends liked me a lot. We did more coke. We watched a movie. Then it was Jamie's turn. This was the way he liked it. Every time I had seen Jamie it was like this. He always found people for me to sleep with. He always set it up. Sometimes he watched, sometimes not. Then later, when everybody went home, he would want his turn.

We took a shower and went into the bedroom. We started having some pretty hot sex. Jamie was cute. He was one of the few guys who could turn me on. Maybe it was all the coke, but that's what all the straight boys say... Things were getting pretty hot and I hadn't come in like three days of sex. I was ready. We were both on the verge. He was ready but I told him to wait for me, just another second, almost there, and then finally...

"Jamie Martinez, open the door! This is the Metro Dade Police Department!"

Oh fuck! Jamie shot a huge load on my belly and ran for the bathroom where he started emptying bags of coke down the toilet. I just lay there in the bed trying to concentrate, trying to come. I saw Jamie, out of the corner of my eye, running past me in a frenzy. He was grabbing empty baggies and mirrors everywhere.

"What the fuck are you doing?" he screamed. "Help me!"

I just laid there on the bed stroking my dick like crazy. Sometimes you just have to come regardless of the consequences. Jamie got the house in order and I heard him talking to the cops in the other room. At that very second, I exploded in one of the greatest orgasms of my life. I saw stars and I saw the moon. It was complete and total release.

"Matthew Lee?"

I looked up and saw a red-faced cop standing in Jamie's bedroom doorway.

"Yeah?"

"Put your clothes on, son. You're coming with us."

B E F O R E
E N L I G H T E N M E N T

Chop wood, carry water. I was never exactly a Zen monk or anything, but I was similar to the uncarved block in my own way, I
guess. Looking back on the way I handled my situation, I guess
it was pretty Zen after all. I just said okay and moved along. The
situations I found myself in were what they were, and there
wasn't much for me to do but deal with them the best I could.
Things weren't bad or good, they just were. Sure, sometimes I got
down on myself and wished I had a so-called normal sex life or
that I was in high school like all the other kids, but everyone has
a different path and this was mine. For the most part, I made the
best of it. And then I met the Buddha on the road...

B U D D H A

So it's hard for me to explain exactly what happened in my last of all rehabs. It's hard for me to tell it, anyway. What people always miss about so-called talk therapy, or any modern Western psychotherapy, is that it works both ways. I mean, the more you talk about uncomfortable or unpleasant memories from your past, the more they lose their control over you. In the beginning, it's difficult to find the words, your mouth becomes dry, your palms get sweaty, and maybe even your eyes start to water just trying to put some past physical or emotional trauma into words. You stumble, you stagger, and you cry and blabber and eventually get it all out in some haphazard fashion. Maybe it's with a therapist the first time, maybe with a close friend or sibling. Maybe even by yourself. That is the worst to me. Some terrible event in my life that's been lying dormant in my mind for years will suddenly surface and I will remember every minute detail as if it just happened again, and suddenly it will dawn on me that whatever it was that happened was pretty shitty. And I'll be all like, "Whoa, that sucked! How did I ever get through that?"

Sometimes I cry, but most times I just get pissed off. "I can't believe that motherfucker did that!" Or more often than not, "I can't fucking believe I let that happen to me!"

It's strange how I can feel more remembering it then I felt during the actual event. Like at the time, I couldn't deal with it, so I didn't. I just said okay and moved on. But then, ten years later...BAM! It all comes back and I get pissed. So I call up a friend and relate the experience or the story, awkward at first, maybe even a little teary-eyed still. Six months later, after abusing all my poor friends' ears, I find myself telling this very same traumatic tale at some party in front of strangers, only now it has a twist of sarcasm and black comedy. And during the telling, I feel nothing. Western Psychology in a nutshell. Talk more, feel less.

And that works great for the bad and ugly things in your life that you are trying to forget. Stop trying to forget them; remember them so much they lose their fangs and become nothing more than silly anecdotes. But one thing I've learned in life is that every angle has its downside. So while I can write about the darkest moments of my life with complete clarity and detachment, I have tears in my eyes now just considering telling you about my journey into adulthood and the people who made that possible.

The man who taught me that I was all right and showed me how to find the strength in myself to do what I wanted to do with my life also taught me the most valuable lesson I've ever learned: the other side of talking. Hold the good things in! And I am so full of them now. I have so many memories inside me that I've never even tried to put into words. When I think of them, it's just a blur. A blur that makes me smile and feel good. Now, when I think about him and the time I spent in that last of all rehabs, I can't put my finger on a single image. I just see a blur of events and moments all at once, and I feel so much. That makes sense; I don't tell that many stories about my time there and I don't even think clearly about it too often. And that's how I'd like to keep it. I like to keep all my good memories stored up inside, only bringing them out when I need them.

I don't ever want to find myself sitting at some dinner party telling the tale of Ralph to ten or twelve friends and not feeling anything during the telling. Like a human tape recorder recalling the facts. That's fine for Paper Cut Bob, the freak to whom I owe nothing, but not for Ralph. When I talk of Ralph, I would like my eyes to always light up and my face to become animated. Writing his name on paper brings tears to my eyes. I promised I wouldn't use his name, but there it is, out now. Too late, I broke another promise. I do that sometimes.

I honestly don't know where or how to begin this. Let me first say that it took me three weeks to write this entire book up until the last chapter and that I've been thinking about these last two chapters for one year now and not written a single word until an hour ago. One hour ago, I was twelve thousand feet over Osaka, Japan, and at this moment I am about thirty minutes from touching down in Taipei. And this is as good a place to start as any. When I met Ralph, I didn't think I'd ever get off of Biscayne Boulevard in Miami, and now I am about to touchdown in Taipei. I mean, it may not mean that much to you, but I was a thirteen-year-old hustler! Think it over while I stow my laptop for landing...

The chanting across the river woke me at 5 a.m. local time. I have no idea of the name of the river or who's chanting across the bank, but it's so beautiful. The bats are just coming home to roost on the roof of my hotel. I am in Colombo, Sri Lanka. Are you starting to get the point? Another Cinderella story, right? I guess you could call it that. It certainly is a *fairy* tale.

I'm in Sri Lanka on business; respectable business more or less, if you can call any business respectable. It's legal, anyway, and doesn't involve my getting naked in any way or performing any lewd or unsavory acts. And how boring is that? Well, sometimes it gets pretty damn boring. It's probably just that boredom that pushed me to write down the stories of my childhood. The business world has done its best to rob me of any individuality or character I may have left, but let me tell you they've done a piss-poor job of it. I may fit into their world on the surface, but just beneath the surface I'm still a thirteen-year-old hustler laughing in their faces. Sometimes I will be sitting in some conference room for some stupid meeting and I will move back inside myself and laugh, thinking, *If they only knew who they are dealing with!*

But they don't know and that's the point. When I met Ralph, I could not fit in with anyone except the extreme outcasts of society. I couldn't look anyone in the eye, and I preferred to be invisible to all but the secret society of older men who cruised by bus stops looking for just such a boy as me. I thought I was the scum of the Earth. Ralph taught me that I was indeed the scum of the Earth, because that's what I thought, and so that is what was real. At first I learned to take pride in being the scum of the Earth and later, that I didn't have to limit myself to this class forever. Not that there's much difference, after all, but back then, it seemed like the universe had finally opened up for me and my possibilities were limitless.

They still are, absolutely limitless. You see, back then, I was bored with being the scum of the Earth, just like I'm bored with being in the business world right now. Only back then I didn't know I could change my lot. I thought we were all doomed to play the hand that was dealt to us. I was wrong.

Since then, I've played many different hands and even

stopped playing altogether. The only constant in my life now is change. But let's get back to how I got here...

RALPH

Jorge had called the police after he had returned home and found a crazy message on his machine about me, a lot of coke, and, of course, Jamie. Jorge knew Jamie too, and I guess he knew what I was up to and wanted me to stop. The police took me to the hospital directly from Jamie's. At the hospital I received one of the great pleasures of Western medicine, a stomach pumping! After which I was administered a lot of fluids through an intravenous tube inserted in my arm. Then I just lay there for what seemed like a week, staring at the ceiling.

It turned out to be only about twenty-four hours. A doctor came in and checked me out and told me I was a lucky boy to be alive. I was lucky they pumped my stomach when they did. He asked me why I had taken so many muscle relaxers. Was I trying to kill myself? I was about to ask what the fuck he was talking about, but then I remembered Jamie being very concerned that I wasn't getting enough fluids and trying to get me to drink a lot of orange juice. That motherfucker! He had always tried to get me to let him fuck me, but I had always refused. I guess that explained the pills. To the doctor, I said nothing. He reiterated how lucky I was to be alive and then left me alone again. After he left, I thought about what he said. Was I lucky? I didn't feel especially lucky. I felt sick. Sick and tired.

The police came back a little while later. It was two new cops — one female and one male, both not too bad-looking. They told me to get dressed, that they were taking me back to rehab again. They also mentioned how lucky I was not to be going to jail. I guess that must have been my lucky day. On the way to rehab, I sat in the back of the police car and fantasized about the two cops driving me to a secluded spot and molesting me. It was pretty hot too.

It's incredible how I operate. There I was, in the back of a squad car with my stomach feeling like it was turned inside out, and still all I could think about was sex. The whole trip, the female cop was lecturing me on the evils of drugs, which I didn't mind because it sort of fit into my fantasy, added realism if you know what I mean. So the male cop was forcing me to perform oral sex on the female cop, me being handcuffed of course, and down on my knees in front of her. My pants were down and the big male cop kept hitting me in the ass with his nightstick, not too hard, just enough to let me know he was still there. And she was lecturing me about saying no to drugs while I ate her out, it was all incredibly erotic, and then...

"What in the hell are you doing?!" the female cop screamed at me.

Her face was as red as a tomato.

"What's he doing, Debra?" the male cop asked.

"He's got his hand in his freaking pants," she yelled.

The male cop pulled the car over, put on surgical gloves, and came back and opened my door.

"Come on, get out, and put your hands behind your back."

Then, he handcuffed me and shoved me back in the rear seat and we were off again. We rode the rest of the way in silence.

At the rehab, the usual: blood samples, vital statistics, and an interview with a doctor.

"How do you feel?"
"All right."
"Are you down?"
"A little."
"Do you think about hurting yourself?"
"Nope."
"What drugs were you doing?"
"Whatever I could get."
"What do you think led you to relapse?"
"I don't know."
"Can you stand up for me?"
"Sure."
"Come over here to my side of the desk, please."
"Okay."
"Drop your pants."
"Okay."
"Why is your penis hard?"
"I don't know."
"Does this turn you on?"
"A little."
"How would you feel if I sucked your penis?"
"All right."

"Do you like that?"

"Yes!"

"Matthew? Matthew? Matt!"

"What, Doctor Thomas?"

"You've been daydreaming again. Have you been listening to me at all?"

"Yes."

"Okay, then what did I just tell you?"

"I don't know."

"I told you that we can't keep you here very long. We feel it would be detrimental to our other, younger clients. We are trying to get you admitted to an adult rehabilitation center. You have an interview scheduled there in the morning. They don't accept minors, but we are hoping they will make an exception in your case. It's important that you concentrate during the interview and try to be as honest as possible. If they don't let you in, I'm afraid we will have to turn you back over to State Child Services and you know what that means."

"Back to jail?"

"That's correct, back to jail until your eighteenth birthday. So you see how important this interview tomorrow is?"

"Yes, I can see that. I'll try to concentrate."

I could tell right off that this place was going to be different from all the previous rehabs. To begin with, all the other rehabs were in hospitals or psychiatric hospitals. They were all in nice suburban neighborhoods, and they looked clean, and the grounds were always well maintained by professional landscapers. This place was in a rundown part of the city called Little Haiti. It was a dump. When we pulled into the driveway there were all these people picking up trash and raking leaves out front. They did not resemble professional landscapers in the least. They all looked like pimps and crackheads who had won a shopping spree at Goodwill. A few of them were unloading day-old bread and pastries from a rusty white van. Others were barking orders and writing notes on clipboards.

They took me inside and sat me in an office. Everything inside also looked like it came from Goodwill. I sat down on a threadbare couch that was most likely older than me, and looked around. I made a point of always checking out what books my doctors were reading, so that's the first thing I did. Whoever this office belonged to was not your average therapist. William Burroughs, James Baldwin, Hillman, Bukowski, John Fante. It seemed like a strange collection of books to me. Most were written by junkies, drunks, or perverts.

A few minutes later a man walked in. He was a big guy with long hair, dressed in dirty jeans and a T-shirt.

"Who are you?" he asked.

"Matthew. I'm waiting for a therapist to interview me."

"Me too," he said and sat down on the couch next to me.

"What are you here for?" he asked.

"I told you, I'm waiting for the therapist to interview me."

"No, I mean what brought you here to this rehab?"

"Oh, I do a lot of drugs when I can get them."

"You look pretty young for this place."

"I am. I'm only seventeen. The kid rehabs don't want me anymore. I guess I've got more problems than most kids."

"Oh, do you think they'll let you in here?"

"I hope so. Otherwise I have to go to jail."

"So you're just here to stay out of jail?" he said, laughing.

"Yeah, I guess so."

"Have you met this therapist yet?"

"Nope, but he's got a weird name," I said.

We both laughed, staring at the nameplate on the desk.

"He's got cool books though," I added.

"Have you read any of those books?" he asked, pointing to the bookshelf.

"Some."

But immediately I thought of *Giovanni's Room* and the implications of having read it and I regretted what I had just said. It was too late.

"Which of those books have you read?" he asked.

I wanted to lie, but then I figured he was just another fuck-up like me who liked books, so I told him.

"I started *Giovanni's Room* but never finished it. I've also read *The Western Lands* trilogy, *Junkie*, *Another Country*, *Ask the Dust*, *Post Office*, and *Ham on Rye*. Oh, and of course *Lolita*. That's my favorite book."

"Wow, that's impressive. How old are you again?"

"Seventeen."

"What's your name again?"

"Matthew."

"What do your friends call you? Matt?"

"Whatever. I prefer Matty, though."

"Okay, Matty. Why don't you get that driver to take you back to the hospital and get your stuff. I'll expect you back here tonight in time for Ralph's group at seven." The he got up and started to walk out.

"Wait," I yelled. "I don't understand."

He was already through the door. I got up off the couch and followed him out. He was heading down the hall at breakneck speed.

"Wait a minute," I yelled. "I don't understand."

He turned around.

"Matty, my name is Sherwood Forest, but my friends call me Woody. I'll see you tonight."

Now I understood. Sherwood Forest was the name on the placard on the desk.

I got back to the dumpy rehab at six forty-five. I was shown upstairs by two men who took me to a room that I would share with three other men for the next nine months of my life. I was told to drop my stuff off quickly and get downstairs to the living room for Ralph's group.

"Who is this Ralph?" I asked.

"You'll see."

They both laughed. I put my stuff on the only empty bed and followed them down the stairs to the living room.

When we walked into the living room, I had second thoughts about the place immediately. Jail might not be so bad after all. In the living room, forty people were sitting around the room in a circle, in metal folding chairs. The guys I was with took their seats and I just stood there for a moment looking for a seat for myself. My eyes had to adjust to the low light. The entire room was only lit by two small lamps in opposite corners covered by scarves.

"You got a problem with fat people?" someone asked very loudly.

Everyone laughed, and then I realized that the woman was speaking to me. An enormous woman, sitting next to the only free chair in the room.

"No," I said meekly.

"Then sit your ass down, honey!"

More laughter. I walked over and sat down next to her.

"I'm Cynthia," she said. "But they call me Sin."

"Hi, I'm Matty."

Then we just sat there for what seemed like eternity. All of us just sitting quietly and staring at each other in the dim light. And then he arrived...

I guess I was expecting some extremely large, intimidating man, but he wasn't. He was slight and only average height and when he spoke it was with the most gentle and reassuring voice.

"Good evening, family."

"Good evening, Ralph," they all replied in chorus.

He began speaking to people around the circle individually but loud enough that the whole group could hear, yet without raising his voice. He seemed completely tranquil to me. All my fear evaporated. Take away the dark room and the mystery, and here was just another therapist. I had his number. Pretty soon he would be asking me how I was *feeling* or telling me to put a note on the mirror that said, "I love you, Matty" and look at it every time I brushed my teeth. I was daydreaming and staring at my feet when I noticed two more feet in my view.

I looked up and there he was standing extremely close to me with his crotch right in my face. I looked up at his face and what I saw there scared the shit out of me. This was no ordinary therapist. His gaze was piercing, yet soft and reassuring at the same time. He was sizing me up and that scared me to death. I felt naked. Nobody had ever looked at me like that before. And he just stood there for two minutes longer staring at me. I looked away, but he just kept staring. Then out of nowhere he said one word very loudly.

"Trick!"

"What?" I asked.

Everyone laughed.

"You heard me. I called you a trick!"

Again he used the loud voice which was such a contrast to his voice a few moments ago.

"Have you ever slept with a man for money, trick?"

"Huh?" was all I could muster.

"I understand," he barked triumphantly.

The whole room erupted in laughter. I guessed I had just been *outed*. There was nothing I could do or say. If I argued it would only make me look guiltier. I bowed my head and tried to disappear. That seemed to work too. He started talking to someone else and the whole group forgot about me. I sat there for the next hour, wondering what had just happened, while he talked to other people about God knows what.

Did they all know? All of these people, even the girls? Fuck! I was getting out of there as soon as everyone went to bed. I didn't need that crap. That wasn't therapy, it was harassment. How had he known? I guessed he must be gay. That was it; he was just another faggot trying to get into my pants. I had to get out of that place as soon as possible! And I pretty much spent the rest of the next hour formulating my plan of escape for later that night.

He spent the rest of the hour talking with other people. The group all seemed to be enjoying themselves. They were all laughing and hanging on his every word. I didn't get it. I was going to split as soon as lights-out came later that night. Once I had that settled, I tried to listen a little, but I couldn't concentrate. I just kept feeling embarrassed and mad. Then as the group was winding down he walked over to me again, and I prepared for the worst. I was going to tell this faggot to fuck off! But he didn't say anything; he just looked at me with this sympathetic look on his face, which almost made me cry. He looked very kind and nurturing then, not at all piercing and violent like he had been before. How did he change his face so much from moment to moment?

"You're correct," he said softly.

"About what," I asked.

"I'm a faggot, a cocksucker, and a queer—all three wrapped into one. To be blunt, young man, I am a homosexual. Didn't you know?"

"I suspected," I said weakly.

"And why did you suspect? Do I look like a queen to you? Am I swishy?"

"No, not exactly."

"Well, what is it then about me that made you think I was gay? Or, is it something about you? Something that enables you to pick us out from the crowd? Have you ever asked yourself that? You've heard the saying "takes one to know one," haven't you?"

I was about to cry.

"I'm not gay," I shouted.

"Of course you're not, sweetie," he said sarcastically.

But then he looked into my eyes and became very serious. Very quietly, so only I could hear, he said, "I want you to know that I believe you, and I want you to know that I understand that this is not the life you wanted. It's important for you to remember that sometimes we all need to take what we can get." Then raising his voice slightly, "There's one final thing I want you to know before we end this group tonight. You don't have to climb out the window after everyone goes to sleep. There are no locks here. You are free to go whenever you like. But if you choose to stay, I think we can work this out for you."

"Work what out?" I asked.

"I think one day you might be happier sleeping with girls. That's all. Thank you all very much for a very enlightening group. I will see you tomorrow." And with that, he was gone.

That night I had the first wet dream of my life. When I woke up, I went through what I would come to know as the routine: garden work, breakfast, more work, lunch, some groups, some free time, then dinner and more groups. All day I kept wondering if what he said was possible. Could women actually appreciate me the way men did?

It was hard to believe, but until I found out more I wasn't going anywhere. Just before dinner they told me Ralph wanted to see me in his office. When I arrived he was sitting behind a desk reading some papers.

"Sit down, Trick."

That was the name he would call me for the next nine months.

"I see you made it through the night, and you're still here. I'm glad you decided to stay."

"For the time being," I said.

"Of course," he repeated. "For the time being."

"Is there anything you'd like to ask me?"

"Well," I answered, "there is one thing."

As I started to speak he stopped me with his index finger and said, "Out of the question."

"What's out of the question?"

"We will never sleep together," he answered matter-of-factly.

"What?" I screamed incredulously.

"You and I will never become lovers."

I wanted to tell him that I had no intention of us ever being lovers but just like the night before, it seemed futile.

"Any more questions?" he asked.

"No," was all I could say.

"Good. Then I would like to invite you to a group I'm doing tonight in the rec room. It's called Sexuality and I think you might enjoy it. It starts at seven sharp. Please be on time."

And I was. Did I have a choice? The rec room was just a smaller version of the living room, and the setup was the same as the night before. Only the chairs were different. In the rec room everyone was sitting in La-Z-Boy recliners in a circle with all the lights out except one small lamp in the corner. The other difference was that it was a much smaller group. Maybe ten or twelve people, and everyone in this group was laughing and joking and they all smiled in recognition as I walked in. Sin looked at me from her La-Z-Boy and smiled.

"There's a seat over here next to the fat lady if you want, baby."

"Thanks," I said and sat down.

At exactly seven sharp Ralph walked in and everyone got quiet.

"Good evening, and welcome to Sexuality. Since we have some new faces here I will go over the rules. Rule Number One: This group is called Sexuality. You can deduce from the name that it deals with sexual-related issues. If you don't have sexual issues or are unwilling to share them with us, then this group is not for you and you may leave now."

Dramatic pause.

"Rule Number Two: Take what you get. We are all living in glass houses here, but I assure you that stones will be flying."

Another dramatic pause.

"Rule Number Three: *Nothing leaves this group!* What's said in this room stays in this room. No exceptions."

The last one he repeated every week. And I apologize, but I'm a stickler for rules. As far as Ralph's sexuality group and what went on there, I cannot and will not say. Not now and not ever. One of the things I learned from Ralph was that there are certain things that must remain uncompromised if you are to retain any respect for yourself. There must be certain rules you set for yourself that cannot be bent or broken. Unfortunately, this is one of them, and as much as I would like to reveal to you the details of the group, I simply cannot. I can, however, tell you how it changed me.

I came to appreciate myself; not some vision of myself that I fantasized about, but who I was right then: Matty the hustler. When I walked into that room the first time, I hated myself more then I've ever hated anyone in my life. To this day I've never felt hate like that again, not for anyone. I had no idea what men saw in me. I assumed they were desperate old men who couldn't do any better and that was all. I thought all girls instinctively knew what a freak I was and avoided me like the plague. I could never look a woman in the eyes. When I left that first night, for the first time in my life I thought I was pretty cool. Don't ask me how this happened, I'm not even sure myself; I just felt better about myself and somehow unique and yes, even a little cool.

Slowly, I began to think that what I had done did not make me some kind of freak, but instead a unique individual. The more comfortable I became with the things I had done, the more others became comfortable with it as well. It wasn't long before I was bragging about it. I also started to grasp that I was either gay or straight and that was it. If I liked girls, then sleeping with all the men in the world would not change that. That was a relief. Before, I had thought that eventually the thoughts of girls would melt away as I got more and more into men until I was eventually gay. But I also learned from Ralph that being gay was not a problem either. It was incredible after how many men I had slept with how homophobic I still was. Finally, I started to get over that.

I started reading *Giovanni's Room* again and this time I finished it. I loved it. After that book and going to Ralph's groups twice a week for six months, I started wishing I was gay. I forgot all about my desire to be straight. It wasn't that I felt gay or even that I was more attracted to boys exactly. It was more like a desire to drink wine when you're very young; it seems romantic and full of allure and mystery. Never mind the taste for now. I just started to see that there was truly nothing wrong with desiring to sleep with a man as opposed to a woman or vice versa. On the contrary, I started to believe that it made you special and unique as opposed to the popular opinion that it was deviant. I spent a lot of time reading, particularly ancient history, and I was amazed at all the references I found to homosexuality.

I found out that some of the greatest thinkers and writers in human history were gay, or at least had experimented with the same sex. It was obvious, and it was everywhere, if you knew where to look. I discovered that this outlawing and stigmatizing of homosexuality was only a recent thing. That other older and, I think, wiser cultures had accepted this behavior as completely normal. I also started to read Edmund White and other contemporary gay writers, and I began to see that others shared my struggle. They had also lived in secret and in shame due to an uptight society that didn't allow for completely natural desires and that termed them abnormalities. In short, I started to like myself.

For six months I went to Ralph's groups and read and educated myself. I had no contact with my family or any friends on the outside. In rehab, I surrounded myself with a gay or at least a gay-friendly crowd. Most of my closest friends there were gay men or lesbians.

At the same time, I also started to get a little insight into the straight world through the older straight men. I never had any adult males in my life that weren't gay. At rehab I shared a room with three black men in their thirties. All three of them were larger than life to me. Dennis was six foot four and weighed like two hundred and twenty pounds. He was in his early thirties and had such a deep voice that women, and sometimes men as well, would melt in his presence. He had extremely strong features and was all man, for lack of a better description. Charles was from Jamaica and the accent alone was enough to get most women going; add that to his very light skin and piercing blue eyes and you had one incredibly hot dick-swinging Caribbean Don Juan. Lucious was your typical Southern inner-city black male; black as night and just as beautiful, six feet tall without an ounce of fat on his body, charming and soft-spoken with a hot temper lying just beneath the surface. They were without a doubt the hottest straight guys at rehab. I think Ralph and Woody must have stuck me in their room on purpose. Well, everything they did had some purpose—it just took me a while to figure it out.

These three men taught me more in six months than an army of fathers or older brothers could have. They taught me to shave. They taught me the courtesy flush. They taught me that it was okay to jack off and that it was normal at my age to want to fuck every girl I saw. They let me know I was not some freaky pervert but just a guy like them. In short, they taught me to be a man. At night we would lie awake in bed with the lights out and talk. That was my favorite time of the day. Invariably the talk would always turn to sex. What we all thought of the new girls, what we thought of the female staff, and other more interesting stuff.

One night Lucious and Dennis were talking about this new girl.

"Shit, man, I'd love to eat her dirtbox," said Lucious.

And by the way, whoever told you that black men don't eat pussy is full of shit.

"What's a dirtbox?" I asked, and they both started laughing.

"That's the forbidden fruit," said Lucious.

"Her asshole," added Dennis.

Charles got freaked by this.

"Lucious, you're sick, mon. Dat's nasty! And dat girl just come off da street too."

Dennis and Lucious both laughed.

"You've never eaten no ass, Charles?" Lucious asked.

"Sure I's eaten some ass but only my lady's ass, mon, not no crack ho's ass!"

It was all new to me. I had no idea before that straight people had good sex too. I honestly would have never guessed that straight guys ate their girls' asses. Incredible!

"Hey, Matty, you ever ate you some ass?" Lucious asked.

I just laughed.

"Na," Dennis said. "Matty likes the girls to eat his dirtbox!"

Then we were all laughing. In the morning, when I would tell all the queens what we talked about the night before, they would get so jealous.

"Oh, honey, I've got a dirtbox here for him to eat—only I prefer to call it my manpussy."

So I continued to learn and grow and, in short, discover myself in the eyes and hearts of others. Dennis taught me how to notice a woman flirting.

"Aw-ight, Matty. That new girl Sharon has got her eyes on you."

"You're crazy," I said. "She never even looks at me!"

"Man, don't you know nothing? That means she likes you. Man, girls don't just walk up and tell you they like you. Well, not fine girls, anyway. They just check you out on the sly and shit. You gotta look for the signs. Most likely you'll never even catch her looking at you directly, but, if the bitch is showing up where you at all the time, that's a sign. Like if a woman is constantly disagreeing with you, that's a sign."

"Oh," I mumbled. "Well, why don't they just tell you?"

"That's nature, Matty, as old as time. If they just came up and told you, then there wouldn't be no hunt. It's not a real hunt. It's symbolic. You dig?"

"No."

They all laughed.

"Okay, Matty. Let's put it like this," Dennis said. "Man is the hunter. Woman is the prey. Every woman wants a strong man, a good hunter, so to speak. They want to be pursued, desired. It makes them feel good. If you were out fishing and you saw some sick fish floating on top of the water, would you try to catch it?"

"No," I answered.

"Exactly, because it's sick. The good fish are down below under the water. You got to catch 'em. That's the point: you got to catch you a fine woman. If she's just floating on top of the water, then she most likely ain't no good to eat anyway."

"Okay," I said, "but that still kinda sucks."

Later that night I thought about it, and there was some truth to it. When men drove their cars past me, they were hunting. I let them know I was game, but never made it too easy for them. It made sense. Otherwise it got boring. Other times, I was the hunter and they were the prey. I shot arrows in them as they drove past, and if they turned around it was like I got a kill. These things started making sense to me, and I began to add it all up. The bottom line being that if I could do well with men, then I could do well with women too.

About six months into my stay Ralph called me into his office. "Tomorrow you go out and look for a job. Are you ready?"

"I think so."

"Let me ask you a question. Try not to picture sex. Try instead to think of romance. If you picture yourself lying on a bearskin rug in front of a fireplace in some Swiss château, who is there with you, a boy or girl?"

"A girl, definitely."

"Then why do you think that you sleep with so many men?"

"Because up to this point they have been what was available to me."

"Do you think that will be different now?"

"I hope so."

"Hope keeps the misery in place! What's different now?"

"Well, for one, I'm not as afraid of girls anymore. Two, I'm not as ashamed of myself as I used to be. And three, I kinda like my own sexual confusion. I think it's pretty hot and I think some girls might think so too... I hope... Ugh, sorry, like I'm learning to use my sexual prowess with men on women too."

"And how's that working out for you?"

"Good so far. I mean, sometimes I still feel like a troll, but other times I feel like David Bowie."

"Good. One more question. Has anyone ever made love to you?"

I was dumbstruck.

"You mean sex? Sure."

"No, I don't mean just sex. I mean has anyone ever made love to you tenderly. Gently kissing you, holding you, making love to you softly?"

"I guess not."

I felt incredibly depressed, as if I had been missing something all along, something wonderful.

"I have to go now," Ralph said. "Good luck on your job search tomorrow."

A F T E R
E N L I G H T E N M E N T

Chop wood, carry water. So I went out to look for a job the next morning. We were only allowed to have daytime jobs so we could return to rehab at night to attend groups and sleep. Most of the other clients got to get a job after three months, but they kept me in the house longer due to my age. So there I was in downtown Miami, seventeen years old and looking for a job. I kept thinking about what Ralph had asked me yesterday. It really bugged me. Why would he let me get myself all built up where I almost liked myself, where I was almost proud of my sexual adventures, and then drop that on me?

"Did anyone ever make love to me?"

No, of course not. That was the answer and he knew it. Nobody had ever made love to me. And now I was pissed and upset again. I felt like I had missed something about this whole sex thing right from the start. He was talking about the kind of sex they show in Hollywood movies. The four letter word. *LOVE.* I never associated that with sex. I loved small animals, I loved my grandpops, I loved the smell of Lucious after he put on Palmer's Cocoa Butter, I loved my new friends at rehab, and I loved Ralph. All of those had little or nothing to do with sex. I kept telling myself, "He wants me to feel this way. He wants me to feel like I'm missing out on something. He wants me to seek out and find love."

I went to the mall at Bayside, and tried to go into some stores to apply for a job, but every time I got near the door I would look in and start thinking, *They won't hire someone like me, not in a million years.* Then I started thinking the same about love. *Who could make love to someone like me?* Sex yes; love...not a chance.

So I got a cup of coffee with my next day's job hunting bus fare and went down to the docks and sat down by the water. There was a huge old sailing ship in the harbor. It was a replica of the infamous *HMS Bounty* that was now touring the world as promotion for the new Mel Gibson film. It was so beautiful to me, and I began to imagine that I was Fletcher Christian sailing to Fiji and about to overthrow the evil Captain Bligh. There was this young sailor on the deck cleaning and stowing ropes and shit. He was dressed in white old-time navy bell bottoms and a red-and-white striped shirt. He had long black hair slicked back over his head and huge dark eyes. He was built like an Olympic swimmer. I thought for a minute of Giovanni and I fell in love.

I don't know if what I felt for that sailor was real love, but it felt poetic. I felt warm inside and like Ralph said. I just wanted to be near him, to hold him tightly. I didn't want to suck his dick or anything but nevertheless, I got that old fear again.

I'm gay! That's why Ralph asked me those questions.

Then the fear went away, and I just accepted that I was gay and for once it was all right. But it was so difficult to imagine. I mean I wanted to love the sailor, but I didn't want to fuck him. I had never slept with a man out of love. I hadn't even slept with that many men whom I thought were attractive. All this was a little overwhelming, and I just wanted to get back to rehab and safety. I went to the bus stop on Second Avenue and waited approximately four minutes before some old Colombian man in a rental car stopped and signaled for me to get in.

Without thinking I got in his car. We drove up behind the cemetery and he blew me right there in the front seat in broad daylight. He gave me twenty bucks and I got out and started walking back. What, did you think I was cured?

I felt fine when I got back to rehab. Same as with all the tricks after the first one, no sooner finished than forgotten. As soon as I walked in, I saw Ralph standing at the end of the corridor. He looked at me for the first time in months with that penetrating stare he had used on me the first night. It didn't take him long. About fifteen seconds and he knew; I was sure of it. No communication was necessary.

That night I walked into his group and he was already there, waiting. Waiting for me, I was sure. He never arrived early or late, just seven on the dot every time. My suspicions were correct: as soon as I walked in he asked me to close the door behind me and take a seat. Then he gave me the stare one more time, this time for about thirty seconds. I couldn't take it. I was about to burst out with it, but he saved me the trouble.

"And what did you do today, Trick?" This with a very loud, accusatory voice.

"Nothing. I looked for a job."

"And did you find one?" Again in the same accusatory tone.

"No."

"Oh, I think you did. I think you plied your trade again, Trick! How much did you make this time?"

I'd had enough. I burst out crying and somehow managed to whimper, "Twenty bucks."

I cried then for about ten minutes all alone. Nobody spoke. Ralph walked over to the window and stared out into the night. Finally he walked over slowly and stood in front of me.

"Is that how much you're worth now, twenty dollars?"

"I guess so." Still sobbing.

"And me, how much is my time worth?"

"I don't understand."

"How much is my time worth to you? Do you think that twenty dollars would cover six months of my time? And the rest of the staff here, would that same twenty cover them as well? What about your friends here, would you sell them for twenty bucks?"

"No!"

"Interesting."

"And was it worth it? I mean did he get what he paid for?"

"I don't know, I guess so. Why don't you ask him?"

"He's not here now, Mr. Lee, but you are, and I'm asking you. Was it worth it to you?"

I couldn't answer. I just burst out crying again. I could not understand why this was affecting me so much. I had done this like a million times, and it never made me cry. But then again, nobody ever talked to me about it either. Why was I crying so much? Did it really mean that much to me? Some guy sucked my dick. I pretended I was somewhere else for a few minutes and then came in some stranger's mouth. I got twenty bucks. What's the big deal? Why couldn't I stop crying? Ralph kneeled down in front of me and for the first time ever he touched me. He slowly pushed my hair back out of my eyes and softly touched my cheek.

"Mr. Lee, you are worth so much more than twenty dollars to me."

And for a moment I thought he was going to cry too.

"I'm finishing this group early tonight. Enjoy the rest of your evening."

Then he was gone.

Cynthia walked over to me after Ralph had left the room.

"You better think about what you done. Ralph's never ended the group after fifteen minutes. You fucked him up, Trick. The shit you do now ain't just on you. I don't give a fuck if you don't respect yourself, but you better get some respect for that man. That man's trying to help you and you steady fucking it up! Now you went and fucked up group too. You act like the last six months don't mean shit to you. You better think about what you done!"

I got a lot of mean stares from the rest of the group, but nobody said anything else. I went upstairs and lay in bed staring at the ceiling. It was obvious Ralph was upset. I had done that. I'd never even considered that what I had done would have any effect whatsoever on others. It made sense to me now. I was a selfish little prick. I thought about my mom. How would she feel if she knew what I was doing all that time? I know she wasn't the best mother, but I also knew she loved me and if she knew, it would hurt her very much.

I thought about my sisters and how one time, when I was very young, my sister Stephanie had beaten some guy up who she found fondling me in the park. I knew earlier someone had most likely fondled her, but she wanted to protect me from all that anyway. If she knew about all the hustling, she would be heartbroken. I have never felt so guilty in all my life as on that night. I stayed up all night thinking about what a selfish kid I was and that it was time for me to grow up.

R U S T Y

The next morning I got a call on the pay phone. I rarely received calls at all and never early in the morning. I was exhausted when I picked up the receiver.

"Hello."

"Matty, it's Jorge."

"Jorge, what's up? How you been?"

"Up and down, man. Have you read the *Miami Herald* today?"

"No, you know I don't read the paper."

"Well, you should read it today."

"Why, what's up?"

"On the cover. The headlines, man. It's about Rusty!"

"Rusty who?"

"Rusty, man. The kid you were sponsoring at the NA meetings."

"Oh, cool, is he famous?"

"Sure he's famous now. I gotta go. Just read the paper, man."

"Okay. Hey, Jorge."

"Yeah."

"I miss you, man."

"I miss you too, Matty. I'll see you when you get out."

"Later."

"Later."

I hung up the phone and went to the front office to see if they had the paper. The clients in charge of cleaning the staff offices saw me picking up the *Miami Herald* and yelled at me.

"That's Woody's paper, man! Leave it there."

"Come off it, man. This is important, my friend is in here. I'm just going to read it quick then put it back."

"Okay, but hurry up. He'll be here in less than an hour."

"No problem."

I went outside and sat on the front porch to read in private. It was a beautiful sunny day. The sky was that deep clear blue you can only see in the Caribbean. The birds were chirping and palm trees were swaying in the breeze. I was starting to feel better. It was nice to hear from Jorge again. I had the clear idea in my head that I could work through this, that I would never let Ralph down again. Maybe I still didn't value myself that much, but I valued him and he valued me. Maybe one day I would value me too. There is this Buddhist saying that goes like this, "If you meet the Buddha on the road...kill him!"

Don't get me wrong, I'm not a Buddhist or anything. I just like the saying. It means worship yourself. It means stop looking outside yourself for a guru, savior, or analyst. In short it means become your own Buddha. The final earthly words of Siddhartha, the historical Buddha, were "Be a lamp unto yourself and seek your own liberation with diligence."

I was finally beginning to understand. I needed to kill Ralph! Not literally, but my greatest compliment to him would be for me to tell him "fuck you" and make my own choices and live with the consequences.

I took the paper out of its protective baggy and unrolled it. The headlines were two inches high.

Teen Stabs Senior Citizen 28 Times!

They never mentioned his name in the article, but I knew it was him. I knew in my heart that Jorge was right. They found the body after five or six days when some girl told her mother that one of her friends had a dead old man in his apartment. Rusty had been bringing his friends over to show them all that time, driving the old man's car, using his credit cards. He must have snapped. Later on, I found out from friends that the old man had been feeding him cocaine for two or three days and then cut him off. Rusty didn't want to stop. He tried to beg, seduce, and threaten with blackmail, but when all these failed, he got the knife.

After he killed him, he realized that the old man didn't have any more coke anyway. So Rusty cleaned out the apartment and loaded everything worth anything into the old guy's Cadillac. After he pawned the stuff, he scored more coke and then picked up a few friends and took them back to the apartment to see the dead guy. They partied there for five or six days with the dead old man in the bedroom. I guess Rusty had really lost it.

The papers didn't mention anything about sex or cocaine, of

course. The police probably wanted to spare the old guy's family. They just described it as a home invasion that went terribly wrong. The unnamed youth was being held at the Miami Dade Correctional Center without bail. Due to the severity of his crime, he would most likely stand trial as an adult even though he was barely fifteen. The finality of what I had just read nearly stopped my heart. This was no unnamed youth; I knew his name and we ran in the same circles. And more than that, he had once turned to me for help. Now there was nothing left. He had signed a full confession. It was over. I knew what I would do if I were him. I could see no other way out.

If he chose to live, what life did he have left? He was fifteen. If he was lucky he would be someone's punk, if not... He could not take back what he had done. Not ever. He had crossed the line that I had danced on so many times before. Even if they let him out in his late thirties, what life would he have then? A life of remembering and trying to forget. Who could ever forget stabbing someone twenty-eight times? Who could forget spending twenty or more years in prison? No, for him it was over. Right then, when he picked up that knife.

For the next seventy-two hours I thought about lines. I didn't sleep, I barely ate, and I couldn't speak to anyone. I just thought about lines; lines that I've crossed. I crossed the first one by force when I was just a kid. The first time an adult male laid his hands on me; that was a line. I couldn't go back. I didn't need any hypnosis to remember; I couldn't forget. When I made the choice to go back to the Havana Hotel with that first-ever trick, I crossed a line, with thirty-five cents to mark the passage; thirty-five cents to remember it by. There were more, so many more. Some I crossed without even knowing, others I tiptoed over only to jump back to the other side before it was too late. Now, Rusty had crossed one ahead of me, giving me a glimpse of what was on the other side: nothing, emptiness, terrifyingly dark and quiet. For the second time in my life I felt terror, real terror.

The first time was when I was fourteen. Some blond cowboy type had picked me up in front of the library one night. There was nothing remarkable about him, but the moment I climbed into his pickup truck, I was terrified. I felt like I had to do something quick to get out of there and away from him or I was going to die. I could not explain the feeling, but I could not shrug it off either. He was being very pleasant and accommodating and offered me one hundred bucks right away. In a panic I pretended that I was going to vomit. He pulled over quickly and I jumped out and ran.

I never looked back, and I stayed away from the library for months. A few weeks later I heard the police were looking for a blond cowboy who sexually assaulted some young men off Biscayne Boulevard. He allegedly gave them sleeping pills, then while they were unconscious, he inserted Coke bottles in their asses bottom end out. He would then place the pointy side of a large nail on the bottom of the bottle and strike it with a hammer, which would cause the bottle to shatter into a million pieces. They never caught that motherfucker either. I guess the cops weren't too busy looking for him. You know, just a couple of fags is all...

That was a line too, but I didn't see it that way. I just felt lucky and smart. I cringed when I heard the story, but that was all. It didn't stop me. But this thing that Rusty had done was different, and I was different too. I was afraid and it wasn't going away. All I could think about night and day was Rusty. I kept repeating to myself, *I don't want to go that way*, over and over in my head. *Please don't let me go that way!*

Ralph left me alone, everyone left me alone. After three days I fell asleep. When I woke up I felt peaceful. Something had changed in me. I was still sorry for Rusty, but as for me, it was over. I would not go that way. I would never cross that line. And I never tricked again.

B R I A N

A few days later everything went back to normal. Ralph, I think sensing the change in me, began to speak to me again. I found a job; yeah, a normal job. I worked at a deli in Miami's Interior Design District; great choice, right? I now spent eight hours a day surrounded by wealthy gay men. But somehow, I managed not to hustle any of them. I got plenty of offers over the counter, and I refused them all.

"How would you like to make a hundred bucks?"

"Sorry, if you haven't noticed I'm already employed."

When I asked one tired old designer if he planned on tipping me, he replied that the only tip he had for me was the tip of his dick. Nice, huh? And that's what I started to notice. Most of the guys who were looking for that kind of sex were fucking crude assholes. Not the young ones, of course; they were nice, they still had time. But there were those lines again. Slowly they crossed them one by one until one day they crossed the final, noticeable one. After that, there was no going back. After that, street sex was all they had left. This left them with a slightly bitter attitude, I guess. I don't blame them for this; they couldn't see the lines. If they had, they would have stopped. It's not like they ever wanted to wake up one day and be a dried-up old prune that paid twenty bucks to suck some detached kid's penis. Nobody chooses to end up like that.

The hardest part was walking to and from work. It was in my muscle memory to watch every car that passed, and to make eye contact with every potential trick. I had to literally repeat the word *no* over and over and over again in my head whenever I walked anywhere. Sometimes I still do, not that anyone's tried to pick me up in the last ten years, but just for old time's sake.

That actually worked too. A car would go by and the driver would slow down, he would lower the window, the power ones too, and all the while I am going, *No, No, NO, NO!*, and miraculously the car would drive away.

Of course I would look around for it, hoping it might be circling the block to come around again, and feeling a little rejected that they never did. I guess I was just putting out different vibes or something. But that was really it! No more hustling. Just a simple two-letter word that's made all the difference in my life. NO.

"You need a ride?"

"No."

"You want to make some money?"

"No."

You get the idea, right? Strange how it took me so long to find such a simple answer.

And life rolled on. I worked, I read, I talked to Ralph, I went to some Narcotics Anonymous meetings, I turned eighteen, and I stayed off the streets. After four months, it was like I had never even been a hustler. I never stopped noticing the cars, but I did stop getting in. Things were good. I still had some confusion as to my sexual preference, but doesn't everyone? Woody told me it was time to start thinking about moving out and getting my own place. I was scared, but I agreed. We set a date for four weeks later. Meanwhile...

At work, these two guys named Brian and Rene kept flirting with me. Brian was young and beautiful; Rene was older but also good-looking. He was also much cooler than Brian. He wore cool clothes, he drove a cool car, and he acted like he didn't really care if I liked him or not, which drove me crazy.

One Friday Brian asked me if I wanted to go to the movies with him on Saturday and I accepted. I ran right home after work to tell Ralph. I was so excited. I was gay and that was all there was to it. Ralph just smiled and told me to have fun, which I did. Being gay and *out* was fun. If you've never tried it, you should.

Saturday afternoon Brian came by and picked me up. We went to a mall downtown and discovered we were an hour early for the film. So Brian, who is openly gay, says, "Let's go pick up some girls!"

And we did. I couldn't believe it. We just went walking around the mall talking to all the pretty girls we saw. Brian was hysterical with laughter after every encounter, and I was in shock. At first I let him do all the talking, but then, after noticing his success, I joined in and even led once or twice. I kept thinking, *This is incredible. I'm getting lessons on picking up girls from a fag!* Incredible but true. I got more numbers that day then I had ever gotten in my life. Actually, I had never really gotten a girl's phone number before.

Needless to say, I fell in love with Brian immediately. He was so sure of himself—I guess because he had nothing to lose—but it worked like a charm. Girls were creaming over him. Un-fucking-believable, and all I wanted to do was take him home and fuck him! Actually it was more like what Ralph was talking about: I wanted to take him home and make love to him. So I did, sort of.

The problem was I just couldn't do it. He was very beautiful, he was charming, he was young, but there was one problem. He was a he. I just could not get past it. I wanted so badly to be gay. I wanted to kiss him and hold him, but when I did, it just wasn't working for me. For the first time ever, I couldn't even get hard. I don't know about you, but when I was eighteen, that was a huge issue. I was in shock. He was sweet about it. He told me we had plenty of time and that we could work it out. He said we could just hold each other. I fell asleep in his arms that night and got into big trouble when I got back to rehab the next day. But I didn't care; I felt I was on the verge of knowing myself for the first time. Of course, I wasn't.

R E N E

Brian kept coming to the deli and even asked me out again. I politely declined a few times and one day just explained to him that I wasn't so sure if I was gay after all. He took it well and went on with his life. We were friends for a while, and then we kind of lost touch. Years later we ran into each other again on Miami Beach where he was attending his ex-boyfriend's funeral. We talked for a few minutes but then he had to go. As I watched him walk away, I couldn't help thinking that it was my loss.

I finally moved out of rehab and into some tiny dump in Little Haiti. I still went back to see Ralph a couple of times a month and sometimes even helped out there on the weekends. To be honest with you, for the first time since I was like eleven or twelve, sex did not occupy all of my thoughts. I went whole days without even jacking off.

I was in awe of all the little things that normal people take for granted like paying the rent, opening a bank account, and getting the lights turned on. I seriously didn't even think that those kinds of things would work for me. I imagined if I went into a bank to open an account, that they would simply have some document or important paper that I did not have and could not obtain, and therefore I would not be allowed to open an account. So I went down to the bank and secretly pocketed a checking account brochure. Seriously, I stole it! I thought they wouldn't let me just walk in there and take one.

"I'm sorry, young man, but those free brochures are for customers only."

"Okay."

So I stole the fucking thing! I waited until I thought nobody was paying attention and then I stuffed the brochure in my pants and left. I went home and made some chamomile tea, then sat down and read the brochure. Apparently, you needed two forms of photo ID and one hundred dollars to open a totally free checking account. Wow, was that all you needed? But I didn't even have one piece of ID. I scanned the list of what the bank considered valid photo ID.

Driver's license.

Shit!
Passport.
Shit!
State ID.
Shit!
Social Security Card.
Shit!
Birth Certificate.
Shit, shit, shit, SHIT!
I didn't have any of them. Obtaining them seemed impossible to me. *Shit!* How come a library card didn't count for anything?

I calmed down and tried to think. It looked like I was going to have to deal with some government office no matter how I looked at it. I borrowed my neighbor's phone book and looked in the front for government offices. I found the Department of Motor Vehicles and from the pay phone in the hall I gave them a call.

"DMV, good morning."

"Yeah, hi, what do I need to get a driver's license?"

"Your birth certificate, social security card, and twenty-six dollars."

Shit! I slammed the phone down. They were going to make this impossible, weren't they?

To make a long story short, I called the Social Security office who sent me downtown to their main office where I paid six dollars and was told my social security card would arrive by mail in five to seven days. Then I called the Department of Vital Records in Pennsylvania, where I was born. They would mail my birth certificate immediately after they received a check from me for fourteen dollars. *Shit!*

"But I don't have checks! I need my birth certificate to open a checking account!"

"I'm sorry, sir, but we don't accept cash payments via the mail. You're welcome to come to our walk-up window in Scranton and pay cash there or charge it on a major credit card."

"But I'm in Florida and I don't have any credit cards!"

Shit! Shit! Shit!

"Does it have to be a check from me?"

"No, sir. As long as the check clears, we'll mail out the certificate."

"Okay, thanks."

"Thank you, sir, and have a nice day."

Now where the fuck was I going to get a check? I was stumped again.

I was obsessed with opening up a checking account and getting a driver's license. The next day at work I was feeling down about my lack of progress.

"What's wrong with you?"

It was Rene; he looked as happy as ever. I don't know if it was just when he came into my deli, but Rene always looked like a mischievous little boy.

"I've never been born."

"Wow, that's serious!"

"I know. I don't even know if I can get you a sandwich today. If I can't prove I was born, then I guess I don't exist!"

"Well duh! Why don't you just get a birth certificate and then you can make me a tuna melt on rye."

"That's my problem. I need a birth certificate to get a driver's license, and I need a driver's license to open a checking account, but I can't pay for the birth certificate without a check."

"Haven't you ever heard of a money order?"

"A what?"

"Forget it. How much does a birth certificate cost?"

"Fourteen bucks."

"Wait."

He left. Five minutes later he came back.

"Give me fourteen dollars."

"For what?"

"For the new Chanel eyeliner I want... For the check, dummy!"

"Oh, okay."

And that's how my first-ever real gay affair started. Rene handed me a check for fourteen dollars signed but blank on the Pay To line. I handed him fourteen dollars cash.

Rene checked back with me every couple of days to see if I was born yet, and finally, I was. He asked me if I wanted to use his car to take the driving test and I said yes. Of course, Rene drove a black Maserati Biturbo. What a car to take the driver's test in!

"I guess you should at least take it for a spin first to get used to it."

"Are you sure it's okay?"

"What time do you get off work?"

"Five."

"Okay, I'll pick you up out front at five fifteen tonight."

"Okay, thanks a lot, man."

"Later much."

Rene always said that, but it was still the eighties so cut him some slack.

I was outside at five holding my breath. Ten minutes later Rene pulled up in this gold 1970 Volkswagen Super Beetle.

"Hey, what happened to your Maserati?"

"It got repossessed. Get in."

We drove to a Kmart parking lot, and I got my first driving lesson. Thank God it wasn't a Maserati or he would have killed me. He drove me to the DMV the next week and later we went out to celebrate, even though I had failed the written exam and would have to return the next week to take the test again. Okay, so I never was much good at studying. I had a great time that night despite my personal failure. He took me to some very arty café where we had arty food served by arty waiters all dressed very, well, arty, I guess. The next week he drove me to the DMV again, where this time I passed the written and the driving tests, and of course we went out to celebrate again. This time we went to some art-house cinema and saw a foreign film. It was my first time seeing a foreign film. It was a French film called *Betty Blue* and I loved it. I think it was that night that I fell in love with Rene. I thought he was so cultured and fun to be around. He had such great taste and style, and he let me drive his car all the time.

We had a few more outdoor dates, which weren't really like dates per se, but more like hanging out. Then one day when he asked me if I wanted to come over to his place for dinner and a movie. I accepted without considering it a real date. His house was just like Rene: fun, stylish, and artsy—think early eighties New York City, hardwood floors painted black, Warhol- and Lichtenstein-type art on all the walls. These may have even been real, but I didn't know art back then at all; and still don't. All I know is that it was way cooler than any apartment I had been in up until then. Rene made some pasta for dinner, and we talked for a few hours. The nice thing about Rene was that he listened to me. He said he was used to doing all the entertaining and talking and with me he could just relax and listen. He said I entertained him. I really liked that, it made me feel special and more grown up.

After I had exhausted myself talking, Rene put in the movie *The Night Porter*, which was incredibly hot. Then we watched some art film set in the Middle Ages where Paloma Picasso played some lesbian pseudo-vampire princess. First this cute girl/boy maid would dress her up and then they would ride on horseback to all the villages in her kingdom and inspect all the virgin females. The girls would all line up and Paloma would scrutinize their faces and bodies. Then she would select five or six girls from each village and move on to the next one. Before long she had this incredibly long train of beautiful young virgins following behind her horse on foot. When she had nearly a hundred girls, she led them all back to her castle where they all bathed and dressed up pretty for her.

They had an enormous banquet where all the virgins became a little drunk and started fooling around with each other. It turned into a giant orgy, the climax of which was when the boy/girl maid arrived with a huge sword and started cutting all the virgins to pieces. Then the maid collected all their blood in buckets and poured it into this humongous golden bathtub where Paloma was sitting. The last five minutes of the film were just a naked Picasso rubbing blood all over herself. Rene explained that the film was quite controversial because they used real cow's blood for the final scene. Apparently this did not go over too well in America, home of the Big Mac.

After those films all I could say was, "Motherfucker!"

I could not believe they made movies like that. Movies where young Jewish girls fell in love with their Nazi tormentors and the daughter of a famous artist bathed in the blood of young virgins.

"Did you like the film?"

"Fuck, yeah, I did!"

"What about the first one?"

"Fuck, yeah!"

"Do you want to spend the night?"

"Sure."

All the way to the bedroom I could not stop talking about the films. It was as if some whole new world had been opened up to me. I had read books that were on the edges of what society deemed decent and even some that went over the edge, but I didn't know that somebody had the balls to make movies like that too! I was amazed.

But you want to know about Rene and me, right? Well, there isn't that much to tell. We slept together that night; nothing freaky, nothing that would make me blush anyway, just straight sex, shaken not stirred. Was it love? It's hard to say. He was not like all the others, that's for sure. I think he was making love to me. And how did I feel? I imagine I felt like a middle-aged housewife who loves her husband to death but just isn't sexually attracted to him anymore. But I knew the chemistry was there for him and that he was enjoying it and that made me enjoy it too.

After that night, I practically moved in with him. We did everything together for the next six months. He showed me so many things, I can't even remember them all, but it's safe to say that a large portion of who I am today is nothing but a pale reflection of Rene. I wore all his clothes, drove his car, listened to his music, watched his films, and read his books. He introduced me to sushi, ceviche, Thai food, Middle Eastern cuisine, independent films, travel, underground nightclubs, death rock, black-and-white photography, art, and the pure driving pleasure of the Volkswagen Super Beetle. There is so much more, I couldn't possibly list it all. In short, Rene was my first love.

Those six months were the happiest of my life up to that point. No drugs, no hustling, nada. I even eventually opened that bank account. Each day I fell more in love with Rene and each night, well, I got used to it. We never fought or even argued. It was to me, an ideal relationship. To Rene it was something else. I believe he was in love with me too, but our sexual situation was troubling and sometimes frustrating to him. I guess he could always feel my reluctance.

Sometimes we had great sex, but there was always something missing for him. I was never the aggressor. He never came home to find me naked in bed waiting for him. I never ripped off his clothes when he walked in the door. To me this wasn't a problem because none of the other men I had been with ever complained. But Rene wasn't those other men. He knew who he was and what he wanted. He had dignity, I guess—something I didn't know too much about back then. He knew I loved him, that was obvious, but what he wanted was more than that. He wasn't looking for a young trick; he wanted an equal partner. After six months, I guess it became apparent to him that I wasn't ready for that yet.

We woke up one Sunday morning and had breakfast on the terrace as usual. After breakfast, we sat around smoking, drinking coffee, and talking for an hour or so. I was finishing up my coffee when I noticed that Rene had been staring at me for several minutes without talking. He looked so serious that I asked him what he was thinking. I wasn't at all prepared for the answer.

"I was thinking about you."

"Oh, yeah, what were you thinking?" I said, laughing.

"I was thinking that you are lying. Either to yourself or to me."

I stopped laughing.

"What are you talking about?"

"If you're lying to yourself, then that means you're gay but you're not quite ready to admit it yet and that's the reason you don't initiate sex with me. If that is true, then I can stay with you and help you work through it. If you're lying to me, then you're straight, and that I can't help you with. If that's the case, then I'd like you to leave now before we go any further."

I sat there for what seemed like forever. Not thinking, just sitting there completely empty. My mind was as blank as it's ever been. To leave right then and there seemed unthinkable. To leave Rene at all seemed unthinkable. I slowly began to try to reason my way out of it.

Sex—was it really that bad? Not at all. Rene was very good-looking and passionate, but could I be what he wanted? Sure I could—what were my alternatives? Could any girl ever replace Rene? This I doubted, but more importantly, could I ever really have a girlfriend? This I also doubted. I mean, sure, I had spent my entire life fantasizing about having a girlfriend, but I had only slept with one or two and that had been awkward at best; a girlfriend, that was a whole different story.

I thought about living with a girl the way I was living with Rene, and it just seemed impossible. What girl would want to live with me? The idea was so appealing to me but at the same time unattainable. That was a dream, a fantasy. The carrot dangling on a stick always just out of reach. I've always been a realist, and that just didn't seem like a realistic alternative. I had pretty much made up my mind that I would tell Rene that I was truly gay and that I would try harder, but something happened.

I had been sitting with my head in my hands, concentrating. When I lifted my head to tell him my decision, I saw the tears in his eyes and something happened to me. For once in my life, I felt somebody else's pain. I thought about what it would be like to be Rene. He was in love with me and I knew it. What would I want if I ever did manage to find a girlfriend? What if I found my perfect girl: the smart and sexy librarian of my dreams? Would I want her to try? Would I want her to stay with me even though she wasn't in love with me? Would I want us both to pretend that something wasn't missing? The answer was no. I would want it all. I would want her to be in love with me on all levels or not at all.

"I'm lying to you, Rene. I'm sorry. Can we...?"

"Goodbye," he said, interrupting me.

"Goodbye."

R E T U R N

Several years later I returned to my beloved South Beach. I had
spent a year each in New Orleans, New York, and London, and
then another few just traveling around. So much had changed
since I left, both in me, and in the city where I grew up. The
morning I arrived, I called Rene and we agreed to meet for
dinner that night on Lincoln Road. I spent the day wandering
around trying to be nostalgic. I walked passed the library, the
apartment I grew up in, the bus stops and the hotels. It was the
same place, just born again with new life. They were renovating
all the old hotels, and new cafés and bars were springing up
everywhere.

The biggest difference was the people. Where once there
were only people remembering, now there were people dreaming again. A park that used to be crowded with junkies was now
full of children and people with dogs. The sidewalks of
Washington Avenue were overflowing with life and people. All
the rundown television-repair shops were now exotic boutiques,
and the bakery where I once worked was now a nightclub. On
First Street, where the racetrack had been, there was now a giant
sports bar crowded with frat boys listening to reggae.

And I have to admit that I liked it. Well, not the sports bar,
but no matter how hard I tried to tell myself that they had killed
the life and soul of the old South Beach, I just couldn't be bitter.
They might have killed the old life, but they had brought new
life, and the new life wasn't all that bad. I tried to be nostalgic
and sad, but I couldn't help smiling. I think it was the hotels that
got to me. They all looked stunning! My favorite had always
been the Delano. When I left, it had been on the brink of destruc-
tion. More than 80 percent of the rooms were empty and the ones
that were still occupied reeked of death. I used to imagine the
news footage that would eventually cover the demolition. It
would bring tears to my eyes, picturing its great Art Deco tower
collapsing as the entire building imploded into itself and finally
settled into nothing more than a cloud of dust. But when I got to
17th Street and Collins Avenue, instead of a vacant lot, I found the
new Delano Hotel, a truly miraculous restoration. It was once

again the crown jewel of South Beach. It was so beautiful that I almost cried.

When I got to the restaurant, Rene was already there. He looked great too. As with Brian, I couldn't help but think that it was my loss. We talked again as if no time had passed at all. He told me about his new boyfriend and I told him about New Orleans and London. He said I still looked the same. I laughed and told him I thought my boyish charms were fading fast. He said it was never my looks that attracted him to begin with. I still don't know if that was a compliment or an insult, but I like to think positively. We ate, we talked, we laughed, and then he left. As he was walking away I had only one thought: my loss.

I walked down Lincoln to Jefferson and then headed back up to 17th Street. As I turned the corner on 17th, I saw two incredibly good-looking men leaning on a car and making out. I couldn't help but stare at them.

"What's the matter, you've never seen two guys kissing?" one of them asked.

"I have," I answered, "but never two so beautiful."

I can be so corny when I'm happy...

So what am I up to now? Gay, straight, bisexual? Does it really matter? Are they really all that different after all? I truly don't believe in labels. At least 50 percent of the men I've slept with claimed they were straight; yeah, whatever. I don't give a fuck what you choose to call yourself or whom you choose to sleep with—that's your business. All I know is that if you pretend to be something you aren't, sooner or later it will catch up with you.

In the final analysis, it's not any supreme being we have to answer to, it's ourselves. So, if you meet the Buddha on the road...you know what to do. And Ralph, from the bottom of my heart:

Fuck You!

Matty Lee received his GED from the Dade County School Board some time in the late eighties. He went on to attend Los Angeles Community College but lost interest after Spanish I. He's been employed as a tree climber, a bartender, a medical-research patient, a deckhand, a telephone repairman, a salesman, a fabric librarian, a night watchman, a customer-service representative, and on and on. He currently lives in Los Angeles, where he loves to surf, read, and play with small furry animals.

The Beautifully Worthless by Ali Liebegott. $12.95, 0-9746388-4-6. A brilliant novel in verse about a runaway waitress and her Dalmatian, Rorschach, who leave Brooklyn on a postmodern odyssey through an American landscape to find hope in a town named Camus, Idaho. "Ali Liebegott is just what the world of books needs...I do believe she is a genius..." —Michelle Tea

Burn by Jennifer Natalya Fink, $16.95, 0-9710846-8-8. Set amidst the sexual and political repression of the 1950s, Burn tells the story of the flamboyant Sylvia Edelman and Sylvan Lake, a socialist Jewish colony in northern Westchester. A fable for the Bush/Rumsfeld era, Burn will scorch the reader with its Faulkneresque tale of tomatoes, torture, and tangled love.

Killing Me Softly: Morir Amando by Francisco Ibáñez-Carrasco. $16.95, 0-9746388-1-1. Twelve genre-blurring and gender-bending tales from the author of *Flesh Wounds and Purple Flowers*. "If you scraped the rainbow paint off your pride rings with a dirty thumbnail, you would find Francisco's world, skillfully rendered and beautifully imperfect." —Ivan E. Coyote

One of These Things Is Not Like the Other by D. Travers Scott. $16.95, 0-9746388-6-2. Suicide, homicide, fratricide, incest—it's a love story. A thriller from the author of *Execution, Texas: 1987*. "...[S]urreally incestuous brothers and sexy parapsychological polymorphs...a jagged and multifaceted backwater noir, filled with revelation and life." —Stephen Winter

Origami Striptease by Peggy Munson. $16.95, 0-9763411-9-0. "I was intoxicated by the prose of this book in which love, sex, illness, writing, girls and boys who are girls roil around in a steamy, bubbly drunk-making stew. Munson is a stylist extraordinaire and the story she tells will leave you wide-eyed, spent, unnerved. You have been warned." —Rebecca Brown

Pink Steam by Dodie Bellamy. $16.95, 0-9746388-0-3. A collection from the author of *The Letters of Mina Harker* and *Cunt-Ups*. *Pink Steam* reveals the intimate secrets of Dodie Bellamy's life—sex, shoplifting, voyeurism, writing. "Bellamy is David Lynch in print, teen porn under fluorescent lights, a sandpaper jumpsuit sandy side in." —Lynn Breedlove

Pulling Taffy by Matt Bernstein Sycamore. $16.95, 0-9710846-3-7. Moving from mid-nineties Boston, to post-grunge Seattle, to Giuliani's New York, *Pulling Taffy* inhabits the boundaries between fiction, autobiography, and truth. "I admire the candor and the reticence in this beautiful, anguished, funny novel. I have seen the future and it is *Pulling Taffy*." —Edmund White

*Satyriasis: Literotica*² by Ian Philips. $16.95, 0-9710846-5-3. From the award-winning author of *See Dick Deconstruct* comes a new collection of literotica that leaves no prodigal son unspanked and no udder of any sacred cow untweaked. "In this madcap, pansexual, and polymorphous perverse collection of short stories, everybody has to pay the piper." —Patrick Califia

A Scarecrow's Bible by Martin Hyatt. $16.95, 0-9763411-4-X. *A Scarecrow's Bible* is about what happens when love occurs at the most unexpected moment. "Lyrical and anguished, this is a stunning first novel about the despair of addiction and the hope provided by love. The writing is so skillful it's hard to believe that this is a debut." —Edmund White

Supervillainz by Alicia E. Goranson. $16.95, 0-9763411-8-2. Rump-smacking good action-adventure trans fiction that boots transgender literature out of the classroom. A hard-edged tale of passion, revenge, and low-rent apartments, *Supervillainz* has romance, car chases, brutal superheroes, epic battles in dyke bars, and a climax that will have you reaching for the tissues.

Toilet by Thomas Woolley, foreword by D. Travers Scott. $12.95, 0-9763411-2-3. "Both cheery and cantankerous, the stories and rantings of *Toilet* are linked by a battery-acid tone and a smart, atomic energy. Thomas Woolley is a wholly engaging original, and injects his humor with equal parts horror and sad, eerie nostalgia." —Scott Heim

The Wild Creatures: Collected Stories of Sam D'Allesandro, edited by Kevin Killian. $12.95, 0-9763411-1-5. Brings together all the stories of Sam D'Allesandro, a young voice whose life was tragically snuffed out at age 31 by AIDS. "...[M]ore than the resuscitation of a brilliant, out-of-print writer. It's that rarest of things: a true literary event." —K.M. Soehnlein

For more information on Suspect Thoughts Press and our authors and titles or to request a free catalog and to order directly from us, visit our website at www.suspectthoughtspress.com.